Roland Moore is the award-winning series creator and script-writer of the BBC1 period drama *Land Girls*. He's delighted to be able to expand on that world in a new series of novels for HarperCollins.

His lovely wife is a great source of support and his son often comes up with helpful suggestions – even if they mostly involve laser beams and robots.

@RolandMooreTV,
/landgirlstvbook
rolandmoore.tv

Christmas on the Home Front

Roland Moore

OneMoreChapter

One More Chapter
a division of HarperCollins*Publishers*
1 London Bridge Street
London SE1 9GF

www.harpercollins.co.uk

A Paperback Original 2019

A catalogue record for this book
is available from the British Library

ISBN: 9780008204457

This novel is entirely a work of fiction.
The names, characters and incidents portrayed in it are
the work of the author's imagination. Any resemblance to
actual persons, living or dead, events or localities is
entirely coincidental.

Set in Birka by Palimpsest Book Production Ltd,
Falkirk Stirlingshire

Printed and bound in Great Britain by
CPI Group (UK) Ltd, Croydon CR0 4YY

*To Annie, a grandmother who loved books
and who taught me the power of stories.*

Prologue

It was one day before Christmas. And Joyce Fisher wondered whether she would live to see it.

This winter-bleak thought wasn't borne of fatigue from living through so many years of war. It wasn't even the result of having lost so much along the way. No, Joyce knew, totally rationally, that today was one of those days that can change a life forever; a crossroads in which taking the wrong path could cost everything. She wished with all her heart that it wasn't the case, that there was some rosy alternative, another path to take. But she couldn't see any way out of it.

She hadn't planned for it to turn out that way, of course, but the trouble was that you rarely had any warning which days would be the ones to change things. You could plan for saying yes to an invitation or moving house or getting married. But other life-changing events could leap out in front of you, like a distracted deer on a country lane, giving you no opportunity to prepare, no opportunity to weigh up the options. Sometimes there was no time to think about consequences. Sometimes there was only time to act and then hope that things turned out for the best.

Joyce's hands were bunched into fists, her fingernails impressing bleached crescents into her fleshy palms. She had never felt this scared, this nervous or this numb. The torrent of emotions overwhelmed her making every thought struggle for air like a swimmer lost in the currents. It was hard to think straight. And yet that's what she had to do. All the energy had drained from her body; her legs moving slowly, heavy and disconnected. She'd been through enough to know that she was in shock and that more tears would come later. When this was over she could give in to grief. For now, whatever defence mechanisms and natural survival instinct she still possessed had kicked in.

Joyce was a capable, resourceful young woman, and at twenty-four, she was one of the older Land Girls at Pasture Farm. Not as opinionated as Connie Carter and not as naïve as Iris Dawson, Joyce kept everyone on an even keel, offering the gentle, understated guidance of a big sister for the other girls. She enjoyed the farm work. She enjoyed doing her bit for the war effort. In fact, Joyce was motivated to an almost unhealthy degree by the need to do her bit. She believed every bit of allied propaganda, every edict from the War Office about how civilians should be behaving, what they should be doing.

Dig for Victory? Yes, of course.

Don't waste water? Naturally.

Loose lips sink ships. Not Joyce. You could count on her discretion.

Joyce never questioned what she was doing, never questioned her orders like her friend Nancy Morrell had. Joyce needed the order and rigidity of service to hold onto like a lifeline. It made sense of everything that had happened in her life, everything that they were going through individually and as a nation. She'd lost her mother and sister in the bombing of Coventry and the war effort gave her a purpose; a chance to bring something positive out of those events.

She was in her bedroom at Pasture Farm where she had been billeted since she had joined the Women's Land Army. She paced the familiar small room with its mismatched carpet and curtains and faint smell of mould; a room in which she had observed every detail during long evenings after work. The peeling skirting board, the thinning threads on the main drag of the carpet, the patch of damp in the corner above the window (a constant reminder that Farmer Finch, the landlord of the house, had failed to keep his promise to fix the guttering) and the creaky floorboard by the door. In the drawer was an article from the *Daily Mail* about the train crash that had happened a few months ago. Joyce kept it because although it naturally focussed on her friend Connie's heroism, there was also a quote in there from her. It was a small claim to fame; some recognition of the part she'd played. She'd imagined showing her kids one day, if she had any.

Sometimes the room was full of laughter as the girls got ready for nights out; doing each other's hair, trying on each other's frocks, borrowing each other's makeup. But it had been an unhappy room too, the sadness hanging in the air during the long days when John had gone temporarily missing in occupied France and she had been waiting for news. But all those times seemed so long ago now. Joyce heard herself give a small dismissive snort for those days that had gone. What did they matter now?

She glanced down at the neatly-made bed. On the floral-patterned eiderdown were two items: a small parcel with her name and address on the front, and Esther's breadknife.

Ignoring the parcel, Joyce reached towards the knife and picked it up, feeling its familiar weight in her palm. Esther had always warned the girls that the knife was sharper than a breadknife had a right to be, and Connie Carter had ignored that warning and cut her finger with it on at least three occasions. Esther had berated Finch for sharpening it up. But today, Joyce was glad of it.

Joyce could hear her own heavy breathing and was aware she was taking too much air into her lungs. Her vision started to swim with floating stars.

Could she really do this?

Then Joyce glanced at the parcel with its unfamiliar handwriting. Who had sent her this? It wasn't from anyone she knew. What did it matter now? Parcels didn't matter. Nothing mattered now. She already knew what she had to do.

Why was she hesitating?

Come on, they were waiting. They might be dead already if she didn't go now. Come on!

Joyce knew the terrible truth. Gripping the knife she had smuggled upstairs and hidden under her pillow, she knew she didn't have the strength. She'd been through so much these last few days. She wanted to curl up under that eiderdown and let sleep wash over her.

But she had to act, didn't she? Of course, she did.

Time was running out.

She knew that everything was about to change.

And yet, she couldn't find the energy, the sheer motivation to continue.

Decisions.

She couldn't hear any voices downstairs. Where were they? What were they doing?

Her left hand tensed, feeling the handle of the breadknife, unyielding and warm with her perspiration.

She thought about Finch, Esther, Connie and all that had happened. A world ripped apart, the war finally landing on the bucolic doorstep of Pasture Farm. Nothing would ever be the same again. She yearned for the time before, the time, years before when the war was only starting, and it hadn't blighted her life. A time when making different decisions may have led her somewhere, anywhere, other than this bedroom at the farm, on this day. Every crossroad had led her here, and every day had brought her nearer to this inevitable and dreadful decision.

Had she taken the wrong turning?

Joyce found it impossible to carry on.

She dropped the knife to the floor. It clattered on the bare boards near the door. She didn't care if they'd heard it. She couldn't go on. She couldn't be a part of what was about to happen. Her resilience had finally gone beyond threadbare to empty. She had nothing left, and no way of finding the strength to carry on.

She'd stopped at the crossroads.

But then something made her look back towards the bed,

towards the package. Joyce picked up the parcel and tore it open.

When she saw the contents, nestled in the ripped brown paper, Joyce stopped in her tracks. How could this be? It must be a hallucination. It made no sense. Her fatigued mind fumbled to make sense of this impossible package. The contents changed everything; snapping her out of her stupor; providing new impetus and purpose.

Some days change your life forever. And Joyce Fisher knew that today would be one of those days.

With new determination, she picked up the knife.

Chapter 1

It was eight days before Christmas.

The smell of burning coal and hot oil assailed Joyce Fisher's nostrils as she moved from the ticket office to the platform of Helmstead station. She brought a handkerchief from her pocket to cover her nose, to breathe through it and protect herself until she got used to it. A large steam engine was waiting, its carriages filling with an impossible number of passengers and their luggage; the hubbub of excited conversation of people going away. Joyce was wearing a long-skirted yellow dress with a delicate flower print, and had a cardigan pulled around her shoulders. She was regretting her decision not to bring a coat since the warm December morning had suddenly turned to a typically wintery December afternoon, even though the sun was high in the clear light-blue sky. She scanned the platform, looking at the sea of faces, for her beloved husband, John. The station was unusually busy, but not unexpectedly so. These lucky people were on leave for Christmas and they were heading off to visit family and friends. Churchill would cite the importance of the celebrations in his speeches, knowing how important they were for morale. A few days with loved ones while you tried to forget about the sacrifices and unpleasantness of war could do wonders and people would return to their duties with renewed vigour. For some of them they would have to be back to work before Christmas – so their families would move the celebration to suit. For a war that had been going on for so long, any such respite was important. Joyce hoped that she would be able to spend this Christmas – Christmas, 1944 – with John, but she knew he had to go to his brother, Teddy, in Leeds who had fallen from scaffolding the week before. Teddy wasn't married so in his encumbered state he was relying on the generosity of neighbours to provide him with meals and do his washing. He'd apparently slept on his sofa downstairs since the fall, and clearly he couldn't rely on his neighbours' kindness forever, so John had agreed to go to him for a few days until he was, literally, back on his feet. Joyce hoped that Teddy's ankle would heal quickly.

The train horn momentarily blotted out the chatter of people saying their goodbyes to their loved ones.

She caught sight of John making his way towards her from the end of the platform. He'd been to check the train times to see when he'd get to Leeds and he looked smart and dashing in his best suit, the buttons on his coat gleaming, his shirt collar immaculately pressed, a kit bag from his service days slung over his shoulder.

'I'll be back as soon as I can.'

'Just give him my regards, won't you?' Joyce replied. 'And get him to lay off the drink until he's up and about.'

'That's easier said than done. As if he needs an excuse to

drown his sorrows,' John said, hoisting his kit bag up further onto his shoulder.

They both knew that Teddy liked a pint or two and neither John nor Joyce doubted that alcohol may have played a part in Teddy's fall. The fact that the accident had happened soon after lunch only added to that suspicion. Still, accusations wouldn't help the situation now. Joyce knew it was best for them to knuckle down and do what needed doing. The sooner John got there, the sooner he could get back.

As she stood with him, she noticed a red paper lantern hanging in the guard room window behind him. It was the sole concession that the station had made to Christmas, but at least some small effort had been made.

Joyce thought how Finch, at Pasture Farm, was planning to mark the occasion. He'd asked his daughter-in-law, Bea Finch, to bring his grandson with her so they could stay for Christmas at the farm. But she'd told him that she was settled in her new life in Leicester, so she'd invited Finch to come to them. After a moment of disappointment, Finch realised the benefits of this arrangement. He was cock-a-hoop at the prospect of spending time with them both before Christmas and then returning for a celebration with the girls at Pasture Farm. It was the best of both worlds for him. Two Christmas celebrations.

'Try to be back for Christmas dinner, eh?' Joyce straightened John's tie. 'If Finch can manage it, you can too.'

'I hope to. Depends on Teddy. But I'll write to let you know what's happening. When I see him, I'll know what the score is.' John opened the door of the train carriage. The guard pressed his whistle against his lips and blew a warning that the train was about to leave.

Since he'd left the RAF, Joyce felt comfort that John was now working as a farm manager on a neighbouring farm. After worrying about each and every flying mission he went on, she could at least get a good night's sleep knowing that he was sleeping safely in a similar room under two miles away. Joyce tried to put her feelings into perspective. Any separation they had to endure now was hard, but not as traumatic as when he'd been in the forces and flying who knows where.

She hoped in her heart that any real danger to him had passed. It seemed inconceivable now that the nights of insomnia and days spent with an inability to eat were over. Once, every waking moment had been taken with fearful anxiety about John's safety while he was navigating for the RAF. Now the most she had to worry about was whether she could get away with staying overnight at Shallow Brook Farm without being caught by her Women's Land Army warden, Esther Reeves. Esther was more lenient than some wardens she had heard about, but she still drew a line about Joyce spending weeknights with John. She wanted Joyce at Pasture Farm, ready to work, not gallivanting off with her husband. Fridays and Saturdays were different, with Joyce allowed to stay over at Shallow Brook Farm on both those nights. But if she wanted to sleep in his arms in the week, she had to risk being caught creeping out of Pasture Farm at night and returning at first light. Joyce enjoyed that manageable level of danger though. She knew that even if she was caught, it was unlikely that Esther would give her an official warning for her behaviour. The worst outcome would be a firm telling-off followed by unimpressed scowls for a week or so as Esther made her point. But whatever the outcome, Joyce knew it was easier simply to not get caught.

John pulled down the carriage window so he could crane his neck out to give Joyce one last kiss. She hooked her arms around his neck and pushed her lips softly against his.

'You take care, you hear?' Joyce tried to stop herself welling up.

'You too!' He smiled back.

The train remained stationary for a moment. Joyce and John looked at one another, with a moment of amused awkwardness, as they waited for the train to leave.

'It's never like this in the pictures, is it? The train always goes straight away after they've kissed, doesn't it?' Joyce was enjoying a few extra seconds with her husband.

'Or sometimes it goes as they're kissing, and they have to stop halfway through. Lovers torn apart and all that.'

The small delay, the shared joke, had helped. Joyce felt herself relax. It was all going to be alright. John would chivvy Teddy to a speedy recovery and then they'd share Christmas dinner together back at the farm in a few days.

'See you very soon!'

'You're seeing me now. Given the time this takes to go, I'll probably still be here next week!' John replied. As if John's comment had been overheard by the driver, the train started to edge forward.

The guard blasted a final volley on his whistle to warn

people to stand back and the train belched out smoke as it crawled out of the station. Joyce watched the other women running alongside, waving goodbye. But she remained still, waving from where she stood. She was struck by a sense of déjà vu, remembering the other times John had left on the train from this station; usually with a brow furrowed with worry and a kit bag full of his RAF uniform and home-made cake for the journey.

Joyce watched as the train receded into the distance, aware of the other people drifting away around her like ghosts disappearing from view. She pulled her cardigan around her shoulders and braced herself for the walk back to the farm.

A starling swooped down low in front of her as she ambled along the country lane, a light drizzle adding to the already wet ground and making the leaves of the evergreen hedgerow glisten. Lost in her thoughts about the impending Christmas celebrations, Joyce walked the well-remembered route without really thinking where she was going. She'd done it so many times, it was automatic. She could recite it with her eyes shut: the walk across the road from the station; the town square, the vicarage, the little bridge by the newspaper office leading to the fields beyond. It had been nearly forty minutes since Joyce had seen him off at Helmstead train station and she assumed he'd be well into his journey by now.

The blue sky was fading to grey as evening fell. She rounded a corner and trudged across a muddy path to the stile that would lead her to the back of Pasture Farm. She remembered when she had first made this journey, burdened with suitcases and a complaining Nancy Morrell. What had happened to

Nancy? She'd been her first roommate in the Women's Land Army; a cantankerous sometimes entitled young woman who didn't enjoy getting her hands dirty. She'd even tried to get Joyce to carry her suitcase from the station. Flaming cheek! Joyce had flatly refused. She smiled to herself at the memory. It seemed like a lifetime ago now. She had seen so many things in her time here, found solace in her new family of Esther, Finch, and the other girls. She had seen great, life-affirming times of friendship. Even through the bad times the resilience of her friends, her surrogate sisters, had helped her pull through, finding her inner strength to face whatever problems came her way.

The grey sky continued to half-heartedly drop its drizzle. Joyce thought the chances of snow this Christmas would be slim. There had been freezing fog in the lead up and some of that still hung around, but there wouldn't be snow. That would be fine. John would have more chance of getting back in time if there wasn't any snow on the tracks.

Joyce reached the back door of the farmhouse. She could hear muffled voices from within along with the sound of the radio. She sloughed off her muddy boots on the step like a snake shedding its skin and opened the door to the kitchen, enjoying the warm air as it greeted her.

'Did he get off all right?' Esther asked, her hands in the sink, washing some carrots. The stalks and leaves were spilling over the edge of the basin, leaving trails of muddy dirt on the top of the counter.

'Yes, that's him gone.' Joyce sat at the table, pulling off her sock to deal with a small stone that had got lodged inside her boot.

'Don't you worry, I'm sure as soon as he's spent a couple of days with his brother, he'll be back on that train,' Esther remarked. 'And we've still got eight days until Christmas day.'

Eight days.

'Better put the sprouts on to cook soon then.' Joyce was making the best of the situation and finding her humour. Esther threw a tea towel at her in mock outrage.

'Flaming cheek!' Esther let the rebuke land and then added, 'I'll have you know they went on last week.' The women giggled, good-naturedly.

The sky was a bruised purple colour as night fell outside the window, the colour refracted and warped into hallucinogenic patterns via the large raindrops on the pane.

Shortly, Esther and Joyce put on their coats and boots and left the warmth of the kitchen to walk into the village. As they crossed the bridge into Helmstead, Joyce could see the lights of the village hall. The small rectangular building with its corrugated iron roof seemed designed to be too hot in summer and too cold in winter.

'Is Martin already here?' Joyce asked as they approached.

'No, I don't know where he's gone,' Esther replied. 'He went off mooning after Iris. He's wasting his time with that one. Thinks he might start courting her. He's got his hopes up because they'll be at Shallow Brook Farm together.'

'While John's away?'

'Yes, Martin and Iris are going to take up the slack until he's back.'

'Ah it's going to be quiet at the farm without them both,' Joyce had reached the door to the village hall where Connie

Carter was talking to two American soldiers. From the men's postures – one holding the door frame, the other primping his hair – Joyce could see they were flirting with her. She could also tell from Connie's posture that she was having none of it.

'Why can't we come to the party?' One of the soldiers drawled, to the amusement of his friend.

'I never said you couldn't come.' Connie spotted Joyce and Esther and shot them a smile of sufferance. 'And you boys are welcome to come along, providing you're both over sixty.'

'Sixty?' The American looked bemused.

'Yes, it's a party – a meal – for the old folk.'

'I don't think I'm that old.' The soldier smiled before changing tack. 'But how about I take you out for our own party?'

'Yeah, sounds good. I'll just ask my husband,' Connie grinned. Knowing when they were beaten, the Americans shrugged and walked away. Connie turned to the watching Joyce and Esther.

'Can't blame them for trying, can you?' Connie raised an eyebrow archly, 'You coming inside then?'

Esther nodded.

'We thought you could do with some help.' Joyce unfastened her coat.

'Henry could, that's for sure.'

Inside, they found her husband, the Reverend Henry Jameson. The good-looking and earnest young man was struggling to move a trestle table. 'Where have you been, Connie?'

'Some people wanted to know if they could come along.'

15

Connie raised her eyebrow slightly in Joyce's direction. It was technically true, Joyce supposed. 'But I don't think they were quite old enough yet.'

Connie turned her attention to sticking up a piece of bunting that had drooped. Joyce grabbed the other end of the trestle table and they lifted it together. Esther and Connie started to put out chairs. Each year, Lady Hoxley would donate money to a fund run by the church to organise a Christmas meal for the old people of Helmstead. Local business people and good Samaritans would contribute beer, wine and food; a lot of it grown on the fields and houses around Helmstead. A lot of people in the village, from Mrs Gulliver and the other busybodies to the local butcher would pitch in to arrange the meal. Finch had promised them a bag of spuds to help them along.

And the meal wasn't the only attraction for the old folk in the village. There would be songs at the piano and maybe a little dancing. Sometimes the event happened on Christmas Day itself, but this year it was happening earlier. The lunch was organised by Henry Jameson for anyone who wanted to spend the day with the community. With so many loved ones away overseas, Christmas could be a lonely and sad experience, so this event distracted everyone from their problems for a day. And Henry liked to think he'd gain a few new parishioners at the Sunday Service as a result too.

As Esther, Connie and Joyce helped Henry set up the hall, their conversation turned to who would be at Pasture Farm for Christmas.

'Connie and I hope to have the day together – after I've

finished my service and my visits to parishioners.' Henry placed a beer mat under a wobbly table leg.

'That means he'll be home at five in the evening and I'll have been on my tod all day.' Connie rolled her eyes to her husband's amusement.

'So what about Dolores?'

'Oh, she's got nowhere to go, so she'll be there,' Esther replied. About twelve years older than the other girls, Dolores O'Malley kept herself to herself. Joyce remembered Connie playing a game over the summer, to try to find out details – any details – about Dolores's life. Connie would try every trick she knew to get Dolores to divulge even the smallest detail. What colour did she like? What was her home like? Was she courting anyone? But as skilful as Connie was in digging, Dolores proved equally adept at deflecting. She was as closed as a clam in deep water. Joyce felt that Dolores deserved her privacy.

'At least I don't think she's got anywhere to go,' Esther mused. 'You never know with that one.'

'And that's the point, innit? We'll never know.' Connie laughed.

Joyce stood on a chair to put some more bunting up. The streamers had been cut and assembled from strips of old magazines, giving the bunting a colourful and varied effect.

'And of course, Martin and Iris will be back with us for the big day,' Esther volunteered, spooling the bunting up to Joyce. 'Fred will be back by then too.'

'We'll have a good time.'

'Will we?' Esther pulled a sceptical face.

17

'Yes,' Joyce grinned. 'Especially if we persuade Fred to open his carrot whisky.'

'Joyce Fisher! I never had you down as being naughty.'

'It's living with him what's done it!'

A distant rumble distracted her. It wasn't thunder. Joyce's laughter died in her throat as she noticed a flash in the sky which illuminated the glass of the window pane, making the rain drops glisten like pearls for a brief moment. There was another flash and a distant bang, further away. If there wasn't a war on, Joyce would have marvelled that they might have been shooting stars or some strange firework show.

Esther, Connie and Joyce peered through the window their hands cupped over their eyes to help them see outside. In the sky, a small grey shape moved quickly across the horizon, with two other similarly-sized shapes following. A flash went off to the right of the first object. It was the last stages of a dog fight. Joyce squinted to try to work out whether it was an allied or German plane being chased. The first plane banked round, and Joyce glimpsed the markings. A yellow band around the rear fuselage and a black cross told her all she needed to know. It was a German bomber and it was being gained on by two Spitfires. One of the allied planes reeled off machine gun fire.

Henry came over to watch and they all peered intently, trying to glimpse the action.

Joyce instinctively ducked down slightly from the window. Esther put a comforting hand on her shoulder. The truth was that they were far enough away to be out of danger. The bullets wouldn't reach the village hall from that distance. But a basic innate need for survival meant that they shied away nonetheless.

Joyce craned her head. At the corner of the window frame, the second Spitfire looped round, cutting off the escape path of the German bomber. The Spitfire fired its guns and there was a flash of fire on the wing of the bomber. It banked sharply away, an erratic movement that told Joyce it wasn't an evasive manoeuvre but a sign it was out of control. Sure enough the bomber spiralled down and away, with the awful whining sound that signified an imminent crash. Joyce could just about make out a plume of black smoke from the rear of the plane. Fire was gripping the rear section. It disappeared behind some trees several miles away. The Spitfires pursued it over the canopy to check they had completed their task. After a few moments, a smoky mushroom of fire billowed up from behind the trees. Esther looked solemnly at what she had seen.

'There's one for our boys.' But there was no hint of celebration in Esther's voice. They knew it could have so easily been a loss to the allied side. They both knew that death wasn't anything to celebrate. Instead this was a grim tallying up of a minor victory in a war that was dragging on above the skies of Helmstead. Another mother would be getting a telegram.

Joyce continued to put up the celebratory bunting; an action that seemed darkly poignant now. But for now, she didn't think any more about the German plane or what had happened to it.

Twin paths of blackened, smoking grass etched their way into a copse of trees on the edge of Frensham Fields. And there, its nose smashed into an ancient oak tree was the German plane, one of its engines whirring in a death throe of aviation fuel and smoke. The fuselage was already sparking with fire and the fuel caught alight suddenly, sending a dense cloud exploding into the sky like some nightmarish purple and black peony. The men in the cockpit were frantically trying to escape. One of them smashed open the canopy, sending it cascading down the side of the plane. He was up and out, falling over the side onto the singed heather beneath. His partner quickly followed, but being nearer the fuselage, he found his arm engulfed in burning fuel.

The man screamed and fell hard onto the ground. The first man was on his feet, scrambling to his aid, rolling the burning man over and over until the flames subsided. Then he pulled the man away from the wreckage, getting only twenty feet away before he collapsed on his back from the effort.

'*Kapitän?*' The younger man had concern etched on his face, terror in his eyes. His name was Siegfried Weber. He was twenty-two and although this has been his third mission, he had never been to England before.

The older man winced and clutched his right arm. His name was Emory Mayer. He was forty and this had been his eighteenth mission. He had worked as a tailor in England for two years in the 1920s and if sartorial thoughts were foremost in his mind right now, he'd have registered the state of his uniform, which was partially burnt away around the arm, the skin underneath blackened. Siegfried couldn't tell whether it was from the burn or from dirt from the fuel. He didn't want to rub it to find out. Instead, he lifted his captain as best as he could and shuffled them both even further away from the plane. It was burning brightly, and Siegfried knew it would be a beacon for anyone trying to find survivors. They had to get away.

Siegfried hoisted Emory's good arm over his shoulder and walked them across the scrubland, inching slowly away. Every now and then he would risk a look behind him, hoping that the wreckage would be a small dot on the horizon. But the progress was such that he stopped looking behind him, knowing that the continued proximity of the plane would sap his morale and rob him of the impetus to keep going.

The plane exploded in a final, epic fireball, plumes of black smoke reaching fleetingly into the sky before disappearing forever. Siegfried risked a look back, feeling a burst of heat on his face. And then the fire was gone, the hulking remains continuing to spew black smoke into a black sky. He hoped that the explosion had signified the end of the plane acting like a beacon for the enemy.

In the distance, Siegfried could hear dogs barking. They sounded close, but he had no idea how close. How could the search have been coordinated so quickly? Siegfried tried to calm his nerves, taking deep breaths as he hauled his captain along. No, the searchers were probably a long way away and the sound of the dogs had carried in the wind.

Siegfried knew that he couldn't be certain of any of that. He knew that his life was hanging by a thread. He had to find shelter soon; a place to give medical treatment to his captain. They had to find somewhere safe.

Joyce Fisher stood on the front step of the village hall, staring up at the sky. She thought she'd heard an explosion in the distance, far off in Frensham Fields. But it could have been soldiers on night manoeuvres. Esther came out to join her and they looked out into the night sky together. A chill wind was blowing gently, carrying a faint rainfall and Joyce felt her face getting slightly damp. It was oddly refreshing and she didn't immediately think about going back inside. Sometimes it was good to feel nature and enjoy a light rain against your face.

'We should be getting back to the farm,' Esther commented.

'I know,' Joyce replied. She and Dolores would have to be awake by six and out working by half-past. Late nights weren't something you could keep doing when you were a land girl, not unless you wanted to fall asleep on your shovel.

By the time they got back to Pasture Farm it was nearly ten o'clock. Joyce locked the back door. The light flickered slightly.

'Probably the rain,' Esther commented. 'I keep telling Fred that the junction box gets submerged when there's too much water.'

Joyce turned out the light and she and Esther trudged up the stairs to the bedrooms. Joyce could hear Dolores murmuring in her sleep and she wished Esther a hushed goodnight and went into her own room.

'See you in the morning,' Joyce whispered.

'I wish it was really the morning. It's still the middle of the night when we get up, isn't it?' Esther replied. They shared a smile as Joyce closed the door behind her.

She dropped her dress to the floor and carefully folded it over the back of the chair. Walking to the window, Joyce closed the curtains. Outside she could hear the plaintive cries of a fox somewhere in Gorley Wood. She got her washbag and sat on the bed, waiting for the sounds of Esther in the bathroom to fall silent before she ventured out to see if it was free.

Joyce stared at the dressing table. A dog-eared photograph of John was propped next to her rollers and hairbrush. Seeing his face warmed her heart and made her smile. She hoped he was resting and taking it easy and not having too many chores to do for Teddy. But more than that she hoped he would be back soon; back on the train.

She hoped he'd be back in time for Christmas.

Chapter 2

S even days to Christmas.

It was chilly in the fields with a winter frost covering the ploughed soil as Joyce, Connie, and Iris trudged out to repair a fallen fence; the earth cracking under their feet like frozen chocolate on ice cream. They competed to see who could produce the biggest bloom of cloudy air from their lungs until they all felt dizzy and had to stop. Iris wanted to find out who had the widest stride and started taking huge steps on her way to the field. Connie tried too. Joyce thought this was unfair as her legs were shorter than both the other women, but they joked and cajoled her into having a go.

'Well, make sure you're watching!'

'Go on, Joyce. See if you can beat Iris's record.'

'Yes, I managed to get all the way from that furrow to this one.'

'It was never that far.' Joyce suspected they were trying to put her off by fibbing. This was psychological warfare. 'You'd have to be on stilts to do that.'

'Excuse me. My legs are exactly like stilts.'

'Hush now, I've got to focus.'

Joyce concentrated as the other women watched expectantly. She lifted one foot and pushed it forward as far as it would go before planting it on the ground. At the last minute she realised she'd overstretched, and while Connie and Iris had managed to do the manoeuvre elegantly, Joyce lost her balance and fell over. Connie helped her to her feet, and they walked the remaining distance across the field giggling at the ridiculous competitions they invented. It was a way to pass the time; a way to have fun in these difficult times.

Reaching the fence, they started to sort the planks of wood and posts on the ground into a rough approximation of the fence they planned to build. Joyce counted out nails as Connie idly swung the mallet round like a gunslinger from a western.

'Here, do you think I could test your reflexes with this, Iris?'

'Not flaming likely. You'd break my leg.'

Iris and Connie dissolved into a fit of giggles.

'Will you two stop mucking about? I want to finish this job before Christmas day.' Joyce was grinning too as she placed the nails into different pockets ready for the assembly.

They had lived through five wartime Christmases and it was getting hard to remember the ones before. Or at least it was getting hard to remember them without them being painted as halcyon days when everything was perfect. But there was no denying that those pre-war Christmases had plenty of food and presents; they were times you didn't have to scrimp and save your rations for the big day; when turkeys and chickens hung in the butchers' windows and you could take your pick; times when you could put on a pair of stockings without having to think about faking them with an eyebrow pencil to draw the seams.

Each Christmas since had seemed to present more challenges. As people became adept at scouring the shops for sought-after rations, basic goods for Christmas became harder to source. You really did have to be an early bird. This year, like the ones before that she'd spent on the farm, Joyce had put aside some of the sixteen shillings she was paid by Finch since September. This nest egg, together with money from the other girls, could enable them to buy a decent ox heart or some beef cheek from the butchers – plus other food and drink for the Christmas period. But it wasn't always easy to save.

'Sorry I haven't put any into the pot for a few weeks,' Joyce looked apologetically to the others. 'Finch said there's been a delay in getting the wages from the government.'

'Ah there's always a delay.' Iris shook her head. 'But we're all in the same boat. Finch pays some of us one week, and the others the next. He's always catching up with himself.'

'I think he's betting it on the horses.' Connie offered a devilish smile. They laughed, but in reality they knew that the one thing Finch would never be dishonest about was their wages. He valued what they did on the farm and was happy that it didn't personally cost him anything to have them doing it.

They worked in silence for a few minutes, concentrating on excavating the holes for the fence posts. It was hard to dig down into the frosted soil; the clay underneath was solid and unyielding.

'Oh, I had a look for some dried fruit,' Joyce said, apropos of nothing. 'For the Christmas cake. We've got enough sugar put by for the icing, but there will be no point doing it without fruit in the middle.'

'If there's none around, my mum cuts up apple and puts in a few raisins.' Iris mimed the act of cutting an apple, just in case they didn't understand what she was saying.

'Where did we get it from last year?' Connie asked.

'Finch got it from Birmingham. Mind you, he had to wait forty minutes in the queue for it. Do you not remember all the swearing when he got back? Very festive!'

Connie laughed, shaking her head. 'I don't listen half the time.' She lodged a fence prop into the first hole.

'Very wise.' Iris held the base of the prop. 'Some of those words were an education.'

'So can we send him over to Birmingham this year?'

'There's no way he'll do it.' Joyce hammered in the post as Iris and Connie kicked in earth around the base. 'Is that vertical? It doesn't look very vertical.'

'Yes! It's vertical.' Connie squinted at the post. 'It looks wonky because your head's at an angle!'

Joyce smiled and straightened her neck and assessed her handiwork with a fresh perspective. The post stood proud and upright in the hole. She watched as the other women finished tamping the earth down around it.

'Maybe there will be dried fruit in the village?' Iris ventured; her open and childlike face full of hope.

'No, Mrs Gulliver and all those harpies will have snatched it all by now.' Connie frowned. 'Face facts, one of us will have to go to Birmingham at the weekend.'

'Sounds like you're not volunteering?' Joyce smiled.

'You're correct. I don't mind drawing lots though. Loser spends all day waiting in the queue.'

'Deal.' That sounded a good arrangement to Iris.

Joyce considered for a moment and nodded. 'Go on then.'

Connie scoured the ground for some twigs and found three of a similar size. She broke one of them, so it was shorter and bunched the three in her closed hand for the others to pick.

'Whoever gets the short one has to go.'

'Who goes first?' Iris asked.

'Shall I do it?' Joyce volunteered.

'Go on, Joycie, be lucky!' Connie proffered her hand with the sticks clenched in her fist. 'Or don't! Actually don't be lucky at all. I don't want to be lumbered!'

Joyce took a deep breath and pulled out a twig. To her relief, it wasn't the short one.

'Thank goodness for that.' She jumped up and down and taunted Connie and Iris with her twig.

'Look at her! It's like she's won a flaming Oscar!'

'Just you and me then, Connie.' Iris's face was taut with concentration.

'You and me, Iris.' Connie moved her closed hand towards the youngest Land Girl. Iris mumbled to herself as she looked at both the twigs. For her part, Joyce had no idea which was the shortest but she was just glad she was out of the running.

Iris cautiously plucked a twig from Connie's hand.

It was the short one.

Connie laughed and Iris's face fell in mock anger. Joyce suspected that Iris didn't really mind the prospect of a trip to Birmingham. It would be a chance to look in the shops. She could queue for the dried fruit and then perhaps stop for a cup of tea and a cake in Butler's Tea Rooms near the station off Stephenson Street.

Butler's Tea Rooms.

Joyce hadn't thought of that place in years.

Why had it popped back into her head now?

She'd only been there once herself back in November 1940, before she joined the Women's Land Army. And although the tea and cake had been lovely, that visit had turned out to be an unhappy experience. She thought back to that time. It had been the day before she discovered that her home in Coventry had been destroyed in the blitz of the city. So by rights, that afternoon in the tea room should have been the last time she'd been truly happy; unburdened by the effects of the war, unburdened by loss. But something else had happened in the tea room that had marred even that final sunny day.

She'd been away in Birmingham with John. Ostensibly it had been a business trip as John was scheduled to see a motorbike parts manufacturer for a discussion about supplying the Triumph factory where John worked in Coventry. But John and Joyce had used the opportunity to turn it into a mini-honeymoon – after all, they'd not managed to get away after their wedding. They'd stayed in a small hotel and John had gone to his meeting leaving Joyce alone. She'd looked at the wallpaper with its busy design of roses and vines, flicked through the bible on the bedside table and, bored of waiting, had decided she needed some air. Butler's Tea Rooms had been visible from her window and she'd seen a steady procession of well-dressed people amble inside for afternoon tea. Joyce decided to put on her best clothes and join them. Why shouldn't she live a little?

When she arrived at the tea rooms, Joyce was dressed in her smart dress – an eggshell blue frock with a white collar and a white belt blooming out to a full skirt. She sat at a table for four, her handbag occupying the seat next to her. She imagined she was a toff as she surveyed the smart and impressive establishment with its central atrium where a grand piano stood on the black and white tiled floor. Tables were arranged all around with a selection of large potted plants to add a splash of colour. For some reason the lower section was closed, so Joyce was seated on a table on the balcony that overlooked the atrium. All around her, other patrons sat around tables, chatting and smoking. On the plate in front of her was a business card for Butler's Tea Rooms. Joyce put it into her purse as a memento. And while a proper toff wouldn't have done that, Joyce didn't care. Then she perused the menu and ordered tea and a sponge cake. The elderly waiter explained in a low voice that would have conveyed the reverence of a funeral parlour that the cake was made with dried egg and honey due to rationing. Joyce had assumed that would be the case and said she didn't mind.

Joyce smiled at some people who were crammed in around a table nearby. She indicated the three free chairs at her own table, wondering if they would like to spread themselves out, but they were too busy chatting to notice her gesture. To her surprise, when Joyce turned back to her menu, a woman was already sitting down with her. The woman was catching her breath as if she had run from somewhere and had seemingly appeared out of thin air. She was a similar age to Joyce but stick-thin and glamorous despite her shorter hair and lack of makeup. She wore a simple black suit with trousers. On her shoulders sat a fur wrap, making her ensemble a curious mix of business and evening attire. Joyce noticed the worn cuffs on the woman's jacket and wondered if the woman was down on her luck.

'Hope you don't mind.' The woman had an accent that was hard to place. Was that a faint Manchester twang? 'Say if you mind and I'll move. But they didn't have any other tables, see?'

'I don't mind.' The truth was that Joyce would enjoy having someone sit with her. It would save her having to keep reading the menu to pass the time. 'I'm Joyce Fisher.'

'I know.' The woman stared straight into Joyce's eyes.

Joyce felt her mouth fall open in total shock.

'How could you——?'

'No, I'm joking,' the woman laughed. 'I'm always doing that. You should have seen your face!'

'Yes, well,' Joyce replied grumpily. She didn't enjoy practical jokes. She remembered when her brother-in-law, Charlie, had excitedly claimed that John had won a prize in the Mayor's raffle and made him get dressed up for a non-existent prize-giving ceremony. John had found it funny, but Joyce hadn't appreciated it.

'I'm Alice Ashley.' The woman extended a black-gloved hand across the table.

'I know,' Joyce countered half-heartedly, feeling slight irritation at this woman's manner. Hopes of passing the time with someone's company she might enjoy were diminishing.

Alice smiled back, amused at Joyce's comment and seemingly not noticing any weariness in her new companion's voice. Alice promptly collared the passing waiter and ordered a pot of tea.

'Why were you running?'

Alice looked perplexed for a moment as if she'd forgotten how she had arrived. 'Oh, it was raining.'

'Was it?' Joyce hadn't seen any rain on the windows and there had been no sign of drizzle on Alice's shoulders or hair. She contemplated picking up the menu again and shutting out her irritating guest.

'Sorry if I annoyed you.' Alice had obviously picked up on Joyce's mood. 'I'm always annoying people. I think I'll say something funny and it normally backfires on me. Sorry!'

'That's alright. I suppose we all need a laugh, don't we?'

'Yes, we do!' Alice grinned, lines appearing at the corners of her mouth. Their tea arrived and the waiter arranged the pots and cups and saucers for them. He nodded and glided off to another table. The chatter in the room provided a reassuring and convivial ambience, but it made Joyce acutely aware of her own lack of conversation.

'So, what do you do, Alice?' Joyce poured them both a cup of tea.

'I work on a production line. Hence the gloves.'

She pulled one of her long black velvet gloves off to reveal a set of stubby fingers adorned with sticking plasters and small cuts. 'I move around a lot, but at the moment I'm here in Birmingham. They move me where I'm needed. What about you, Joyce Fisher?'

Joyce did her best to hide her annoyance. She never liked it when people used full names when they didn't have to. It reminded her of being back at school.

'I work in a salon,' Joyce lied. She wasn't sure why she said it. Perhaps it was to make it sound grander than it was, when the reality was she did the hair of friends and neighbours in her mother's front room. Perhaps she felt a little embarrassed that Alice was doing proper war work and she wasn't.

'You never do!' Alice exclaimed.

Was she accusing her of lying or was she surprised?

'Yes, I do.' Joyce felt a little uncomfortable. Alice must have sensed that she had crossed the line again and endeavoured to put things right.

'Oh sorry, I wasn't saying you didn't. I just – well, I'm in need of a hairdresser.'

Joyce glanced up at the woman's hair and decided that what it needed was to be given a thorough wash. Black strands hung limply down from where they had escaped a carelessly affixed hairband.

'Well, if I had my things I could help you, but they're back in Coventry.'

'Coventry?' A frown crossed the woman's face.

'Yes, have you been?'

'No. It's just—' Alice seemed distracted, troubled even. And then it seemed she didn't want to talk at all. 'Sorry, I should be getting back to work.'

'Oh right, yes, of course.'

Alice stood up and downed the rest of the tea in her cup. She pulled her fur wrap close around her shoulders.

'It was nice to meet you Joyce Fisher.' Alice offered her gloved hand for a shake. Joyce obliged, rising slightly out of politeness.

'And you, Alice Ashley,' Joyce sat back down again and watched the thin woman snake her way around the tables towards the exit. What a curious woman.

It was only when Alice had gone that Joyce realised she hadn't left any money for her tea. The cheek of the woman! Had it been intentional? Some older businessmen, with shirt buttons straining because of too many expensive dinners inside them, were making their way into the café. Joyce realised that the establishment was gearing up for the evening crowd. She'd better go to meet John and find out how the meeting had gone.

Joyce called the waiter over.

'Can I pay please?'

The waiter nodded and totted up the total for two pots of tea and a slice of cake. Joyce pulled her handbag across onto her lap and opened it.

Her purse was missing.

Joyce felt her heart sink.

'Penny for them?'

Joyce was aware of Connie waving a work-gloved hand in front of her face. They were huddled around another new fence post and Joyce had been working without engaging in what she was doing; her mind firmly back in 1940. She batted Connie's hand away.

'Oh, I was just thinking back.'

'You don't want to do any thinking.' Connie looked horrified. 'Henry says I should read more books to make me think more. But I can't lose myself in a book like he can. I joked that we'd have to pulp all his books for the war effort.'

'I was remembering when I last went to Birmingham.'

'That's alright then. That sort of thinking's allowed.'

'The next day I went back to Coventry and saw what had happened.' Joyce looked lost in her memories.

Connie touched her friend's shoulder. 'I'm sorry. It can't get any easier thinking about that, can it?'

'Not really, no.'

'We should raise a glass to your mum and your sister, eh? At Christmas lunch. The least we can do.'

'That would be nice. Thank you.' Joyce still couldn't believe that her family had been wiped out in such a devastating way.

The women worked in silence for a bit. By lunchtime, half of the fence had been done and they trudged back to the farm for a sandwich and some hot soup.

The car hadn't moved in years. Three of the tyres were missing and the fourth was flat; its rubber caressing the contours of the woodland track underneath. Bindweed grew around the chassis, poking through the radiator grill like insistent green fingers. And even though one of the back doors was missing and the seats were mouldy with fungus, the car had provided somewhere for Emory Mayer and Siegfried Weber to snatch a few hours of sleep in relative shelter. The woodland around them was similarly overgrown and Siegfried doubted that anyone came out here often. He'd still slept lightly, half-listening for any sounds; the call of foxes in the night startling him at several points. Emory had been on the back seat, covered with a filthy blanket that they'd found in the boot of the car. From the seats in the front, Siegfried couldn't see if his captain had slept, but whether he had or not, Emory had stayed still for several hours. Similarly, Siegfried had tried to conserve his energy. His teeth had chattered throughout the night and he'd prayed for the sun to come up quickly.

Now it was seven in the morning and daylight was beginning to push back the winter darkness. Siegfried sat still in the driver's seat of the car, his circulation coming back to his cold fingers. Idly, he wished that he could drive the vehicle all the way back to Germany. He thought of the work he'd done early in the war; the blissful safety of the dairy farm in his hometown of Coswig on the bank of the Elbe. All he had to worry about then were the sores on his hands from the milking equipment and the barking voice of the farmer who would talk about meeting quotas at any opportunity. Such easy times!

Siegfried imagined that the fields beyond the woods would suit dairy farming. The terrain didn't look too different from Coswig and it was easy to imagine himself at home. Oh, how he wished he was at home.

Emory stirred in the back of the car, his mouth moving as if he was eating food. Siegfried glanced back as his captain's bleary eyes focussed and a look of resigned disappointment spread on his face; as if he'd forgotten where he had gone to sleep the night before. He winced at the discomfort in his right arm as reality came rushing back.

'Anything to report?' His voice was croaky and dry.

'I haven't seen a soul,' Siegfried shrugged. Now that he knew Emory wasn't sleeping, Siegfried allowed himself to stretch in his seat to ease the soreness in his back. He took the canvas bag from the passenger seat and removed a small metal canister. Unscrewing the top, he offered it to his commander to take the first drink. Emory took it and glugged down a big swig of water. He handed it back and Siegfried did the same.

'We need food,' Emory stated. 'And we need to find some clothes that don't stand out like our uniforms.'

Siegfried nodded. They were wearing their standard issue Luftwaffe uniforms. It was one of the first priorities to ditch such uniforms if a flyer found himself behind enemy lines.

Soon the men had got out of the car and were stretching their legs in the frosty early morning sun. Competing birdsong from the trees filled their ears. Siegfried took a pocket compass from his bag and passed it to Emory.

'Seems to be a rural area,' Siegfried offered.

'Less chance of them finding us. We should move mainly at night. We need to send a message. Get help.'

'Who will help us here?'

Siegfried found the notion that the British would help them absurd. Surely any British person would want to imprison or harm them?

'There are networks. People who sympathise with us.' Emory's attention was taken by a plume of smoke in the distance. A cottage, perhaps a mile away, was burning a fire.

'Isn't it too risky?' Siegfried followed his commander's gaze. 'We don't have an option. We'll steal what we can and get away. Ready?'.

Siegfried nodded and the two men set off across the field, the most direct route to the small cottage. Siegfried felt conspicuous in his uniform, but Emory was striding forward across the ploughed ground seemingly without such concerns.

Soon they had reached the perimeter of hawthorn hedge that surrounded the cottage. Within the perimeter, the grass was overgrown, and machinery parts were sprawled about. The cottage itself was a single storey building with a thatched roof and two windows and a green door that needed repainting. Emory and Siegfried crouched behind the hedge, watching for signs of movement.

The door opened and a burly, bald-headed man in a cable-knit sweater appeared. Siegfried didn't fancy their chances against him in a fair fight. But then he saw that Emory was gripping his service-issue knife. It wouldn't be a fair fight. Siegfried got his knife out too and gripped it tightly. The man from the cottage stood still for a moment, a plate of potato peelings in his hand. Had he spotted them? Then he arched his back and belched before moving across the garden. When he reached the end, he tipped the peelings into a compost heap and went back inside.

'What do you think?' Siegfried whispered.

'He would have clothes.'

They both knew it was risky to venture inside. What if the man was not alone? And even if he was alone and they over-powered him, Siegfried knew that the alarm would be raised, and people would be on their trail. No, they had to be careful and not leave a trail of destruction. Not unless they had no other option.

'He's growing something near the compost bin.' Emory pointed to where potatoes and cauliflower were growing. 'That would keep us going until we find something better.'

Siegfried nodded. He liked the idea of stealing a cauliflower more than the idea of facing that man in a fight. Emory indicated for Siegfried to move forwards. There was no gate, so Siegfried moved into the garden, keeping low and near to the house so that he couldn't be seen from the windows. Emory was keeping look out. Siegfried reached the edge of the cottage. There was no choice now. He had to go across about ten feet of open garden to reach the vegetable patch. Taking a deep breath and clutching his dagger, Siegfried ran in a crouch across the area. He reached the patch, not daring to look back. He scanned the food on offer and pulled up a cauliflower. Tucking it under his arm, he ran back to the comparative safety of the side of the cottage. He waited a moment, listening for any movement. When he was satisfied that no one was going to burst out of the door, Siegfried ran back to the perimeter opening. He ran through and Emory joined him in a sprint away from the cottage. When they reached the abandoned car, both men were out of breath and giddy with the excitement of their small victory.

Siegfried tossed the cauliflower to his commander, who used his knife to break it apart. They ate hungrily, crunching down the raw vegetable. Siegfried suspected he would get indigestion, but it was better than being hungry.

When they had finished, the men got back into the old car. They would wait until dusk before venturing out again. Siegfried gripped the knife and allowed a light sleep to take him. He could feel the cauliflower settling uneasily in his stomach. But it didn't matter. He knew they would both feel better for their meal. The men took turns to nap and keep watch. Siegfried was soon bored of looking at the cramped confines of the car and felt that he knew each inch of the dashboard and steering wheel; each rip on the musty leather seats. But eventually after the longest day in his life, dusk began to fall.

And when it did, Siegfried became aware of a tiny squeaking sound in the distance. It was too rhythmic to be a mouse. No, it was a bicycle. He roused the dozing Emory and they listened together. Someone was nearing the end of the lane. Quietly, Siegfried got out of the car. Emory followed, gripping his knife. The unseen rider's foot slipped off the pedal and Siegfried heard them spin without resistance. A moment later the rider had control of the bicycle again – and was getting closer and closer. There was no avoiding the inevitable confrontation. Siegfried picked up a small branch. It might be a better weapon to use at a distance.

And they waited.

A few minutes later a dark-haired woman with pale skin and deep brown eyes cycled into view. She was dressed in a crimson coat and had a magazine tucked under one arm. Abruptly, she stopped cycling when she saw the two men waiting.

A look of fear crossed the face of Connie Carter.

Chapter 3

Six days to Christmas.

When Joyce woke she was aware that it was later than it should be. The sun was higher than she expected, and the sky was a vibrant slate-blue colour that signified it was far beyond dawn. Usually when she awoke, it was as if the sky hadn't been coloured in for the day. There was no denying that she had overslept and, disorientated, she fumbled for her wristwatch from the bedside table and squinted to make out the time.

Nine o'clock.

Why hadn't Esther woken her?

Joyce swung her legs out of bed and padded over to the window. Pulling back the curtains, she could see the morning sun dappling the south field. The tractor stood parked in the distance, its rotavator blades raised skyward as if in silent prayer. There was no one working in the fields and an eerie quietness all around.

Joyce pulled her sweater over her head, walked out the room and made her way downstairs.

'Esther?' She shouted.

No answer.

Joyce reached the kitchen. It was silent and empty. A solitary plate sat on the farmhouse table with a single piece of buttered toast. The toast had a single bite mark. Next to it was a mug of tea, half-finished. Joyce ran her fingers against the mug and found it was still warm. Whoever had left it hadn't left it long ago.

'Esther?' Joyce asked the question more quietly this time, a sense of foreboding in her bones. There was something odd about this.

She reached the back door and opened it. The chill of the morning air wrapped round her bare legs and she pulled her nightie down as low as it would go. She slid her feet into her boots that were still on the step from last night.

'Martin?' Joyce called across the yard, as she squished her right boot up and down to bring it up at the back as she walked. The yard buildings stood silent, their stable doors open at the top, impenetrable black rectangles that refused to reveal their secrets even to the rising sun.

'Come on now!' Joyce shouted, turning round in the yard, looking for any sign of movement. 'Where is everyone?'

But there was no answer.

Joyce walked along the outside of the stables. She was always unnerved by their dark interiors and resolutely refused to look at them as she passed. She reached the entrance to the farm. The old tin postbox had some letters sticking out of it. The postman had been. And no one had collected it. That was odd.

Joyce took the small bundle of letters. One for Finch. A bill.

44

One for Esther. And one for herself. She placed the other two letters in the crook of her arm and tore open the letter addressed to her. She knew the writing. It was John. He must have sent it nearly as soon as he'd arrived in Leeds. How romantic! For the first time since she had woken up, she felt a smile returning to her face. She scanned the contents of the letter quickly. She would reread it at her leisure later, but for now she wanted to get the gist of it. Feel his words and hear his voice.

John wrote that he was already missing her. He said that he'd arrived in Leeds to find Teddy's house in a dreadful state. The plates and pots were unwashed and Teddy himself had been wearing the same clothes for longer than was decent. John gave allowances for Teddy's injury – he couldn't blame his brother for not being able to do those things – but it was a blessing that he'd arrived when he had so that he could sort things out for him. John recited a litany of the odd jobs he'd done since arriving and Joyce's eyes scanned the list, aiming to reread it later.

She was reading the rest of the letter, when a chicken burst out from behind the end stable, squawking loudly with a hysteria that spooked Joyce. She dropped the letters and fell backwards against the gate, catching her right wrist on the latch. She felt a stab of pain in her arm and noticed a cut to her wrist. Soon a rivulet of blood snaked its way down to her elbow.

'Damn and blast,' Joyce muttered. She scooped up the letters and raised her injured arm and ran as fast as she could back to the farmhouse.

Inside the farm kitchen, Joyce let cold water run over the

cut. Despite the amount of blood, it wasn't a deep cut and the water soon ran clear as the wound clotted. Joyce bound her wrist with the makeshift bandage of a tea towel and looked under the sink for Esther's first aid supplies.

Twenty-three minutes later, Joyce carefully picked up the hot kettle from the stove with her bandaged hand and poured the water into a tea pot. She was dressed in her Women's Land Army uniform of trousers, shirt and jumper, her boots laced securely on her feet. She stirred the pot, thinking about the mystery of the deserted farm. It had never been so silent in all the time she had been working here. The small farmhouse was normally alive with chatter and the odd argument, the sounds of Esther berating Finch for his slovenly behaviour. Where was Finch? Esther? Connie? Dolores? Frank?

Of course – Frank!

Joyce remembered that Frank Tucker, Finch's erstwhile game keeper, would be found only one and a half miles away at Shallow Brook Farm next door. The plan had been for him to take over with Iris and Martin while John was away.

Her brewing tea forgotten, Joyce got to her feet, marched across the yard, out the gate and made her way to Shallow Brook Farm.

When she got there, she was out of breath and the cold air was catching on the back of her throat.

'Frank?' Joyce called, her voice sounding croaky. 'Frank?' She tried again and this time her voice didn't fail her.

The darkened windows of the farmhouse resembled blank eyes covered with the cataracts of dirty net curtains. The place had an undercurrent of melancholy and despair about it, forgotten and unloved, unlike the picturesque Pasture Farm. Joyce tolerated being here when John was staying, but when he wasn't around, the sadness and silence of the place made her feel uneasy.

At first, Joyce thought that this farm too was empty and deserted. She called again for Frank, hearing the shrillness of nerves developing with each unanswered call.

'Frank?'

'Yeah?'

A reply came from a side-building and Frank Tucker ambled out, wiping oil from his hands on an old rag. He was a wiry man with thinning grey hair, eyes that didn't quite go in the same direction and a face that had a lived-in expression. But there was kindness in his craggy face and his hazel eyes burned with an unexpected intelligence. This was the man who had taught Iris Dawson to read and who had preferred negotiation to violence when he was goaded into a fight with Vernon Storey all those months ago.

Joyce composed herself. The truth was she had assumed she wouldn't get a response and she hadn't thought about what to say if she did.

'Where is everyone?' She managed.

Frank scratched his chin, inadvertently leaving a smudge of oil on it. His eyes looked serious, his face grave.

'Haven't you heard?'

'Heard what?'

Frank swallowed hard. Joyce had seen that type of expression before.

She guessed that he was about to tell her bad news.

There was a gnawing feeling in his belly that Siegfried Weber didn't like. He wasn't entirely sure if it was down to hunger or whether fear was driving his stomach into knots as well. Nervously his eyes scanned the woodland around him. He was cowering in a ditch, on a bed of the fallen leaves of autumn, his shirt getting wet from the cold ground. He gripped the dagger in his hand. The tape around the handle was fraying and Siegfried felt that it was slippery and hard to hold. He stared at the rabbit in front of him, tantalisingly twelve or so feet away to his left. He moved his free arm, using it to propel himself slowly and steadily across the ditch. Nearer and nearer to the rabbit. Siegfried paused, allowing the rabbit to sniff its surroundings. He didn't want to alert it to any danger and he didn't want to spook it. When the rabbit ducked its head, seemingly less concerned about any imminent threat, he decided that it would be prudent to move forward, edging ever closer, knife in hand.

He thought about Emory. His captain was hungry too and waiting for Siegfried to come good on the hunting skills he blithely promised that he had. He didn't want to let the older man down, and he wanted to keep his spirits buoyed, but the fact of the matter was that the only rabbit he'd ever got close to was the pet of the farmer at Coswig. And he'd never dared to hunt and catch that.

He pulled forward, feeling a twig snag in his shirt.

Anticipating that it might break off noisily if he continued, Siegfried reached slowly down and gently broke it off. The rabbit looked up again. How sharp their hearing was! Siegfried waited patiently for it to relax and after a few agonising moments it returned to sniffing the ground.

He edged slightly closer, scarcely daring to breathe. He was close enough to see the individual hairs on the rabbit's chest, the light shining in its big, brown eyes, its cheeks continually inflating and deflating as it sniffed the air. Siegfried brought his knife up on the rabbit's blind side. Then he realised that he needed to be a little bit closer to avoid making it a stretch when he brought the blade down. That would diminish his chances of landing a blow that stopped the creature in its tracks. Siegfried moved on his belly, his shirt sodden now from the damp. He stopped, motionless for a second. This was the moment of truth.

Siegfried whipped out his free hand to grasp the rabbit as he brought the knife hand down. But as his fingers connected with the rabbit's fur, it bolted for freedom. Siegfried brought the knife down, but plunged it uselessly into the mulch. His free hand managed to feel the pads of the rabbit's feet as it propelled itself into the shrubs and away.

Siegfried felt disappointment welling up inside him, his throat burning with the need to cry in frustration. He lay on the woodland floor for a few moments before finding the strength to pull himself up. He looked around as he pushed the knife back into his belt. He knew he couldn't go back empty-handed, but he couldn't rely on catching anything for dinner. And as his hunger and fatigue intensified, he knew that what paltry ability he had as a hunter would also diminish. He had to find food, and soon.

For now though, he had to improvise. As Siegfried ambled away, he looked for anything that might sustain him and Emory. As he reached the clearing of the woods, salvation arrived in the form of a dead crow near a tree root. Its feathers were sticking out at crazy angles as if a child had constructed it in nursery. Siegfried tapped it with his boot. There was no telling how long it had been dead, but he estimated it hadn't been long. He scooped up the body in his hands and wrapped it in the knapsack that hung around his neck. It would be another culinary delight after the raw cauliflower. But nevertheless, dinner would be served.

Hoxley Manor was a flurry of activity. Some American soldiers were parading on the front lawn, against the express instructions from Lady Hoxley. She tolerated the soldiers' presence and the fact that a large part of her house had been requisitioned by the War Office for use as a military hospital, but she appreciated it if they could keep as low a profile as possible. Parading on her front lawn, where any visitor could see them simply wasn't on.

Joyce rushed along the driveway, the shouted instructions from the army lieutenant to his men washing over her like the distant barking of a dog. She pushed past a nurse who was smoking a cigarette in the doorway and went into the hallway. It was cooler inside than out, but Joyce was hot from running.

She rushed past the grand staircase where Nancy Morrell

had first met Lord Hoxley two summers ago and made her way to the military hospital wing. Slowing to a brisk walk, and regaining her breath, Joyce passed bed after bed of injured servicemen, their bandages telling tales of their woes. Some of them called out to her, others moaned in pain. Joyce kept focussed and walked on. Reaching a room on its own, Joyce knocked on the door. The small room had once been Lord Hoxley's reading room, a circular space of curved bookshelves, a leather armchair and a view out onto the back terrace. Now it had a single bed squeezed into the space.

A single bed occupied by Connie Carter.

Joyce moved to her friend's bedside, feeling the heavy concerned looks from Esther, Finch, and Esther's son, Martin on her. They had all assembled some time earlier. Doctor Richard Channing glanced up from his clipboard where he was reviewing some observations on his patient. He was a distinguished man whose handsome face was tempered by an easy look of disdain that often crossed his features. Connie's husband, Henry Jameson was seated on the windowsill, looking gravely at the floor. He was the local vicar, a mild-mannered good-hearted man who would always worry about consequences. Whereas Connie would dive in and have fun, Henry was always pondering whether they should dive in and have fun.

'I'm sorry, I didn't know,' Joyce mumbled. 'I had no idea.'

Esther put a consoling hand on her shoulder.

Connie looked so pale making her smudged lipstick look even more vibrantly red, like a smear of jam across her face. Her eyelids were closed and her usually immaculately neat black hair was like a bird's nest. A white bandage was wrapped tidily around her forehead, making the unruly hair look like it was trying to escape from above and below.

'You weren't to know, lovey.' Esther removed her comforting hand from Joyce's shoulder and gently encouraged her to move closer.

'Can she hear us?' Joyce asked.

'Don't think so.' Finch looked downcast. 'At least she hasn't responded to anything I've said to her. Mind you, she doesn't respond to anything I say when she's awake.'

He offered a nervous chuckle, but no one felt like laughing.

'What happened?' Joyce stared at her friend.

Esther explained that Connie had rode her bicycle to Gorley Woods to deliver a magazine to one of Henry's parishioners. She was found on a dirt track, unconscious, her bicycle by her side.

'Did she fall off then?' Joyce asked.

No one volunteered an answer. Had they all asked the same question already? Doctor Channing shrugged, suggesting that he wasn't about to indulge in pure conjecture.

'She had a blow to the head. That's all we know.'

'Did she hit a branch on her bike? You know, going under a low tree or something?' Joyce could sense Henry shifting uncomfortably on his window ledge. All this talk about his wife was clearly getting to him. Maybe no one was worrying about how it had happened, just about whether Connie would ever wake up again.

'The blow was on the back of the head,' Channing remarked, his manner getting tetchy.

'So someone hit her?'

Channing shrugged. Joyce looked at the other faces for an answer. And if not an answer, she wanted to hear what their theories were. Surely, they wanted to know?

'She might have fallen off her bicycle and hit the back of her head when she went down,' Esther offered, filling the void when no one immediately volunteered an answer. Joyce guessed she said it more to shut her up than because she wanted to enter into a discussion.

Joyce wanted to ask more, but Henry's agitated shuffling stopped her broaching the subject. It could all wait until later when they were away from here. Joyce assumed that Henry felt uneasy not just because he loved Connie but because he may have felt guilty at sending her on the errand in the first place.

'The problem is also that she may have been there for some time,' Henry spoke, his voice wavering with emotion. 'In the cold, lying there.'

His voice broke and Henry squeezed the bridge of his nose to stop himself from crying. Finch patted him on the shoulder like someone petting an unfamiliar dog. The gesture seemed to help Henry pull himself together. Joyce guessed he didn't want to make a scene in front of these people.

'I suggest you all go back to the farm. Await news.' Doctor Channing surveyed their faces and then glanced down at Henry.

'Apart from you, Reverend. You can, of course, stay if you want to.' The offer conveyed the barest hint that Channing would be irked if the Reverend wanted to stay for too long, getting under his feet while there was important medical work to be done. Joyce knew that Channing preferred uncluttered wards. When she did her volunteer shifts, she would hear him lecturing nursing staff on the importance of minimalism in a hospital environment. And that minimalism extended to visitors. He viewed them with the same warmth that he viewed unemptied bins or clutter.

Henry nodded at the half-offer and stared forlornly at his wife, her face motionless, her eyes closed. Joyce dutifully filed out with Martin, Finch and Esther and they stood in shocked silence in the corridor for a few moments wondering what would happen to their friend. Joyce glanced back a final time as Channing shut the door on her. Connie looked so peaceful and at rest. The thought chilled Joyce. She tried to shake it out of her mind. She didn't want to see Connie at rest. Connie was never at rest. She wanted the mouthy, passionate, talking-ten-to-the-dozen, vibrant Connie back.

She wanted her friend to live.

The meat was tough and chewy and Siegfried worried that they hadn't cooked the bird enough. But it stopped the ferocious rumbling in his stomach for a moment, so that was good. It had taken him nearly an hour to pluck the thing and then Emory had rigged up a makeshift spit roast from twigs to suspend it above a small fire. Emory was grouchy. His arm was sore and blistering. He was cold and the shelter they had found – an old storage hut on the edge of an abandoned farm near Gorley Woods – wasn't a secure base for them to wait in. Emory feared they would be found eventually. He wanted to make contact with some sympathisers who might be able to help them escape this country and get back to Germany. Would it be easier to give up? But Siegfried didn't dare voice that opinion; especially when Emory was in such a bad mood.

Emory checked his luger pistol for what seemed like the hundredth time. Siegfried told him that it would have made his hunting easier to have had the gun. But Emory thought they couldn't attract attention to themselves by firing off rounds in the woods.

'What do we do?' Siegfried asked, chewing on a bit of gristle and trying to make it go down.

'*Kein Englisch sprechen!*' Emory snapped.

'We should speak English! And we should get rid of these clothes. We should try to fit in.'

'You are right. I do not think straight,' Emory sighed, wincing at the pain in his arm. 'We should go to find some clothes. Steal them off a washing line or something. Maybe go back to the cottage where that man was. His clothes would fit us.'

'It's too risky to go back somewhere we've been already.'

Emory nodded, conceding Siegfried's point. He got up and stamped out the remnants of the fire outside their hut.

'We'll find somewhere else with clothes,' Siegfried replied. He wanted to talk about the other thing. But he feared that any mention might antagonise his captain. But he knew that their future might depend on it. After all, they had already attracted attention to themselves.

'What do you think happened to the girl?' Siegfried asked.

Emory scowled at him. Siegfried had been right. He hadn't wanted to talk about that.

'Who knows?' Emory spat out a piece of gristle. 'Who cares?'

After an afternoon silently working the frozen earth of the North Field, Joyce submerged her numb hands in Esther's warm sink, her nerves unable to tell if it was hot or cold. Her fingers tingled in protest and Joyce could picture her mother warning her about the danger of chilblains, but it felt so good. After a moment, she pulled her hands out, steam coming off her fingers, the skin a lucid angry pink, and wiped them on a tea towel. Esther was busying herself with a stew. Finch was reading *The Helmstead Herald* at the table, unaware that his arms were pushing the cutlery of the carefully laid-out places into an untidy mess in the centre.

'It's got to be a mistake. No one would sell a pig that cheap.' Finch scrutinised the advert in the paper as if it was a rare Egyptian hieroglyph.

'Maybe it's only got three legs?' Esther smirked.

Finch shook his head, not registering the joke. Joyce assumed that his brain was busy navigating the fine line of whether this was a bargain or a scam. The man had a talent for that borne out of his own attempts to pull the wool over the eyes of the gullible bargain-seeker. It would irk him if someone else was doing the conning and he turned out to be the victim.

'It's got four legs and working snout, according to this.' Finch weighed up the advert and Esther added more seasoning to her cooking.

'Have you heard any more from the hospital?' Joyce asked.

'Nothing,' Esther shook her head.

'No,' Finch closed the newspaper.

'I guess there's no change then?'

'Maybe they're trying to get rid of it for Christmas?'

'What?' Esther was confused.

'The pig!' Finch was already back on his own topic of conversation. 'Here, I could take it to Leicester for Bea and Annie!'

'Don't go on about the flaming pig. Besides they won't want a pig turning up!' Esther snatched the newspaper from the table and put it on the draining board in the hope it might end the matter.

Despite her concern about Connie, Joyce couldn't help but laugh. Finch's hurt reaction, his face showing confusion at Esther's words, was a picture. Obviously, it seemed eminently reasonable to him to take a pig on a train as a gift. He grumbled and turned the page. Joyce sat down for the evening meal, rearranging the pile of cutlery into rudimentary place settings.

The three of them ate in silence aside from Finch returning unbidden to the topic of the bargain pig. By the end of the meal, Joyce would have been happy never to have heard another word about it. But then Finch said something that piqued her interest.

'Here, maybe I'll drive over there tomorrow and have a look at the pig. If I take the van, I could pop it in the back. It's only at a place called Hobson's Farm on the other side of Gorley Woods.'

'Gorley Woods?' Joyce's mind was racing.

'Yes, why?'

'Could I come with you?'

'Why would you want to do that?' Finch looked suspicious.

'Thought it might be useful to perhaps see where Connie came a cropper. Find out if there was any reason for it.'

''Ere do you think you're Agatha Christie, Joyce?'

'It's just nobody has had a chance to look at where it happened, have they?'

'All right.' Finch shrugged, 'As long as Esther can spare you for an hour that is.'

'I'll start an hour earlier,' Joyce ventured before Esther had time to voice an objection. But despite the appeasement, Esther still managed a scowl.

Henry Jameson was dimly aware of a low creaking noise, rhythmic and close. It took him a while to realise it came from his own chair as he rocked gently back and forth as he sat watching Connie's face. He'd been holding her hand for what seemed like ages, gently manipulating it with his fingers as if the sensation might bring Connie back to him.

He didn't know if she could hear him, but Henry spoke to her anyway. Mindful of the other patients outside their room and the lateness of the hour, he spoke quietly, barely more than a whisper. He gave prayers, made jokes and told Connie how much he loved her. Despite their differences, this unlikely couple had made their marriage work. Connie's headstrong and bawdy nature, against all odds, segued with Henry's sensible and empathetic traits. He assumed that Connie felt safe in the relationship, knowing that Henry would act as a steadying influence to her wilder traits. For his part, Connie's unpredictability was both liberating and infuriating. But she was the spark in his life.

He looked forlornly at his wife, unmoving except for the gentle rise and fall of her chest. What dreams was she having? Henry regretted the small argument they'd had. And it had all been about that blasted magazine. The thing that caused this.

'I don't have time to play postman!' Connie had shouted when Henry had suggested she take the magazine while he finished the evening work at the village hall.

'But it won't take long,' Henry had protested.

'But it will take long.'

'You don't have to stay with him for any length of time.'

'He's a chatterbox. I've waited hours for you to come back from your visits there!'

'Please, Connie,' Henry had pleaded. And his wife had conceded with a sparky flash of her deep brown eyes. All right, she'd do it, but he'd better make this up to her when they're both at home. Connie had taken the magazine and Henry had watched her ride off away from the village hall. That was the last time he'd seen her until finding her in a hospital bed.

What had happened in the time in-between?

Henry's thoughts were interrupted by the arrival of Doctor Channing. He gave a cursory knock on the doorframe and entered without waiting for permission. He seemed somewhat irked to see Henry sitting there.

'It may be best for you to get some rest.'

Henry didn't need it spelling out what Channing was

saying. He nodded and collected his coat and hat, before kissing his wife on the cheek and leaving. Channing watched him leave. Then he moved towards his patient, checking the clipboard at the end of her bed.

'What happened to you, Connie Carter?' Channing mumbled to himself.

He took her pulse, timing it against the small fob watch that dangled from his waistcoat. He made a note of the reading and then took a mercury thermometer from his pocket. He gave it a shake to zero it and was about to put it in Connie's mouth, when she opened her eyes with a start.

'Where am I?' She asked, pulling herself up.

'You're at Hoxley Manor. You had a bump on the head,' Channing tried to gently push her back onto the bed. 'It's important you rest.'

'No, you don't understand,' Connie's eyes were darting around the room. She clutched her head suddenly, an excruciating pain forcing her to squeeze her eyes tightly shut.

'Easy, it's all right.'

'No, they attacked me,' Connie broke off to wince in pain, her mouth open in silent anguish as if making a noise would hurt her further.

'Who? Who attacked you?'

Connie's brown eyes widened in fear.

'Who was it?'

'German airmen!' Connie forced the words out amid the pain. And with that, she collapsed back onto the bed, her hand lolling listlessly over the edge. Channing tried to gently rouse her and then he shouted for assistance.

'Nurse! I need some help here!'

He looked worried, but there was something in his eyes that indicated it might not be just concern for the well-being of his latest patient.

Chapter 4

Five days to Christmas.

Joyce was dimly aware of a clanging sound in the distance as it forced its way into her attention and woke her from her sleep. She fumbled for the alarm clock and stopped the clapper from vibrating against the bells. Sitting up in bed, she struggled to open her sleepy eyes. It was four o'clock in the morning.

She slid her legs out of bed and got dressed, being careful not to wake the rest of the house. Her eyelids felt heavy, her eyes scratchy and it was difficult to coordinate her fingers as she slipped her boots on. In lieu of having time to do anything with her hair, she tied a headscarf around it and bunched it tight at the back. Then she made her way to the kitchen on weary legs, yawning so widely that she feared her jaw might lock. She made a pot of tea, poured some and sipped at a mugful before it was neither steeped nor cool enough to drink. But she wanted to get some work done before Finch headed off on his pig chase.

Joyce pulled her long coat around her, clutched her tea in one hand and slipped the latch on the back door. She imagined John, still fast asleep on his brother's sofa. The thought warmed her more than the tea. As she went outside, her breath formed candyfloss in the air, and she felt the mug cooling in her hands. It was a bitter morning, icy with the promise of snow. There had been snow earlier in the month, but the wireless was issuing reports that indicated it wouldn't be a white Christmas. The ground and the sky seemed the same colour, slate grey but for the hint of a rising orange sun in the distance. But even that felt diminished this morning, burning without its usual confidence. Somewhere in the distance a fox let out an anguished cry.

Joyce made her way to the tool barn and collected a solid-handled shovel. After so long here, she knew it was the best shovel on the farm and she felt a curious mix of satisfaction and sadness at knowing this fact. A young woman ought to have more going on in her life than worrying about which farm tool was best, but as always, Joyce contented herself with the comforting caveat that there was a war on. This wasn't a normal time. Thousands of men and women were missing out on their twenties for the greater good – and any small victory was worth celebrating.

Joyce walked into the North Field, feeling its eerie stillness for the first time. Usually she entered its cavernous space with a group of women, chatting and laughing about the small victories of living on a farm in wartime. She'd never noticed the bleakness of it before, four sides of churned brown soil stretching to horizons of darkened trees. In the dawn light, Joyce spooked herself by imagining movement in the spindly trees, some of them holding on to the last of their autumn leaves. She put such thoughts out of her head, found the spot where she had been working yesterday and concentrated on the trench in front of her. Some of the row was a darker colour, the fine soil having been turned and broken up. Joyce pushed the shovel into the ground and heaved it out with a thick wedge of clay soil on it. She flipped it over as if it was a pancake and battered it down into the trench, breaking it up as best she could. With the exertion, Joyce let out a small sigh and managed to spook herself again. Did she imagine a twig snapping in the corner of the field?

She wedged her shovel into the ground and peered into the distance. The edge of the field was thirty or forty feet away and she couldn't make out the trunks of the trees clearly in the gloomy morning light. But did something glint?

'Hello?' Joyce asked, quietly, hoping that there wouldn't be an answer. No sound came back, and nothing moved. She realised that she had unwittingly tipped off that she suspected someone was there.

Joyce planted her spade in the ground and took a hesitant step towards the trees. Then, deciding it might be prudent to have a weapon, she went back for the spade and carried it with her to the edge of the field.

'Who's there?' Joyce shouted.

No reply.

Her eyes scanned the sparse foliage and the criss-crossing maze of branches for any movement. She didn't dare blink, fearful that she might miss something. After what seemed like an age, she decided that there was nothing there. She turned round to head back to her work – and found a man standing in front of her.

Joyce went to scream, but then realised it was only Finch.

'What are you doing, creeping up on me?' She fumed, letting out her pent-up feelings on the hapless farmer.

'Who's creeping? I wasn't creeping,' Finch protested.

'You gave me a start!'

'I only came to say I was heading off now, if you want to come.'

'All right.' Joyce's anger was subsiding into mild annoyance. Maybe she had stressed herself out. And as she stared at his bewildered face, she felt a little foolish for snapping at him. 'You can help me take the tools back and then we can head off.'

'Yes, sir.' Finch gave her a mock salute.

'That's the wrong hand.' Joyce smiled.

'Is it? Maybe I've been watching them do it from behind.'

'What are you talking about?'

Their voices trailed off as they walked away from the trees, collecting tools as they went. Their playful bickering continued to the gate of the field, and when they disappeared, Siegfried Weber felt it was safe to breathe again. He let out a lungful of air and looked around him. There was no one around. He moved along the edge of the field until he could see through the gate at the end.

In the distance was a farmhouse. The woman and the farmer were heading towards it. Siegfried waited for them to leave the area and then he waited a few moments more to be sure that they wouldn't come back. Deciding what to do, he disappeared back into the undergrowth and scurried back to report what he had seen to his captain.

By the time they drove to the edge of Gorley Woods, Joyce was regretting not having more to eat for breakfast. A gnawing hunger threatened to distract her from her task, as she tried to look for clues on the dirt track where Connie had been found.

'Are you sure this is the right spot?' Finch checked his pocket watch. He was keen to see a man about a pig and wasn't worried about disguising his impatience.

'Esther said it happened at the fork of the main track and the path that leads to the woods.' Joyce scanned the ground in an attempt to find a clue. She didn't know what she was looking for, but she knew that something hadn't been right about what had happened to Connie. She was hoping that something would leap out at her.

'There's nothing here, is there?'

'There might be something.' Joyce wasn't going to be rushed. She was determined not to give up before she'd started. A scuffed area of ground gave a possible place where Connie had fallen, but Joyce couldn't be certain. But then she saw something that piqued her interest. A section of branch, sturdy and broken, lay on the ground near the disturbed area. Joyce picked it up and examined it.

'Look.'

'It's a branch.' Finch smiled, pleased with himself.

'I know it's a branch. It might be what knocked Connie

off her bicycle. She might have hit it with enough force to break it off the tree.'

Along one edge was a section where the bark was missing, revealing the young beige wood beneath. Could it have been damaged when Connie whacked her head on it? The section looked slightly red. Could it be blood?

'We need to show this to a policeman.' Joyce decided that this is what Miss Marple would do. The police would know if it was blood.

'You'll have to go a long way.'

'What do you mean?'

'PC Thorne has been moved to Birmingham.'

'So who is running Helmstead Police Station?'

Even before Finch offered a shrug, Joyce knew that the answer was probably no one. Since conscription had taken most of the policemen, they had been left with one bobby to service three villages and two towns. And now it looked like he had gone to an area of greater need.

'Besides, even if he was here, he wouldn't have time to look at that. We know what happened. The poor girl was riding along and walloped her head on this.'

'But I think we should tell someone. It might be useful in treating her or something.'

'Tell Doctor Channing about it. Can we go now, then?' Finch shifted his weight from leg to leg like an impatient toddler.

'You go. I can walk back to the farm.'

'Are you sure? I mean, I thought you wanted to see this porker with me?'

'No, it's all right.' Joyce tucked the club-like section of

branch under her arm and watched Finch return to the van. He got in, shaking his head to himself as if he didn't understand women. Who wouldn't want to come to see a pig? Humming to himself, he started the engine and reversed the vehicle back onto the lane.

Joyce was about to set off when she saw the abandoned car under the canopy of trees. She walked towards it and peered in the window. There was no one inside, but she noticed a blanket on the back seat. Had someone been sleeping here? Behind her, she saw a patch of charred ground. Someone had been here, but she had no way of knowing how long ago. Joyce clasped the stick and moved back to the lane and set off for Hoxley Manor.

'They have chickens and a lot of land. And it's out of the way. I didn't see many people there.'

Siegfried outlined the results to Emory of his reconnaissance mission to the outskirts of Pasture Farm. The older man didn't look as pleased as the young man hoped he would. But in his head, he excused the reaction as being down to Emory's exhaustion and the pain he was feeling from his arm.

'Good work.' Emory chewed his lip as he considered what the younger man had said. The two men returned to the abandoned car, missing Joyce by less than ten minutes. They knew they had to move and find somewhere else. Siegfried checked that he had the water bottle and the matches safely stowed in his knapsack. Emory checked that the blanket on the back seat was pushed into the footwell. Siegfried used his boot to cover the evidence of the fire, scraping leaf mulch over the charred ground. And after checking that there was little evidence of them having been here, Emory pushed the luger gun back into his belt.

They would head to Pasture Farm.

At Hoxley Manor, Doctor Richard Channing winced at the cacophonous clatter as the trolley of fresh bedpans made its way around the ward near his office. He reached across his desk and pushed the door shut with his fingertips before returning to his paperwork. A small but insistent headache was forming in his sinuses and he pressed his fingers on the bridge of his nose as he worked. Out of the corner of his eye, he was aware of the door slowly opening. He assumed he hadn't shut it properly and idly reached across to give it a firmer push.

He was surprised to see Ellen Hoxley standing in the doorway. She was wearing a light blue woollen dress with a dark blue knitted shrug over her shoulders. A wry smile teased at the corners of her mouth.

'You forgot, didn't you?' Her tone was playful and light.

'Forgot what?' Richard matched her tone.

'The breakfast meeting.'

'You mean, breakfast?'

With a glance of her eyes, Ellen checked that no one was nearby in the corridor outside before replying. 'Yes, but if we bring paperwork to it, it looks like we're discussing hospital business and not merely enjoying ourselves.'

'Heaven forbid people think that.'

'Quite.' A slight coldness had crept into her voice and the

wry smile was replaced with questioning eyes. 'It's important that we set the right example. And even though people know that we are . . .' She chose her next word carefully to Richard's amusement, 'friends. We shouldn't flaunt that fact as if we were some lovestruck pair from the village.'

'No, of course, you're right. And I'm sorry to have missed our meeting.'

He'd hoped that the apology would return the playfulness to Ellen's eyes, but she looked concerned. Richard realised that he wasn't responsible and that her attention had been drawn by an open folder of case notes on the desk.

Connie Carter's file.

'That poor girl.' Ellen looked genuinely upset for her.

'Yes, we still don't know what happened. I think she probably hit a branch. Knocked her off her bicycle.'

'She didn't say anything?'

'No. She woke up briefly, but she seemed disorientated. Made no real sense, I'm afraid.'

Now it was Richard's turn to control the look in his eyes, conscious not to give anything away; conscious of not revealing that he knew more. Ellen didn't need to worry about what Connie had said. He was protecting Ellen. Yes, that was what he was doing. After a long moment, Ellen nodded sadly. Richard relaxed, knowing he'd got away with it. Lying just took conviction. If you had the confidence to carry it off, you could get away with anything.

She moved towards the door.

'I'll make some tea if you want some.'

'That would be nice, thank you.'

As Ellen left, Richard thought about Connie Carter. She hadn't regained consciousness, hadn't woken since that one time. The Reverend was still with her, praying and holding her hand, for all the good that would do. Richard knew that he had to be alert. Had he done the right thing in concealing what Connie had told him? Yes, it was for the best. He had to be ready. He looked at the telephone on his desk and wondered when it would ring. After a while, he decided that worrying about it wasn't going to help him, so he busied himself with writing up some case notes.

There was a soft knock on his door.

Ah, the tea.

'There's no need to knock . . .' Richard trailed off, before realising that it wasn't Ellen in the doorway but Joyce Fisher. She was dressed in her land girl uniform. Her hair was slightly askew, and the sheen of perspiration was shining on her forehead. She caught her breath as she started to speak.

'Sorry to bother you, Doctor Channing.'

'You're not doing a shift today, Joyce.'

'No, I'm here about Connie. I found something.'

Richard moved from behind his desk and stretched out a hand to gently close the door. Joyce registered it closing but didn't seem perturbed. Why should she?

'What have you found?' He asked, his eyes narrowing as he studied her face.

'This.' Joyce reached into her great coat and removed a length of branch. 'I think this is what knocked Connie off her bicycle. See, it's got some red colouration here, like blood?'

'Ah, yes, perhaps.'

72

'I thought it might be important.'

'I'm sure it might be. And maybe Connie can identify it when she wakes up?' Channing smirked.

Joyce bit her lip and her cheeks puffed out slightly in annoyance. 'Are you making fun of me, Doctor Channing?'

'Not at all. Sorry for making light of it. It does indeed help us piece together what happened.' He tried to appease her with his best warm smile.

Lying is easy as long as you do it with conviction.

'There's something else.'

'Oh?'

'At first I thought, she must have hit it hard because she broke it off the tree. But then as I walked over here, I was looking at it.'

'And?'

'And see the bit where it broke off from the tree? Well, that's all dried and old and dirty. So that made me think, it wasn't on the tree when Connie hit her head on it.'

'Quite possibly,' Channing nodded in a way that he hoped would convey that he was wrapping things up now.

'Don't you see what that means?' Joyce's eyes were glowing now, 'If this is her blood, then it means that she didn't hit her head on a branch. Someone hit her with the branch. And nearby was this old car. Like an abandoned vehicle. And I think someone has been sleeping in there.'

Channing nodded slowly as if he was thinking about what Joyce had said. But in reality, he was thinking about what he could say to make this irritating woman, this amateur Miss Marple, go away.

'I will keep this.' Channing tapped the stick. 'And see if I can contact PC Thorne. Is that all right?'

'Well, no. He's away. Finch told me he's gone away,' Joyce's brow furrowed and she turned towards the door, seemingly bent on another course of action. 'Maybe Lady Hoxley can do something?'

She reached to the desk to pick up the length of wood.

Channing put his hand over her wrist, stopping her.

She looked at him, confused, perhaps a little scared.

'I can do it.' Channing's smile was warm, but it didn't extend to his eyes. 'Now we'd better both get on with our jobs, don't you think?'

'Yes, all right.' Joyce backed down. Channing thought her voice sounded unsure, as if this wasn't a satisfactory solution. But he held her gaze until she moved towards the door.

'Thank you for bringing all this to my attention, Mrs Fisher.'

Fly away, Joyce. Fly away.

When she had gone, Channing looked at the length of broken branch in his hand. It was entirely possible that the end was stained with blood. Connie's blood. He opened the filing cabinet by his desk, pulled the bottom drawer out as far as it would go and placed the branch inside. Then he closed it as the door opened.

This time it was Ellen with a cup of tea. And this time, Channing managed a smile that shone in his eyes as well.

'Ah, just the ticket.' Channing took the cup.

Emory and Siegfried moved across the edge of Gorley Woods, sticking religiously to the hedgerows and avoiding the actual roads and lanes. They became aware of voices in the distance. Peering over a yew hedge, Emory could see three soldiers talking to a group of old women. The women were pointing in various directions, perhaps trying to tell the soldiers where they had seen evidence of the airmen. The soldiers themselves were old men, dressed in uniforms that didn't quite fit and which Siegfried didn't recognise. Emory said that they were in the Home Guard and that part of their job was to find airmen like themselves. He removed his pistol from the holster. Siegfried wasn't sure that they could win against three armed men when they only had one pistol and a knife.

'They are old.' Emory continued to watch through the hedge. Siegfried hoped that the soldiers and the women would disperse so that violence wouldn't be necessary. Emory seemed keen to engage the enemy, whereas Siegfried wished he was still back in Coswig and that the war could be finished and over with. One of the soldiers lit up a rolled-up cigarette and inhaled the smoke noisily as another one coughed in apparent sympathy.

After what seemed like an age, the soldiers began to move away. Siegfried heard one of the old women laugh and shout to one of the soldiers that she'd have an apple pie ready for him. The women moved away, talking excitedly amongst themselves about their encounter. Emory watched and waited to see what direction they would go in. Eventually after a bit of discussion, and one of the soldiers moaning about his leg, they set off in the direction that Emory and Siegfried had been heading. Emory relaxed and put his gun away. He sighed in relief. Siegfried wondered if he didn't want to fight either.

'They are heading towards the farm I saw.' Siegfried's eyes flashed with excitement.

'We'll have to find somewhere else for now. But our priority is to find clothes.'

He moved off along the hedgerow.

Siegfried wished their priority was to find something to eat. He didn't think he'd ever been this hungry. He followed his captain.

'I can't see a pig.' Esther looked out of the kitchen window. Joyce peered out alongside her. Finch was out in the yard, closing the rear door of the van. He straightened up and winced as his back locked. They could see his mouth moving with silent curses, but there was no sign of a pig in the back of the van.

'What's he got there?' Esther squinted.

Finch picked up a long stick that he'd had resting against the door of the van and moved towards the house. At first Joyce thought it was a walking stick, but then she realised it was a shotgun. It had an elegant, sleek, single silver barrel. A Purdey, embossed with engravings down its length.

By the time Joyce had seen all this, Esther was already moving quickly to the back door where she intercepted Finch.

'No, no, no!'

'What, what, what?' Finch looked affronted.

'I'm not having guns in the house. You keep them out there with the tools.'

'Ah,' Finch whined with annoyance and disappointment. 'I don't even know if it works.'

'Well, you'll not find out, testing it in here. You'll blow a hole in the Welsh dresser.'

'You worry too much.'

'And you don't worry enough.'

'Didn't you get the pig?' Joyce asked as Finch was beating a retreat to the yard.

'No, it was a bit of a runt.' He mimed the small size of the pig with his hands, unintentionally waving the shotgun around in the process.

'Stop that! Get out with it!' Esther chivvied him to the door.

'D'oh, anyone would think it was your house!' Finch went outside. Esther rolled her eyes at Joyce. Then Joyce watched as she went to the doorway and called for Dolores, Iris and Martin to come to the table.

Soon the five of them were sitting down to eat the rabbit stew that Esther had prepared. There was plenty of ribbing about Finch and his lame pig escapade, until he did his characteristic thing of bridling with anger at a quip too far. After a period of silence, conversation turned to Christmas. Finch thought that they should eat one of the chickens for the Christmas meal. Thinking about the Christmas meal made him wonder what Annie and Bea would cook for him in Leicester. He was due to leave soon.

'What was that dish that Annie always made?' Joyce knew that Esther would come up with something to wind up Finch.

'Oh, old shoe surprise? That was her signature dish, wasn't it?' Esther scratched her chin as if recalling the details. Finch shook his head in bad-tempered annoyance before she'd even finished the sentence. Everyone laughed. Except for Finch. Maybe he really was worrying about what he would get in Leicester . . .

As the laughter died down, conversation turned to the big celebration. Iris mentioned that she would go to Birmingham to get the dried fruit.

'Oh, good luck with that.' Esther speared her last piece of meat onto her fork.

'I might go with her.' Martin looked anxious.

Iris gave him a curious look.

'In case it's heavy?'

'I can still carry it if it's heavy, thank you very much!' Iris grinned.

Esther looked at her son's disappointed face. He was trying so hard to make an impression on young Iris. She suspected that Iris knew that he liked her and it warmed Esther's heart to see Iris throw Martin a warm smile.

'You can come if you like.'

'Yeah.' Martin nodded, as if he might consider it. 'I might do then.'

'It's nice we'll all be together, isn't it? Fred will be back from Leicester. My John will be home, all being well,' Joyce put her cutlery on her empty plate.

'I won't be here.'

They were so unused to hearing Dolores talk at mealtimes that it took a moment for everyone to register it was her. All eyes turned to where she was pushing her food around her plate, avoiding eye contact.

'What's that?' Esther fixed her eyes on Dolores.

'I won't be here for Christmas day. I asked Lady Hoxley for permission. I'm seeing my sister.'

'You've got a sister?' Joyce was surprised

'Yes.' Dolores sounded indignant. 'I must have mentioned her.' Then Dolores turned her attention to a boiled potato on her plate as if it was the most interesting thing in the world. Joyce rolled her eyes at Esther and Iris and they struggled not to burst out laughing. As if Dolores had mentioned anything about her private life! They'd been trying for ages to find out something – anything! – about her.

When the meal was finished, Joyce helped Esther wash up. As Joyce dried the dishes, she watched the rivulets of condensation that criss-crossed down the kitchen window.

'Martin's sweet on Iris, isn't he?' Joyce placed a dried plate on the counter.

'Yes, bless him. I hope they have a good time in Birmingham.'

'They'll have a whale of a time.'

Joyce hoped that John would be back in time. Yes, she had to hope. But if he wasn't then she would do her best to enjoy things no matter what. And like most things in Joyce's life, she was familiar with making the best out of a bad situation.

As she got ready for bed, Joyce pulled her bedroom curtains across and noticed that Finch was talking outside to the soldiers from the Home Guard. There were three of them, all old men she couldn't remember the names of, wearing uniforms and carrying a variety of salvaged and hand-me-down weapons. With the curtains closed, she didn't give them any further thought. As sleep drifted over her, she didn't make the connection that these men were searching for survivors from the German plane crash.

Chapter 5

Four days to Christmas.

Siegfried wasn't sure that he'd had a wink of sleep. They'd bedded down behind a tree tucked away on the edge of a country lane and it had been so cold that Siegfried was relieved to find that he was still alive in the morning. He jumped up and down and flexed his arms to shake out the cold from his limbs. Emory seemed to take things in his stride, rubbing his hands together to warm them up. Siegfried assumed he was conserving energy, which was the right thing to do. He wished that they could find some food soon. The hunger had gone from his stomach, replaced by a grim determination to keep going.

The airmen made their way along the lane, staying on the edges by the hedgerow. After a mile or so, they spotted another farmhouse on the horizon. Smoke was belching from its chimney. The homely Cotswold bricked property looked inviting and Siegfried was about to enter the gate when Emory pulled on his shoulder.

'Look, over there,' Emory whispered.

In the field to the rear of the building, Siegfried could see people working the land. There were perhaps twenty or so women wearing green and brown uniforms, their heads in scarves. Around them were a couple of men, who seemed to be smoking and shirking their duties.

'Too many people,' Emory decided. The airmen moved silently away into the countryside.

Alfred Barnes prided himself on being the best fertiliser salesman in the Midlands. He'd been doing it since 1937, well before the war started, and he'd amassed a sales record that made him the envy of everyone at Edgar Varish and Sons. He knew he was in line to be a manager soon. Mr Varish had promised that the position would be on the cards soon. Yes, soon. Supplying goods for farms meant that most farmers and small holders knew his name. They'd greet him and offer him a cup of tea. Most of them knew that he didn't partake of alcohol, so they'd stopped offering him a small tipple. That made things less awkward when he had to decline their offer. They also knew that he was no fan of blue humour. In fact, Alfred was happiest if they stuck to discussions about business while he was there.

He didn't much like how things had changed since the war started either. Now he had to liaise with the government department of agriculture to ensure that the fertiliser was distributed fairly and evenly, so that more farms could benefit from it during their difficult times.

Today he had the usual number of appointments, each marked on his clipboard. Only one had been ticked off. He knew this would be one of his last working days until after

Christmas, so Alfred wanted to ensure that he got everything done. He sighed when he realised that Frederick Finch at Pasture Farm was on the list. That man always tried to pull some trick on him. Whether it was fiddling the order so he got extra bags of fertiliser or whether it was setting up some poorly thought out practical joke, Finch was a pain. Alfred made a mental note to try to deal with that Esther Reeves woman. She was always sensible.

He steered his Albion CX6N lorry into the lane leading from Gorley Woods to Pasture Farm, when it spluttered and hiccupped in the road. It was a long vehicle with an awning covering the back and a powerful engine in the cab upfront. Grinding to a halt, Alfred found he couldn't start it again. Damn it. That was going to mess up his schedule. He mopped his brow with the blue and white spotted handkerchief, before cramming it back into his breast pocket. Alfred was known for his flamboyant handkerchiefs. He liked the colours but he also recognised that they could sometimes be a talking point with a customer; a way of breaking the ice. A way to lead to a new sale.

He got out of the cab and flipped open the bonnet. The engine was smoking. He didn't know anything about engines but he was sure they weren't supposed to smoke. Alfred waved his hands at it, like a maiden aunt in a Noel Coward play, until the smoke dispersed. A low hiss was coming from somewhere. Alfred noticed that the radiator of the engine was sizzling.

He looked around to work out which way to walk.

That's when he saw two men walking at the edge of the lane.

'I say! Could you chaps help me?' Alfred waved.

The men looked strangely startled. Then in horror, Alfred Barnes realised that their collars had German emblems on them and that one of them looked injured. These must be the airmen that everyone was looking for. Oh, that wasn't good news.

Alfred bolted to get to the cab of the truck.

Siegfried saw him first. He tapped his captain on the arm, and Emory saw the bookish little man running towards his truck. Emory reacted immediately, setting off as fast as he could to intercept him. Siegfried wanted to say something, perhaps to question whether this was a good idea. Would it be better to run away and hide? But the die was cast and he had no choice but to follow his captain's course of action.

'Stop!' Emory shouted, his thick German accent momentarily stopping the man in his tracks. But then the man found his senses, opened the door to the cab and climbed in. Frantically he tried to start the vehicle. Siegfried knew he couldn't get far, not least because the bonnet was up, obscuring any view from the driver's seat of the road. He'd have to drive blindly along the lane, hoping to put enough distance between himself and the Germans. But as it turned out, he wasn't going anywhere. The truck wouldn't start, the engine cranking over and over, like a coughing man. Slowing down, Emory realised he didn't have to rush. He pulled the man from his chair before he had a chance to close the door.

'Please, please, no!' The man squealed as he fell onto the rough tarmac of the lane. Emory unhooked his gun from his belt and pressed the barrel to the back of the man's neck.

'Who knows you're here?'

'What?' The man stammered, clearly terrified.

'Who knows you are here?' Emory repeated, pulling the man's collar to bring him up to his knees. The man threw a frightened expression to Siegfried and the young German tried to offer a smile of reassurance that everything would be all right if he cooperated. Just do as the captain asked. But the bookish man didn't seem to be comforted, perhaps viewing the smile as a cold indication of detachment.

'My company, they told me to come here. They know I'm here.' The man looked desperate. He was lying. Emory pressed him against the side of the vehicle and shook his head slowly, as if unsure what to do next. Siegfried wished that they had run when they'd had the chance. It was too late now.

Some days change your life forever and Siegfried knew that today was one of those days.

'I cannot let you go.' Emory looked serene, thoughtful as if untroubled by the consequences of the words he was uttering.

'Yes, you can. I won't say anything, I promise. I just want to get home, you know?'

'We are at war. I am the enemy. Of course, you will say something. Do you think I'm stupid?'

The man shook his head quickly. He licked his lips nervously, unnerved by the barrel of the pistol that was pointing at the base of his neck.

'Maybe we should just . . .' Siegfried trailed off, as Emory turned to him. There was ferocity and fear in the older man's eyes. This was all snowballing into a massive and difficult problem for him and he was running on raw adrenaline.

Siegfried didn't trust him enough for him not to lash out at him if he continued to question his actions.

'Just what?' Emory spat, perhaps knowing that whatever suggestion Siegfried was about to make wouldn't help.

'Why don't we give up?' Siegfried closed his eyes so that he didn't have to see the loathing and contempt in the older man's eyes. 'We're starving, we're not going to get away.'

'Yes, we'd look after you. In the camps. You wouldn't have to worry.'

'They will kill us.' Emory glowered at their hostage. 'We give up and they will shoot us like dogs.'

'No, we wouldn't. We'd lock you up, but we'd look after you until the war was over. The camps have food and they're nice.'

'You expect me to believe that?'

Siegfried had heard the tales of what happened to Germans who surrendered, and he was inclined to believe what the bookish man was saying. There were rules about warfare and what happened to prisoners. But he knew that Emory was coloured by his experiences in the Great War; his thoughts skewed by having fought this enemy twice. He feared that Emory believed the German propaganda tales about executions and torture.

'Take off your suit!'

The man looked confused. What was happening? It took Siegfried a moment to realise too. Of course! They needed clothes and this man's suit would roughly fit one or them.

'Take it off!'

'Yes, all right.'

Siegfried glanced into the cab of the truck and noticed that a boiler suit was scrunched in the footwell of the passenger seat. That would be useful.

'We could take that too.' Siegfried indicated his findings.

'Good.' Emory kept his eyes on the man. 'Get it.'

The bookish man removed his jacket, fumbled off his tie and unbuttoned his shirt. He was wearing a vest underneath and Siegfried could see the goosebumps on his arms appearing as the December air reached him. A small paunch extended from the bottom of the vest; his eyes wide with terror. The man looked a pitiful sight.

'You take what you want, I won't say anything.'

Emory ignored his words and collected up the clothing, draping it over his wounded arm. Siegfried noticed that he winced as he added each new item to the load. In his other hand, Emory kept the pistol trained on their prisoner.

The man pulled down his trousers, revealing his shaking hairless, white legs. He stumbled out of the bottom of the trousers and handed them to Emory. The older German handed the gun to Siegfried.

'Watch him.' Emory stripped off his own clothes. As he peeled off his shirt, Siegfried noticed that Emory shuddered as the fabric snagged on his wounded arm. Seeing it without the covering of a shirt, Siegfried could appreciate how painful it must be. The arm from the wrist to the shoulder muscle was badly burnt, the skin festooned with blisters and angry patches of red and purple. Even the prisoner looked concerned when he saw it.

'Have you got food?' Emory fastened the new shirt. 'Anything to eat?'

The man shook his head and then nodded as if remembering.

'Sandwiches. For my lunch. You can have them. They're salad but they're nice.'

'Get them.' Emory nodded encouragingly. Siegfried watched keenly as the man leaned into the cab and reached under the seat. He could make out a small metal lunch box there.

Alfred Barnes didn't know how he'd get out of this one. Coming face to face with the enemy was the last thing he thought would happen. He thought he'd bought himself some time by being compliant and handing over his clothes. And during that time, he'd tried to get his terrified brain to focus on the dilemma of how he was going to get out of here alive.

He knew that his pleas for them to leave and for him to say nothing weren't going to cut much mustard. These were desperate men. They were hungry, dirty, tired and scared. The older one looked like he was injured and he seemed unpredictable. Alfred knew he had to be especially careful of that one.

As he watched the German get dressed in his clothes, he pondered his options. Could he trust that they wouldn't hurt him? Maybe if he complied with everything they wanted, they would run off and let him go. They didn't want to be murderers, did they? Alfred knew that this was a massive gamble. These were desperate men and they'd already sneered at his idea about them letting him go. The young one had smiled in a cold way that Alfred assumed meant that that option wasn't on the cards.

Could he escape? The truck wasn't working, so he couldn't drive off. That meant that if he was going to escape, he'd have to run. He'd have to outrun them. And the young one might be faster than him. Also, they had a gun and could shoot him down before he got far. No, escape wasn't an option.

Could he fight them?

Again, the chances of success with this option seemed slim. There were two of them and they had a gun. Alfred knew he couldn't win. He also knew he was running out of time. The older German was pulling on his trousers and fastening them.

Alfred decided on a course of action. It was the only option that had a vague, slim chance of success. It was all he had – and it crystalized in his mind when the older German asked him about food.

'Have you got food?' the older German asked as he fastened the new shirt. 'Anything to eat?'

Alfred shook his head and then nodded as if remembering. He hoped the moment played like he was too upset to think straight and not that he had a plan.

'Sandwiches. For my lunch. You can have them. They're salad but they're nice.'

'Get them.'

Alfred could feel the young man's eyes burning into him as he leaned into the cab and reached under the seat. Alfred knew that there was a small metal box there. A first aid kit. He hoped that the men would see it and assume it was a lunch box.

Yes, that's what he hoped.

Alfred reached towards it.

And then his hand found the crowbar that he kept under the seat. It was used to open drums of fertiliser. But today, Alfred hoped that he could use it to catch the men off-balance, buying himself enough time to escape. He couldn't fight them, but he could lash out and run away in the confusion.

Alfred gripped the crowbar.

Emory tapped Siegfried on the shoulder and grabbed the pistol off him.

'Hurry up.' Emory was suspicious about how long it was taking the man to reach the lunch box. Siegfried knew it had barely been a few seconds since the man had got into the cab, but he sensed his captain's insecurity. Siegfried was caught off guard, distracted by these thoughts as the man lunged from the cab with a loud cry. Something heavy and metallic was swinging towards his head, and Siegfried only had seconds to bring his arm up and duck to avoid it contacting with his head. It glanced off his wrist, and Siegfried shouted in pain.

It was a crowbar!

As Siegfried fell, he caught a momentary look of confusion on the man's face. He realised that the man assumed that Siegfried would still be holding the pistol. He wasn't. That mistake would be catastrophic. Emory fired off a shot before the man could swing again and find the proper target. The bullet caught the man in the side of his flank, and he fell messily out of the cab, the crowbar clattering from his hand to the tarmac. Emory checked that Siegfried was all right. Siegfried nodded that he was fine and relatively unhurt, before Emory turned his attention back to the man. The man dragged himself to his feet and stumbled down the lane, gasping for air as he went. Siegfried looked sadly at the pitiful sight of the middle-aged man in his underwear. He was reminded of the rabbit escaping him in the woods, only this time their prey was badly injured and not going anywhere fast. The man fell over, dragged himself up, desperate. He was making murmuring, pleading noises. Emory moved towards him, the pistol in his hand.

'Can't we let him go?' Siegfried shook his wrist as the pain subsided.

The man scrambled away, clutching his side, a thin trail of red splattering in his wake. Emory seemed unsure what to do. Events had spiralled out of control. Siegfried looked into his captain's eyes.

'By the time he makes it to a town, we can have got away!'

Emory thought for a split second, before shaking his head. 'We can't risk it.'

He fired the pistol and it hit the bookish man in the back. The man collapsed in a heap on the lane. Emory and Siegfried composed themselves and made their way to the body. The man's glazed eyes stared up at them. Siegfried could hear his own heart beating, his pulse racing with adrenaline and fear. What had they done? Emory straightened his new tie and indicated the truck.

'We need to get him onto the truck.'

'What?'

'In the truck!'

Siegfried took a moment to snap out of his stupor. Then he cupped his hands under the man's armpits that were still warm and dragged him back towards the cab. Emory tucked his pistol into his trouser belt and scanned their surroundings for signs of possible danger. They reached the truck and Emory helped Siegfried hoist the body up into the driver's seat. They closed the cab door, trapping the body inside.

'Get the overalls,' Emory nodded towards the other side.

Siegfried moved round the front of the truck to the passenger side. He opened the door and, avoiding looking at the dead man in the driver's seat, took the overalls from the footwell. He peeled off his shirt and trousers, tossing them into the cab. Siegfried pulled on the overalls and zipped them up.

'Are you changed?'

'Yes!'

'Get away from the truck.' Emory opened the petrol cap on the side of the truck. Siegfried guessed that his captain would set fire to it; cover their tracks. Siegfried walked a safe distance in front of the truck as he watched it crackle with flames. Emory reached him as the tank exploded. Both men instinctively cowered before resuming their escape. The canvas top of the vehicle caught light like a paper lantern, the fireball reaching the front in a few seconds. Walking slowly backwards, Emory watched as the flames consumed the cab. Siegfried felt oddly comforted by the warmth of the fire on his face, but he chose to look away.

After a few moments, Siegfried noticed that Emory was walking away. He ran to keep up. The flames crackled and died behind them and by the time they had reached the fork in the road, the truck was a smouldering wreck.

'Finch will be on his way to Leicester by now.' Joyce glanced idly across to the window. 'He'll be at the station at least. Martin and Iris are spending lots of time together. They don't come back from Shallow Brook that often. And they're off to Birmingham together tomorrow.'

Joyce wished that Connie would gasp and say how surprised she was by this news. But Connie was prone in the hospital bed, unconscious. Lady Hoxley had told Joyce that she had only woken once briefly. Doctor Channing thought that was a good sign and hoped she would wake again soon.

Joyce continued her monologue.

'And Dolores is going to see her sister. Oh yes, you'll be surprised to learn that Miss Mysterious has a sister.' The smile dropped from her face as she continued: 'And my John looks like he'll be staying with his brother over Christmas. That's not what I wanted. So all in all, I need a bit of good news like you recovering, to cheer us all up. So come on.'

Connie's eyelids flickered. Joyce could barely believe it. It wasn't possible, was it? Had she imagined it? She looked closer and, sure enough, they flickered again. There was definite movement. This time she caught a glimpse of Connie's dark brown eyes underneath. It was true! Connie was waking up!

'Doctor Channing! Nurse!' Joyce moved towards the door, stumbling over her chair. Then hastily, she returned to Connie's side and held her friend's hand.

'Connie? It's me, Joyce. Come on!'

The eyes opened again and stayed open this time. Connie's eyes looked like they were trying to focus on the shapes around her. Trying to make out Joyce.

'What happened?' Connie's voice was weak and shaky, the words forming with difficulty in a mouth that hadn't spoken for ages. She looked confused; not recognising her surroundings.

'You're in the hospital at Hoxley Manor.'

A nurse entered and made a beeline for Connie. Joyce recognised her as she was one of the fully qualified medical staff who worked there. Joyce thought she might be called Antonia. She leaned in close to Connie and smiled at her.

'You're back with us. That's wonderful,' Antonia turned to Joyce. 'Keep an eye on her while I go to fetch Doctor Channing, would you?'

Joyce nodded as the nurse left the room.

'How are you feeling, Connie?'

Connie looked fearful, her eyes widening as if something scary was in the room with them. This unnerved Joyce and she hastily looked behind her to see what Connie was looking at. There was nothing there.

'What is it?'

'I was attacked. They hit me over the head.' Connie was piecing together her memories.

'I knew it! I found the piece of branch that hit you. I told Channing it hadn't broken off any tree.'

'What?' Connie couldn't process what Joyce was saying.

'Who was it? Who attacked you?'

Then Connie pursed her dry lips and sat up. 'They were Germans. Airmen. One was old, in his forties. The other was younger. I was cycling up to Gorley Woods.'

'Yes, that's where you were found.' Joyce held her friend's hand. 'What happened with these Germans?'

'I stopped to get my bearings, I think. I was out of puff.

You was always telling me I wasn't fit enough, weren't you?' Connie laughed, but it turned into a cough. Her throat wasn't used to talking, let alone laughing. Joyce poured a glass of water from a jug by the side of the bed and passed it to Connie who drank it down eagerly. Joyce took it from her shaky hands when she was finished.

'So you'd stopped on your bicycle?'

'Yes, and then I saw them. They were standing on the lane under the trees. One of them had a length of branch in his hand. The young one noticed me and looked shocked. Never mind him, I was shocked too, I can tell you. Next thing I knew they were running towards me. I tried to pull my bicycle round so I could ride away and then I felt a wallop on the back of my head. That's all I remember.'

'Oh Connie, that's awful. You must have been so scared.'

'I was terrified. Before they hit me, I tried to cycle away but my legs wouldn't go where I wanted them too. I couldn't steer the bicycle round in time.'

Joyce looked shocked by her friend's account of what had happened. She felt pleased though that she had told Channing about the length of branch and how it had been used. With this new information, he could inform the authorities. Yes, that's what she'd do, she'd tell Doctor Channing and he could tell the War Office about the rogue German airmen. Then they could all coordinate a thorough search for them and catch them before anyone else was injured.

There was a commotion by the door and Antonia returned with Doctor Channing in tow. The medic looked at his patient and gave a concerned smile.

'I'm back!' Connie mustered a little smile.

'It looks like you are.' Channing took her wrist and checked her pulse. 'Very good news.'

Joyce rose to her feet. 'When you've finished, could I have a word please, Doctor Channing? It's just that Connie knows who attacked her.'

Doctor Channing gave her a smile that said she'd have to wait. He attended to his patient, making Joyce wait in the corridor until he was finished. Joyce paced up and down and after about ten minutes, Channing emerged from the room. He seemed surprised that Joyce was still there. She thought he'd probably forgotten about her.

'Now, what did you want to tell me?'

As Joyce walked home it was starting to get dark and as night fell it brought with it a freezing mist. Joyce stumbled forward, the familiar path becoming ever more unfamiliar, as she struggled to see where she was going. As she crossed the North Field, she had to slow down to avoid twisting her ankle on any of the furrows they'd dug in the ground. Joyce could make out the dark skeletons of trees through the fog as she reached the gate and lifted the ice-cold latch. The fog was freezing and that wouldn't be good. She hoped that everyone had got to where they were going and that they weren't stranded on some railway station somewhere. Also, any search for those airmen would be hampered by it. She felt like she was being watched, but she put that down to paranoia; disquiet brought about by not being able to see what was around her; worry about the men who'd attacked

Connie still being out there. Yes, it was paranoia. That was all it was.

Joyce was relieved to find the back door of Pasture Farm. She let herself in and found Esther sitting at the kitchen table, nursing the remains of a cup of tea. She poured one from the pot for Joyce as she took her coat off and settled in. Joyce told her the good news about Connie waking up. And the bad news about her being attacked by German airmen.

'At least you've told Doctor Channing. He'll escalate the search now that they know they are looking for actual survivors. Before that the search was just a precaution.'

'Yes, I'm sure they'll find them.' Joyce enjoyed feeling the warmth of the teacup against her cold fingers. 'Even in this fog.'

'I wonder whether Connie will be out of hospital in time for the old folks' lunch.' Esther drained her cup.

'Even if she is, I doubt she'll be up to helping Henry.'

'Maybe we could invite her here? For the day?' Esther put her cup in the sink.

'That's a good idea. While I'm working, she could sit down and help you make the rabbit pie.' They had a tradition of having rabbit pie on Christmas morning every year and Esther liked to make it in advance so that the jelly in the crust was firm.

'I'll telephone Henry in the morning and tell him that the offer is there for her then.'

After finishing the tea, Joyce went upstairs to freshen up from the day. She returned downstairs with John's letter, intending to reread it at her leisure in the sitting room. Esther was already in there, reading a book and listening to the wireless.

'They're saying that the railways are all over the shop with this freezing fog.' Esther turned a page.

'That's not going to help John get back, is it?'

'Sorry, lovey. Have you heard any more from him?'

'He's still getting Teddy back on his feet. It'll take .time.' Joyce sat down and looked at the letter. Esther smiled warmly at her and returned to her book. Joyce looked at the words of her letter, each one warming her more than the fire in the grate. He was her soulmate and best friend, a man who had been through it all with her. She savoured each and every word, feeling her spirits lift. So what if he wasn't with her for Christmas? They were both doing their duty – him to his brother and her to the Women's Land Army. And soon they would be back together again.

There was an urgent knock at the back door.

Esther and Joyce shared a look. The rapping continued. Someone wanted them to come to the door. Cautiously, Esther rose from her armchair and moved across the room. Joyce frowned and followed, carefully placing her letter on the arm of the chair to return to in a minute.

Who could it be?

As they reached the kitchen, the knocking paused as if the person outside was aware that the door was about to be opened. The glass at the top of the door was frosted so all they could see was an outline of a man. Esther reached for the key that was in the lock – but Joyce put a hand on her forearm, stopping her. She shot the older woman an urgent look. Esther understood what it meant. There were German airmen on the loose after all. They had to be careful; really careful.

Joyce picked up the breadknife from the counter by the sink. It was too sharp for a breadknife, thanks to Finch's insistence in sharpening the blade using his grinder in the tool shed. She nodded to Esther that she was ready.

'Could you use that?' Esther glanced at the knife.

'Hope I won't have to.'

Their eyes darted towards the door. The shape moved to one side as if the man was trying to listen for any sounds of life from the kitchen.

'Who is it?' Joyce used as authoritarian voice as she could manage. The shape moved.

'Home Guard.' It was a man's voice from behind the glass.

Joyce and Esther glanced at each other. Both of them knew it could be a trick. Was there a faint hint of a German accent or was Joyce imagining it?

'How do we know that's true?'

'I'm Horace Winstanley. We see each other at church every Sunday, Mrs Reeves,' The shape moved behind the glass.

Knowing it was genuine, Esther relaxed and turned the key. Joyce put the breadknife back on the counter as they let Horace in. He carried the chill of the freezing fog around him. Horace was a wiry man in his mid-seventies with glasses and grey hair; a man whose baggy Home Guard uniform seemed to wear him rather than the other way around. Joyce was surprised that he was on his own.

'Would you like a cup of tea? It must be freezing out there.' Esther ushered him inside and closed the door on the cold night.

Horace removed his army cap and nodded hello at Joyce.

'I'm all right for tea, thank you Mrs Reeves. And I've got the rest of the men waiting at the gate for me. I came by to give you a progress report.' Horace seemingly chose those last two words carefully.

'Have you caught the two airmen?' Joyce glanced towards the yard.

'Two?' The old man looked curious.

'You know there are two, don't you?'

'No, I didn't know that, Mrs Fisher. That's interesting. How do you know that there are two Jerries out there?'

'My friend said she was attacked by them,' Joyce's mind was spinning. Why hadn't Doctor Channing told them? The stupid man must have forgotten. But how could he forget something so important? 'And she thought there were two of them. They attacked her near Gorley Woods, on the north side.'

'It seems you've got more of a progress report than I have, Mrs Fisher.' Horace removed a large white handkerchief from his pocket and blew his nose that was bright red from the cold.

'What did you come round to tell us then?' It was Esther's turn to look curious now.

'Just to say that we're calling off the search for tonight and that, well it seems silly now,' Horace's voice trailed off. 'But we were beginning to think that we'd call it off for good.'

'You mustn't!' Joyce was worried. 'You must keep looking. They're dangerous and they're out there.'

'Although I don't think they'll survive long in this cold

weather, unless they have shelter somewhere. And we've been asking all the farmers and everyone to check their outbuildings and barns and that.'

Horace pondered his next move as he scrunched up his handkerchief and put it back into his pocket. 'Looks like we'll resume the search in the morning then. Over by Gorley Woods.'

He nodded his goodbyes and moved towards the door. Esther let him out. 'Remember to lock up all the doors until we catch them.' He pulled his cap onto his head and disappeared into the night. Esther closed the door and locked it. She moved one of the kitchen chairs up against the handle.

'That should stop anyone coming in.'

Together, Esther and Joyce went round the farmhouse making sure every window and door was secure. Joyce contemplated taking the breadknife upstairs for protection, but she decided that the house would be secure enough. When they had finished, Joyce and Esther looked at each other, both suppressing the terror that they felt. Joyce felt that if she didn't voice her concerns and fears then they couldn't scare each other. Both of them noticed how quiet the farmhouse was.

Joyce knew she wouldn't sleep well that night. Instead she lay in bed comforted by thinking about her family; a time when they had all been together at the start of the war.

It had been a day of much excitement. A large German bomb had landed on the Triumph factory where John worked. The workers had been marshalled to safety by the army and Joyce had run down cobbled streets to check that John was safe. To her immense relief, he was fine and together, they had watched the bomb being loaded onto a lorry where a soldier sat next to it, listening for any change in sound. They said he was an expert and that he knew all the sounds a bomb could make. Joyce and John waited near the factory gates as the lorry and a motorbike outrider headed slowly off; crawling along the terraced street. Amazingly, the soldier was still lying next to the bomb, holding it as if it was the most precious thing in his life.

'They couldn't disconnect the detonator.' John was scared to speak too loudly in case it set the thing off.

'What's he listening for?'

'He's listening to the ticking of the bomb. He'll warn the driver to get clear if the ticking stops.'

Such heroism! They watched as the lorry edged its way over the brow of the hill. People began to join them, their conversations becoming more animated as if they'd all been holding their breath for the last ten minutes. Finally the lorry disappeared from sight and everyone seemed to breathe a sigh of relief.

Joyce and John walked back to her mother's house. She assumed their silence was due to the shock they were feeling, the relief and bewilderment of a lucky escape. If that huge bomb had gone off . . . it didn't bear thinking about. Joyce supposed it could have demolished the factories and half of the surrounding streets. She didn't resent the silence. For now, holding hands and feeling the warmth of each other's skin was enough. Conversation only resumed over dinner nearly an hour later. Owing to all the houses being evacuated for the bomb, Joyce's mother – Doris – hadn't had time to finish the meal, so they all sat down to a dinner of mashed potatoes, green beans and gravy. John complimented Doris on the meal. Joyce supposed he was trying to be nice and she loved him even more for that. He was always trying to make everyone feel better, and often he would be the main peacemaker in this little house with its crowded walls. They lived there not only with Joyce's mother, but with her sister and her husband too. It was a cosy arrangement! Her sister Gwen was often hard work to share a roof with and her husband Charlie was lazy but funny. Joyce loved them both. Charlie and Gwen were particularly vocal about the events of the day. Charlie claimed that he'd heard the bomb falling and that he'd raised the alarm to get everyone out. Silently John gave a small shake of his head to indicate to Joyce that this might be another of Charlie's exaggerations. Doris would mumble about it all being too much sometimes. She hated his tall stories and would remark to Joyce that she would say it straight to his face one day. But she never did.

Gwen worked at the factory as a secretary. She had heard that the factory would be closed and that alternative premises would be found for motorbike production. If the Luftwaffe knew the location of the factories, it would only be a matter of time before they came back to finish the job properly. And next time, everyone might not be so lucky.

Joyce and John held hands under the table. Where was the bomb now? And what happened to that brave soldier?

'I might go for a pint to celebrate not being blown to bits,' Charlie exclaimed, loading his fork with a large lump of gravy-soaked mash.

'We're supposed to be saving!' Gwen protested.

'But one pint won't hurt.' Charlie looked aggrieved.

'It wouldn't be one pint would it?'

'The trouble is, you don't trust me, do you?'

'Not when it concerns you counting how many pints is one!' Gwen gave him a rueful look.

John and Joyce smiled across the table at one another.

After the meal, the family played pontoon. Doris was cheating but blamed it on her poor memory about whose go it was. No one believed her, but no one like to say anything. They shared a pot of tea and listened to the wireless as they played. It was a nice, relaxing evening after the events of the day.

That night, in their room, John slipped off his braces and prepared to get into his pyjamas. Joyce applied cold cream to her face at the dressing table. Outside in the street, she could hear a woman and man laughing as they tumbled back from the pub. Someone down the road yelled at a yapping dog to shut up. In the room next door, she could hear the sounds of Charlie trying to persuade Gwen to have sex. She wasn't in the mood for it and he was grumbling. Their voices were muffled by the wall but still audible. It was a familiar argument that Joyce had inadvertently eavesdropped many times before.

'How are we going to get you pregnant if we never do it?' Charlie moaned.

'I don't want to get pregnant yet. I want us to be in our own place.'

'Make up your mind. You want a baby, you don't want one.'

'I don't want one until we're away.'

'Come on, it'll take nine months though even if we strike it lucky tonight, won't it?'

'We'll still be here then.'

'Shut up.'

'No, you shut up.'

There was what Joyce presumed was an awkward silence. Then she heard them both get into bed and the bedside light being turned off. There were no other noises and she assumed that Charlie was scowling in the dark about his lot. She turned to see John waiting in bed for her. His boyish face was smiling, relieved to be home, but even more relieved to be in their private corner of the house. But there was a weight around his eyes which she hadn't seen before. It wasn't the result of having completed four long shifts in a row, as he'd done that many times. It was something else.

'I was lucky today,' he whispered as Joyce neared the bed.

She nodded, knowing full well how relieved she'd been when she'd seen he was all right. He turned off the bedside lamp and Joyce slipped into bed next to him and pulled the eiderdown around the pair of them. John hugged her tightly, as if he didn't want to let her go. Joyce wondered if they would make love tonight. She enjoyed it even if it meant having to be quiet. Even though she recognised the double standard, she'd be mortified if Gwen and Charlie listened in on what they were doing. She kissed John, feeling his warm lips press against hers. But he didn't respond by kissing her more passionately. Instead, he stroked her hair away from her eyes as they looked at each other, their eyes glinting in the semi-darkness. This was their time, alone with each other; a silent corner of tranquillity in the hustle and bustle of the world's problems. She knew what was troubling him. She spoke softly in his ear.

'The war's getting closer, isn't it?'

And now, four years later, they were still living through it. She had been right. The war had got closer than she'd ever imagined. The brutal and extensive bombing of Coventry had left the city ablaze and had taken her mother, Gwen and Charlie. The raw desperate pain of the loss had faded, and Joyce felt a strange numbness as she thought about her family. Sometimes she had difficulty picturing their faces and had to concentrate. She wished she had a photograph. Joyce lay in her bed in Pasture Farm, listening to an owl hoot in the distance. She wished that John was back from Leeds. She wished they would be back together again. He was all that mattered now.

Chapter 6

Three days to Christmas.

Siegfried Weber hadn't slept properly but he found himself rousing from a strange, shallow half-sleep, cold and exhausted with a headache pounding in his temples. The overalls he'd taken from the bookish man's truck hadn't given much warmth. Emory and Siegfried slept in a ditch a mile from Pasture Farm. The road was very quiet and the chances of being spotted sleeping in the ditch were slim. The downside had been the inch of icy water in the well and Siegfried had had to arch and wedge his body on the side to avoid it soaking into his clothes. Emory seemed to have had a better night's sleep, supported by some rocks in his area of the ditch. But they had both woken in a bad mood; grouchy and uncommunicative. As Siegfried went off to see what food he could find, he felt relieved to be moving his legs and taking deep breaths. It was easier to be awake than trying to sleep; listening for every sound; nervous of every shadow. Siegfried jumped over a stile into a field. There was one ray of sunlight in all this. He felt less conspicuous in the boiler suit than his uniform.

The dead man's clothes.

He'd been haunted all night by thoughts of the bookish man, scrabbling desperately to escape, his body slumping down on the road. He had to think of other thoughts otherwise the images would upset and overwhelm him. He'd fought back tears as he didn't want Emory to hear him sobbing. It was strange. He'd never thought much about the bombs he'd dropped and the lives that had been lost on the raids. But seeing the grubby and messy death of a man right in front of him had been far more traumatic. Siegfried hoped he'd never have to watch someone die again.

Soon Siegfried came to the fields that bordered the farm. He moved quietly into the yard and reached the chicken coop and knew what he had to do.

After breakfast, as Joyce got her boots on, Esther and Joyce flipped a coin to see who would telephone Henry to invite Connie for the day. The shilling spun on its axis near the edge of the kitchen table before falling king side up. Esther won. She went off to make the call as Joyce headed outside. They had decided to flip a coin as there were two tasks that needed doing. Phoning Connie was the pleasant one. Joyce now had the less-pleasant task of catching one of the chickens. It wasn't something that she had ever done before. On the rare occasions when they'd eaten chicken, Finch had completed the gruesome task of catching and killing the bird. He knew that they shouldn't be eating chickens because of the loss of egg production, but he squared it with himself by only taking the poor layers. Mind you, if the War Office found out, he'd be in a lot of trouble.

Joyce watched her breath billow into clouds as she wrapped her coat tightly around her. The freezing fog of last night had given way to a clear, crisp day. Mist had settled in white blankets in the fields around the farm, but Joyce could still make out the smudged charcoal outlines of the trees on the perimeter. She moved across the yard and came to the chicken coop where the two eldest birds were kept.

To her surprise, the door to the cage was open and there were no birds inside. Maybe Finch had forgotten to close it properly? Joyce looked round. Perhaps a fox had got in? Maybe that fox she heard in the night had done this. But she would have expected to see feathers everywhere, the signs of a struggle amid the carnage.

Joyce turned round, looking for the chickens, but there was no sign of them. She headed towards the lower field to see if she could see anything around the side of the house.

Siegfried had a chicken in his arms; holding it tightly so it couldn't flap its wings again and make that godawful noise. He would have killed it in the coop, but he wasn't sure if that would make more noise. He walked quickly across the field, his boots finding potholes that were invisible thanks to the mist. His ankle had already wrenched in one and he was going carefully now – despite his speed. He knew he had to get away before the theft was spotted. He knew that he had a plan.

When he got to the stile at the end of the field, he clambered over, nearly losing a grip on the bird. Siegfried adjusted his hand to get a firmer grip as he jumped to the ground on the other side of the stile.

Behind, across the field, he could make out the shape of a woman. Was she wearing a Land Girls great coat? She was looking around, searching for the chickens. Siegfried only had one; the others had escaped and run round the back of the farmhouse. He didn't want to follow in case he was spotted.

He had a plan.

He knew that he was too hungry to think properly, and that Emory was in too much pain to think straight. So he felt that a hot meal would revive them both. They couldn't afford to make any more stupid mistakes.

Siegfried didn't want to kill any more people.

He knew that they didn't have long before that murder was discovered. Maybe the soldiers had already found the burnt-out truck and the body. His only hope was that they might assume the truck had caught fire and killed its driver in the blaze. He hoped they wouldn't see the blood further up the country lane that would give a lie to that idea.

He ducked low as he crept away, confident that the mist would obscure him from the girl in the field.

Lady Ellen Hoxley took a small bite from her piece of toast, dusted her lips with a serviette and laid the slice back on the china plate. She was distracted by the morning's post, a small bundle of different coloured letters sitting alongside *The Times*. The newspaper spoke of the latest reports from the fronts. She hoped that this infernal war might be over soon. Some recent victories had seemed to be decisive, but she didn't want to get her hopes up. Ellen picked up the letter knife and ran it along the fold of one of the items of post. It was a letter with a pink envelope.

An invitation to a garden party in Buckinghamshire from Lord and Lady Davenport. Ellen wrinkled her nose. She was under the misapprehension that Lord Davenport had died. She decided she might go if Richard could attend with her. She disliked going to social events on her own. And ones far away from home meant that she could be more open, within the limits of respectability, about her relationship with the dashing doctor.

Where was he?

Another breakfast that he'd missed. Ellen consoled herself that he was fully committed to his job. That was a blessing and she understood that all their jobs had to come first during these difficult times.

She scooped up another letter and ran her knife along it. A small brown envelope.

Ellen's mother had had a saying that no good news ever came from a brown envelope. And sure enough, this one yielded a bill to be paid: a piano tuner's invoice for the work he'd done a couple of weeks ago. It was cheaper than Ellen recalled it would be, so that was a small mercy.

She took another bite of toast before proceeding with the next letter. This one was a letter from her sister, Diana. Ellen flicked through densely written pages of handwritten emotional blackmail.

'If you could see yourself able to send . . .'

'As my sister, I'm sure you don't want to see me turfed out and . . .'

111

'A cheque for fifty pounds or so would make a massive . . .'

Ellen folded it up and sighed. She would read it later when she felt more awake.

She picked up the last letter.

Another small brown one. This one had a postmark from the War Office and Ellen had seen enough of this type of letter in her time. A telegram informing of the fate of a loved one.

No good news ever came in a brown letter.

Ellen wouldn't open it unless it was addressed to her. She flipped it over and looked to see whose name it had on the front. She knew it would be for one of the doctors or nurses that worked in the medical wing.

So it surprised her when she saw the name on the front.

It was addressed to Mrs Joyce Fisher.

Ellen realised that subconsciously she'd taken a deep breath. She didn't feel like eating the rest of her breakfast.

Connie found that she was too unsteady to perch on one leg while slipping her trousers on, so she sat on the bed and hitched them up one at a time. Even the effort of that left her head swimming. Tentatively, she touched the bandage that was wrapped around her head. She still had a headache, but at least she wasn't unconscious anymore. With the trousers finished, Connie scooped the tangle of her blouse up and set about finding the arms.

Through the green fabric screen around her bed, she could make out a blurred shape as if someone had left an indistinct charcoal outline of a man. It was Henry. She could tell this by the way he was bobbing around nervously.

'Are you alright?' He asked for what seemed the twentieth time.

'I'm fine. I'm not made of bone china, you know.'

'But you did have a tumble and you should be careful.'

'I am being careful. I'm putting my blouse on, not defusing a land mine!'

Henry laughed in that way that told her he found the joke funny on an intellectual level at least. He rarely laughed out of helpless spontaneity. Connie supposed it was his prim and proper nature curtailing any desire to let go and relax. Often, she would make it her unspoken mission to make him laugh. And it was always in the hope that she might one day find a genuine amused reaction from him. One day.

Connie finished doing up her blouse. She'd missed one of the buttons, so it didn't do up straight, but she felt too tired to restart. She smoothed the front panels down and got off the bed tentatively. She draped her great coat over her shoulders. Her legs felt like they weren't connected to the rest of her.

'What are you doing?' The voice asked from behind the screen.

'Standing up,' Connie replied.

'Let me help.' Henry's worried face poked itself around the corner of the curtain. Connie let him put his arm around her shoulder to give her support. She was grateful because she felt like her legs might give way otherwise. Henry collected up the small suitcase near the door. He'd placed all her toiletries and clothes inside, along with the large number of get-well cards that people had left for her.

She opened the door for them both and Henry edged her into the corridor.

A wheelchair was waiting. And Doctor Channing was waiting behind it. 'I thought this might make things easier. Just for a few days.'

'I ain't going in no chair.' Connie kicked up a fuss. But secretly she felt she had to make a protest before giving in. It's what they'd expect of her. Probably.

'Nonsense, it makes sense.' Henry ran his hand across the cushion of the chair as if to show how comfortable it was.

'Alright then.' Connie pulled a disgruntled expression as she let Henry and Channing guide her into the wheelchair. When she was sitting Henry put a hand down to scoop up the brake and pushed her along the corridor. Connie was grateful for the sit-down. Feeling as tired as this, she had no idea when she'd be able to go back to work in the fields.

'What are your plans?' Channing opened a door.

'Well, I've got to spend most of the day in the village hall today,' Henry pushed Connie through.

'Ah, preparing for the big lunch,' Channing smiled. 'And I hope you'll be taking it easy, Mrs Jameson?'

'Too right.'

'Connie's had an offer.' He looked at his wife. 'Esther telephoned earlier to invite you to Pasture Farm. They can look after you while I'm hosting the lunch.'

'Sounds a good solution.' Channing smiled.

Connie nodded. Yes, that would be good. It would be nice to see Joyce and the others, catch up on what had been happening.

They reached the end of the corridor to find Lady Ellen Hoxley standing in a dark blue coat with a matching bag. She looked deeply troubled.

'I missed breakfast again, didn't I?' Channing was perturbed. But she shook her head. She took him to one side, as Connie and Henry proceeded to make their way along the corridor. She waited for them to get out of earshot and then she showed him the telegram addressed to Joyce Fisher.

'How do I tell her?'

'Tell her what?'

'Tell her that her husband is dead.'

Chapter 7

Where had they gone?

Joyce tramped around the edge of the gardens surrounding the farmhouse, but there was no sign of the missing chickens. Could trekkers have taken them? They were the displaced victims who had lost their homes in German bombing raids. No, that would be unlikely. Trekkers weren't often seen in these parts, tending to stay closer to the big cities in the hope of casual work.

Another option was that someone else had snaffled them for their own Christmas dinner. That wouldn't be beyond the realms of possibility but who in the close-knit community of Helmstead might do such a thing?

Joyce reached the line of trees at the rear of the farmhouse. An empty coal bunker stood derelict and forlorn, its stained dark interior sucking the light in this corner of the garden. Joyce looked around. An eerie stillness permeated the morning air. She felt a sudden unease – as if her mind was finally succumbing to the one thought she was desperately trying to shut out.

What if the German airmen had taken them?

Joyce ran from the garden and burst into the kitchen of the farmhouse. She planned to tell Esther about the chickens and the lack of any signs of it being a fox that had taken them. But instead she was confronted by two sombre-faced women sitting at the kitchen table, turning to look anxiously as she entered. Esther was sharing a pot of tea with Lady Ellen Hoxley, resplendent in her blue suit. Esther had put out a plate of the oat biscuits she was saving for Christmas day. They were untouched. Joyce knew that something was badly wrong. But what? It must be something to do with the airmen . . .

They spotted Joyce and a look of sadness came her way.

What was it?

It must be something else, something more personal. Joyce heard herself saying, 'No, no, no, no' repeatedly, but the voice was in her head, an anxious internal monologue to ward off the awful, inevitable news that she sensed was coming.

'I'm afraid to tell you,' Lady Hoxley began.

'Sit down, lovey,' Esther offered.

'No, what is it?' Joyce asked, desperate to know.

No, this couldn't be happening.

There was only one thing in her life that meant anything. There was only one thing that this could be. And they were telling her to sit down. They were telling her to brace herself.

Even before Lady Hoxley said it, Joyce knew that John was dead.

She didn't register anything as she slumped to the floor against the kitchen cupboards, shaking her head in blind refusal. Tears came, but they felt like someone else's. Joyce saw the women's faces as they crouched over her, hands on her shoulders, their voices of concern distant and muffled.

She barely realised that they'd helped her to her feet and gently coaxed her towards a chair. A green-blue utility cup of light brown tea was clinked in front of her. Joyce watched the ripples in the tea. She tried to focus on what Lady Hoxley was saying, but she only caught fragments, as if her brain was trying to shut it out. She didn't want to hear the words. They wouldn't be true if she didn't hear them.

A house fire in Leeds.

John was asleep inside.

No, this was so unfair. He'd survived all the death-defying bombing missions when he was in the RAF. He'd survived getting shot down over enemy territory. He'd survived escaping occupied France. And after that trauma and the sleepless, desperate nights it had given Joyce, he'd been demobbed and found work at the neighbouring farm. He should have been safe!

A house fire.

It felt like the blackest and sickest joke Joyce had ever heard. She felt numb and empty as Esther showed out Lady Hoxley and then helped Joyce upstairs to her bedroom. Joyce sat on the bed, crying. She didn't feel the real pain that she knew would come later. At the moment, it was a shaken disbelief.

Yes, they must be wrong.

Maybe she could go to Leeds tomorrow and find out.

'It's unlikely you'd get a train so close to Christmas,' Esther looked consolingly, and Joyce realised that she'd been talking out loud. What else had she said? It didn't matter.

'If Fred was here, he might be able to drive you, at least some of the way. But you can go as soon as the trains are running again. In a few days, eh?'

Esther held her hand and asked her for what seemed like the hundredth time if she needed anything.

'Only John.'

'I know. And if I could do that for you, I would. You poor thing.'

Sometime later – Joyce wasn't sure whether it was minutes or hours – Esther left her and closed the door behind her as quietly as she could. Joyce sat on the bed, her eyes red and her heart torn apart. She realised that she was holding the telegram in her hand. How long had it been there?

We regret to inform you that John Fisher died in a house fire on the morning of twenty-first December. Stop.

And that was it – the bald statement that confirmed the end of his life. A kind, vibrant and funny man. The love of her life reduced to a few lines of typed text. Joyce saw him walking down Friday Street in Coventry with his sandwiches in his hand, turning his head back to smile at her. She remembered seeing him amid the crowd of workers at the factory on the day they found the unexploded bomb. She remembered the trip to Birmingham on business. She remembered so many times.

He was the rock that had always been there for her.

And now he was gone.

Some days change your life forever. Moments played out in the blink of an eye rewriting the path you're on.

Joyce registered the silence of the house. Was it night? Then she noticed the light still coming through the curtains. No, the silence was because it was just her and Esther in the house.

She stared at the words on the telegram, until they became meaningless letters. After a time, she folded the paper in half and put it in the bedside drawer. Other letters were kept in an old cigar box and the telegram sat on top of John's latest letter from a few days ago; a few inked words still visible. Joyce ran a finger over the letter and imagined him touching it. She closed the drawer.

Joyce got to her feet. Her legs felt unsteady, but she forced herself to head to the bathroom. She closed the door and looked at her red eyed face in the mirror. She felt so tired, so sick of this war with its random cruelties.

She splashed cold water on her face and dried herself with the small hand towel near the basin, feeling the coarse fabric against her skin. When she turned off the tap, she thought she heard movement downstairs. She pictured Esther in the hallway, looking up at the sounds of Joyce moving around.

Joyce knew what she had to do.

She had to keep going.

Joyce Fisher had always kept going, in spite of whatever life threw at her. She was a survivor, whose nature had been forged by the need to make sense of the awful things that were happening in the world. Joyce couldn't give up. Everything had to happen for a reason. When she'd lost her mother and sister in the bombing of Coventry, she'd clung to the war effort, in a desperate need to find something to make sense of it all. Joyce was fully aware of how she could sometimes sideline emotion and at least fake the image of the fighter with the stiff upper lip.

Inside she may be crumbling, but outside she looked – what was the word that everyone used? – Stoic. Joyce wasn't certain what it meant, but she assumed it referred to the steel in her heart.

Joyce looked in the mirror. Stoic. Strong but broken inside.

'I have to keep going.' She told the woman in the mirror. 'Mum would want me to keep going. Gwen would want me to keep going. And John . . .'

Her voice faltered. She soldiered on.

'I'm doing it for them until this war is over. Yes, that's what I'm doing.'

Joyce straightened up her pullover, pulled a stray lock of hair from her face and left the bathroom.

'There is hardly anyone there!' Siegfried was almost laughing. He didn't know why he was laughing. He didn't find it amusing. It was just that he had been so tired, scared and full of hysteria that his emotions were coming out as laughter. It had been the release of any response, even one that didn't fit the circumstances. He still felt foolish not being able to control it.

Emory frowned at him. He continued to tear meat off the chicken leg. Siegfried noticed that his commander's burnt arm was dangling at his side. He supposed that it hurt Emory to bend it too much, but he didn't know for sure as the older man rarely confided how he was feeling. The most he'd see would be a wince on Emory's face.

Siegfried persisted in outlining what he had found. 'I saw one woman. She nearly caught me taking the chicken. In fact, I'd have got both if it wasn't for her. She opened the farmhouse door and I heard her.' He laughed again. 'Sorry, I don't know what's wrong with me.'

'You're cracking up.' Emory glared at him with barely concealed contempt. 'You're feeling desperate.'

'Aren't you?' Siegfried struggled to stop his laughter. The more it felt inappropriate, the harder it was to curtail.

'I'm keeping a clear head. Eat more. It will stop you laughing like a fool.' Emory proffered the rest of the chicken. Despite their best efforts at cooking it, some of the meat was still pink. But the taste of the warm meat had revitalised him in a way that he couldn't have imagined. It was easier to think now, his thoughts less muddled. Even his movements felt more coordinated. He ripped off a wing from the carcass, inspected it for signs of being uncooked and then bit into it.

Emory seemed to wait for Siegfried to calm down before asking him to tell him more about the farmhouse he'd seen.

'So I saw one woman. But the others had gone.'

'There can't just be one woman there.'

'That's all I saw,' Siegfried insisted. 'It's the quietest one we've come across, I promise you. Not just in being out of the way, but in terms of having the fewest people.'

Emory brushed at a blob of chicken fat that had fallen on his business shirt. 'We have to be sure.'

'What choice do we have? They'll find us unless we find a safe place, won't they?'

Emory nodded. He knew that they were running out of

time. He stood up and brushed the detritus of the meal from his suit. Siegfried tossed the rest of the chicken carcass into the ditch by the road, stamping out the embers of the fire as he did so. The two men collected up their sparse belongings. Emory checked the pistol, and they headed off back to the farmhouse.

'I don't know if I'll go to the farm tomorrow,' Connie called up the stairs at the vicarage to where Henry was getting changed. She didn't wait for a response before continuing. 'I mean, you'd need me to help, wouldn't you?'

Henry appeared at the top of the stairs, adjusting his dog collar after having a wash. 'I'll be fine, honestly. There are so many people volunteering it'll be a problem finding them all something to do.'

'Couldn't I come to the hall and help out? I could be in charge of rationing out the roast potatoes.'

'You shouldn't be exerting yourself.' Henry brushed past her and went into the living room so he could check his appearance in the mirror. 'I think you should go to the farm. Joyce and Esther will be pleased of the company.'

'Alright then, if you insist.'

'They may even raise a glass to our lord,' Henry offered a cheeky grin.

There was a knock at the door.

Connie went out and opened it. Lady Hoxley was standing there in her blue suit, a sombre look on her face.

'Hello. I'm afraid something dreadful has happened to Joyce's husband.'

At Pasture Farm, Joyce watched the bowl of carrot soup go cold in front of her, a thick film forming on the surface. Esther was busying herself by the butler's sink, although Joyce knew that nothing needed doing, especially now it was the two of them. She knew the real reason was Esther's awkwardness about the situation and not knowing what to say. What could she say? Instead she kept it to normal, functional topics.

'You should eat something, lovey.'

Joyce shook her head. She was trying so hard to carry on, but the wind had been knocked out of her. The telephone rang in the parlour. Esther wiped her hands on her apron and headed off to answer it. Joyce could hear her voice as she spoke on the telephone, hushed tones, full of concern.

'She's not said much. I don't know whether she wants to talk or not, to be honest.'

Esther stopped talking, obviously listening as the person on the other end spoke. Then she continued. 'Poor love, I'll tell her. Bye, then.'

Joyce registered the clunk of the receiver hitting the cradle, followed by Esther's footsteps as she entered the kitchen. Joyce was vaguely aware that she returned more slowly than she had left. Was Esther in no rush because it was more bad news?

'Connie mentioned she'd come tomorrow to see you. She's so sorry and sends her love.' She squeezed her shoulder.

Joyce nodded. She was thinking about John getting on the train at Helmstead Station. He'd looked so dashing. That was the last time she'd seen him. She wished she could have stopped him going to Leeds. It all seemed so wrong, so meaningless.

Maybe he wasn't dead.

Maybe they'd made a mistake.

Yes, she'd go to Leeds as soon as the trains were running, and she'd find him. It would all be some dreadful mix up. She knew that it was hard to keep track of everyone in these times, and that mistakes were easily made. She remembered that woman in the village that Mrs Gulliver told her about. What was her name? It didn't matter. But anyway, that woman had got a telegram telling her that her son had died, and it turned out it had been wrong. Yes, they'd got it wrong then, hadn't they? After being distraught for two days she realised the name of the soldier had a different middle initial. It wasn't her son.

Joyce rode her train of thought, desperate that it might be true. The telegram didn't mention whether John's brother had died, did it? It didn't even give an address.

Esther registered the change in Joyce's face. There was a light in her eyes that hadn't been there earlier, and she was biting her lip as she concentrated on the possibilities.

'What is it, lovey?'

'There's been a mistake. There must have been.'

Esther nodded slowly. Joyce wondered if she didn't want to give too much credence, too much hope to her. But yes, she nodded. So that meant she must agree to some extent. That's what a nod meant.

'After Christmas, I'll go up there. Find out.' She crossed to the window and looked out. Magpies were swooping over the yard, keen to scoop up any remnants of grain.

'Yes, all right,' Esther nodded her consent.

The tone told Joyce that Esther didn't believe what she was saying. She was humouring her. But Joyce didn't care if Esther didn't fully buy into her idea. She knew it was a possibility, a slim possibility. And any vague glimmer of hope to get her through the next few days until she could get a train would be a good thing, surely? Joyce felt exhausted.

'I might go and have a nap.'

Esther nodded, scooping up the untouched bowl of soup from the placemat. She took it over to the stove and tipped the contents back into the pot. Waste not, want not. Esther washed up the bowl, throwing Joyce a warm, pitying smile as she left the room. Joyce supposed that Esther had dealt with the aftermath of telegrams like these many times in her role as warden.

Joyce resisted looking at the telegram a final time before sleep. She took her shoes off and rested on the eiderdown, feeling the rough hem of the fabric on her fingertips. Sleep came surprisingly quickly.

Chapter 8

It was early evening by the time that Joyce woke.

She felt groggy, her eyelids heavy and her mouth dry. A fingernail had snagged on a thread of the eiderdown. Carefully she extracted the cotton. Her nail had a rough groove in the end. She swung her legs out of bed and yawned. She padded out of her room over the landing to the bathroom. Inside she idly picked up the nail scissors from the bathroom cabinet and went to trim her nail.

There was the pounding of someone coming up the stairs quickly. Maybe it was Esther with some news! Yes, maybe they'd discovered the mistake and sent news while she was asleep. Joyce hurried out to the landing, the scissors still her hand. But it wasn't Esther that greeted her.

A young man in overalls was running towards her. His desperate eyes and dirty face were surrounded by matted blonde hair.

Who was he?

It didn't matter. He shouldn't be on the stairs and there was something threatening about him.

Instinctively, Joyce went to go back into the bathroom so

she could lock the door. But the man was too near. He blocked the way back with his hand, forcing her to take a step away from the bathroom door. Joyce brought the scissors up like a dagger and tried to ram them into his shoulder. He grabbed her hand, twisting it back so she dropped the makeshift weapon. The scissors clattered to the floor and the man kicked them away. He held her tightly, pushing her fingers back to force her to her knees. His eyes looked even more desperate now.

'I'm not going to hurt you!' He was shouting but his face looked scared. He was doing a good job of hurting her. 'You stupid woman!'

'Who are you? What do you want?'

'Calm down, calm down!' He gripped her. 'Please!'

She assumed it was a gesture of trust that he relaxed the pressure on her fingers. Joyce was slumped against the wall from where he'd forced her to kneel. She rubbed her fingers. Suddenly she thought she knew who this man was.

The hint of a German accent; cropped hair.

Oh no!

She had to get away.

'Now, we're going to go downstairs. Nice and slowly.' Beads of perspiration were dappling the man's brow. He took a step backwards to allow Joyce to stand up.

Slowly she got to her feet. She knew what she was about to do but hadn't had time to process whether it would be a wise course of action or not. That was best.

She made out that she was brushing herself down and composing herself, watching as the man took a step towards the top of the stairs. Then she seized her moment – and pushed him as hard as she could. The man lost his footing and seemed suspended in mid-air for a split second before tumbling backwards down the narrow staircase. He somersaulted halfway over before getting caught against the bannister. It broke his fall and stopped him reaching the bottom with the same momentum. Having fallen on his back, the man was momentarily stunned by what she'd done. Joyce didn't wait for him to regain his composure. She knew about the element of surprise and how important it was. She leapt down the stairs, jumping over him as quickly as she could. He tried to grab her leg, but she was too fast.

That would teach him to call her stupid.

Joyce reached the bottom of the stairs.

Where was Esther? She had to find Esther and they had to get away.

But as she turned to run into the kitchen, she found an older man, flecks of grey in his short military-style hair, pointing a Luger pistol at her. There was no doubting who these men were now. The German airmen.

'Stop or I will kill you.' His eyes were cold. Joyce knew that he wasn't messing about. She may have been reckless on the stairs, but she knew when she was beaten.

She could hear the younger man getting up and finding his footing. He reached them and grabbed Joyce's arms, pinning them behind her. It was an unnecessary gesture and Joyce assumed it was borne out of the anger he felt at being overcome. He let out an exasperated sigh as he rubbed his head.

'We are in charge and you will do what we say,' the older man eyed them with contempt. 'Understand?'

'Yes,' Joyce scowled, matching his look of contempt.

'You have fire in you. That will not end well for you.'

He nodded to his colleague to bring Joyce into the kitchen. The man in the overalls pushed her forwards into the kitchen. Esther was sitting at the table, her hands bound behind her, the rope passing through the slats of the farmhouse chair. She looked scared but smiled as reassuringly as she could to Joyce. The younger airman pushed Joyce into a chair at the other end of the table and started to bind her hands with a shirt from the airer.

'You lied to us. You told me no one was here.' The older German rounded on Esther.

'Why should I help you in any way?' Esther shook her head defiantly.

For now, the man in charge ignored this. He was interested in facts. He wanted military intelligence. 'Is there anyone else? I will not ask you again.'

'No.'

'If you lie again . . .' He pointed the gun at Esther's temple. She winced and closed her eyes.

'There's no one else.'

The man turned to Joyce. She shook her head. 'She's telling the truth. We're the only two here. Finch is away. It's his farm. Dolores is with her sister and Martin and Iris are at Shallow Brook—'

She trailed off.

'There's no one here,' Joyce finished, realising the words had a bleak finality. It was true. What were they going to do? They were on their own. She felt the shirt – one of Finch's – constrict

132

around her wrists as the younger man yanked it tight around the slats of the chair. Joyce tried to angle her wrists so that there would be some room when he knotted it; so she might be able to wiggle free later. But the younger man noticed what she was doing and forced her hands flat so that he could tie her up properly.

'They're looking for you.' Joyce stared the older man in the eyes. It was odd, but she didn't feel fear. Not in the way that Esther, who was trembling, did. Joyce supposed that too much had happened to her in the last few hours. She was operating on automatic; emotionally volatile with her feelings all over the place. And for now, that was stopping her feel any fear. Part of her enjoyed her defiance. These men wouldn't intimidate her.

'The old soldiers?' The older man smiled, 'Yes, we've seen them with their makeshift weapons.'

'Don't underestimate them. You won't get away, you know.'

'Joyce,' Esther's eyes were wide with terror. 'Don't provoke them.'

'Your friend is sensible.' The older man paused for effect. 'We will stay here until the old soldiers stop their search.'

Joyce's tired brain tried to process this information. What if they were still here at Christmas when Finch and the others came back? Would that be a good thing? No, they might hurt them. That might make things worse.

'We will stay until we can contact people.'

'What people?'

'People who can help us escape.'

Joyce had never thought about it before – but, of course, the

Germans would have some method of getting their stranded pilots back to the Fatherland, wouldn't they? In the same way that France had its evasion lines for getting British airmen home. She supposed that collaborators or Nazi agents hiding in plain sight might help them escape.

'Well, you'd better be quick about it, because we're expecting a house full of people for Christmas day.'

Joyce didn't know where that came from. She had a sense of bravado about her that she never thought possible. Was it fuelled by anger at what had happened to John? Was it because she didn't care what happened to her? She didn't know, but at the moment it felt good to stand up to these men. Her only concern was Esther. She knew she mustn't jeopardise her friend's safety.

'You're expecting people?' The older man paced around the kitchen, seemingly mulling over Joyce's words.

'Yes, they'll all be back soon.'

'Really?'

'Yes.'

'When?'

'I don't know. Depends on the trains and things.'

The Germans looked at each other, perhaps gauging the impact of this revelation on their plans. Joyce wondered if they were thinking of a new course of action. Maybe they would just go and find somewhere where they wouldn't be disturbed. She decided to push them to that course of action.

'They'll all be back tomorrow.'

'Shut up!' The older man raised his hand as if about to slap her. They were dangerous and she knew she had to be careful. Joyce winced and closed her eyes, but no blow came. The man lowered his hand. Esther shot a supportive look to her. Joyce's mind was racing as to how they might escape this dreadful situation.

There was no doubt about it that both men were willing to use violence. Having prisoners that were women meant nothing to them in that regard. They were obviously desperate if they were willing to act in such a way. They were dangerous, yes. And worse still they were unpredictable.

What had they said they wanted?

Somewhere to hide until they could contact people who could help them.

Joyce's mind filled with questions. How would they contact these people? How long would it take? What would happen to the pair of them in the meantime? Indeed, what would happen afterwards – would the men kill them as they left?

Was Esther similarly occupied? Joyce noticed a tear roll down Esther's cheek, her shoulders silently heaving as she was scared to make a sound. Joyce knew that it was down to her to fix things. She tried catching Esther's eyes to send another supportive smile, but Esther seemed to look straight through her; her mind perhaps frozen in terror. The men were looking out of the window and then the older one went out into the yard, leaving the younger one with the pistol. The younger one continued watching out of the window, sparing the occasional glance over to Joyce and Esther.

What were they up to?

Joyce felt strangely calm, numbed. This was an additional

nightmare on top of the one she was currently frantically denying in her head.

'Are you airmen?'

The younger man ignored her.

'I said are you airmen?'

'Yes. So?' The younger man turned momentarily from the window. Joyce didn't reply and the man went back to his vigil, waiting for his friend to return.

Joyce thought about these men – and men like them; the ones who dropped the bombs, causing families to be ripped apart. It was men like these that had torn Joyce's life apart at the start of the war. It was men like these that had destroyed her street in Coventry. She felt a knot of anger rising in her throat.

At the end of the alleyway, Joyce reached the main road. Its surface was glistening black thanks to a ruptured water main pumping across the tarmac. Joyce padded through it, passing a group of people who were watching a fire team put out a blaze in a wrecked factory. The people were huddled in cardigans and grief, their world destroyed and standing in the only clothes they possessed. One man held a painting in a frame. A woman held a tattered wedding dress over her forearm, pointlessly trying to keep it flat. People had taken what they could, the essentials, as they abandoned their homes. A little girl clutched her mother's hand, a small, blackened toy teddy bear under her arm.

As Joyce slowed to navigate the group, John took the opportunity to grab her arm. She stopped and turned towards him, her eyes glazed, looking at him as if he was a stranger.

'Maybe we should find someone first. Someone who knows what happened? An ARP warden or someone?'

'We're nearly there now.'

She had a mission.

'But we don't know what we'll find, Joyce.'

She gently but firmly moved her arm away from his hand and continued on her way. She guessed that John would want to stop her, protect her from what she might find. But she also knew he wouldn't stand in her way. She had to know, and she felt some reassurance that she could glimpse John following in her peripheral vision. He'd be there to support her, like he always was.

As her pace quickened, Joyce slalomed around two old men who were removing a mattress from a wrecked building, carrying as if it were a dead body. She reached an intersection in the road that was vaguely familiar, even though most of the houses were now rubble. As John caught up, she got her bearings, looking up and down, her breathing noisy, jittery with nerves and laboured from the brick dust in the air. It was Friday Street. She looked round to where she lived, bracing herself for whatever sight she saw. Time slowed to a snail's pace as her eyes focused on the street that had been home for all her life.

It had gone.

Some of Mrs Protheroe's side of the street was still standing, the house fronts like blackened movie flats from a *Keystone Kops* set, but Joyce's side was a pile of smoking rubble. A water pipe gushed in the rear of the property, flooding what was once the back yard.

For all their eagerness earlier, Joyce's legs wouldn't propel her forward any further. She was rooted to the spot, her eyes desperately trying to work out where the rooms were in the grey mound of wreckage. She felt something; a hand pressed on her shoulder. She looked up at John's face, etched with disbelief and anxiety. Joyce found the strength to move forward.

'Joyce.'

A warning from John not to go any further.

But Joyce had to know. She scurried across the ruins, glimpsing fragments of her life: a wrecked tin bath; an ornamental clock with its face smashed. Then she found a blue front door. She tried to navigate this alien landscape. Her throat was raw, and she was on the verge of tears as Joyce ran over the mounds of bricks. Joyce twisted her ankle on a metal pipe that was sticking out from some rubble, but she didn't stop. Something snagged her coat, ripping the lining from it. Nothing mattered. Her eyes scanned the ruins, desperately, hopefully.

And then she saw it.

The front of Gwen's radio.

It didn't mean anything. Things could still be all right, couldn't they? Joyce sank to her knees, her hands clawing furiously at the rubble. She felt a fingernail pop as she dug. She cut her hand on some glass. She felt John trying to pull her away. She batted him off, not finding the words to discourage him. Instead a guttural noise escaped her mouth. She was crying now but had no real feeling. John stood back and sobbed, watching the tragic sight of his wife digging at the rubble.

It may have been minutes. Or it may have been an hour when Joyce stopped trawling through the wreckage. She collapsed exhausted on the ground, her hands blackened and bloodied.

In front of her, sticking out of the detritus was a corner of a patterned fabric. It had been the dress her mother had been wearing.

Joyce's eyes were full of tears; a heat rising in her throat. The younger man turned from the window and moved towards her; his own face riddled with questions.

Joyce got a grip of herself. As he approached, she instinctively flexed and relaxed her wrists behind her, in an attempt to loosen the knot. Come on. If he was going to hurt her, she had to be ready to have a fighting chance.

'What is your name?' He rested his hands on the table.

It had been Siegfried's idea to come here. He'd told Emory that there weren't many people in this farmhouse. And when they'd got here, they'd spotted a woman through the window, at the sink. The older woman. At the time they'd mistakenly thought she might be the same woman who'd been out looking for the chickens. Emory and Siegfried had braced themselves before knocking on the farmhouse door. There had been a moment of silence in which they speculated whether the woman at the sink would answer the door, but then Siegfried had heard the key turn in the lock. An attractive woman in her forties, with brown curly hair in a bob looked at them, kind eyes and a pleasant complexion. She was wiping her hands on a tea towel. Siegfried didn't want to hurt her. The woman had looked at the two men – Emory in a suit, Siegfried in overalls and furrowed her brow. Did she think they were salesmen?

'Hello? Can I help you?' Curiosity mixed with a hint of suspicion.

'Inside.' Emory produced the gun from his trouser belt. Siegfried had wanted to stop him being so aggressive, but how could he control the man? And besides, Emory was his commanding officer. He couldn't say too much. The woman looked immediately terrified and backed obediently away.

Inside, Emory indicated for Siegfried to get her into a seat. They bundled her into the kitchen and Siegfried, as gently as he could, pushed her into a chair.

'Bind her.' Emory looked anxiously around.

As Siegfried went to work on tying Esther's hands, he whispered that they wouldn't hurt her. But the woman was sobbing and didn't seem to be capable of taking in what he was saying. She was looking at the man with the gun.

'Are you alone?' Emory scrutinised her face for any hint of a lie. Siegfried finished the knot.

'What?' Esther couldn't process his question.

'Are you here on your own?' Siegfried was being as kind as he dared, his tone reassuring. Esther nodded quickly, her breathing laboured. 'Just try to calm down. Yes?'

'So you are alone?' Emory didn't seem happy with her previous answer.

'Yes, there's no one here.'

'Find a first aid kit.' This had been high on their priorities. Siegfried knew that his commander needed medical attention for his arm.

'Do you have one?' Siegfried didn't know where to look. Esther stared at them as if they were speaking a foreign language that she didn't understand.

'Where is your first aid kit?' Emory was growing impatient.

'Under there,' Esther nodded towards a cupboard under the sink. Siegfried went to open the cupboard, when they heard something that stopped them in their tracks.

A sound on the landing upstairs.

Both men froze. Emory indicated that he would go to investigate, his pistol at the ready. Siegfried saw the fear in the captive woman's eyes and resolved to go instead. His captain was too eager to cause pain.

'I'll go.' Siegfried waved away Emory's attempt to give him the gun. It would be fine.

As he left the kitchen, he heard Emory snarling in a hushed whisper to their prisoner. 'You shouldn't have lied!'

Esther whimpered in fear. Siegfried slowly crept up the stairs, seemingly managing to find every creaky floorboard along the way. Giving up on stealth, he ran as fast as he could up the rest of the staircase, figuring that surprise would still be his advantage. A younger woman came out of the bathroom, seemingly to see what the noise was. She looked shocked, surprised.

Siegfried had tried to give her a look of reassurance, but she was scared. The woman tried to jab something sharp – nail scissors – into him.

And that's when he'd been forced to overpower her. Siegfried hated hurting anyone, especially a woman. But he thought of the excessive force that Emory might have used and salved his conscience as best as he could by doing the bare minimum to control her. When Joyce had knocked him down the stairs and tried to run away, Siegfried had been genuinely worried that if he didn't stop her, Emory would shoot her dead.

And now, here they were in the kitchen with two prisoners. Emory had gone outside to check the surrounding buildings while Siegfried watched the women. He was intrigued by the younger one. She seemed to possess a spirit that was stronger than the older one. And yet she had tears in her eyes for some reason, but they didn't seem to be borne out of fear. It was something else. He went over to ask her name. After all, if he was going to be here for a while, he had to know what to call them.

'I'm Joyce Fisher.' The younger woman scowled. 'She's called Esther Reeves. And you've ruined her Christmas. Mine was already ruined, so I don't care if you're here or not.'

'What are you talking about?'

Joyce didn't want to give him the satisfaction of explaining her situation. It was none of his business.

'Not going to tell me your name, then?'

'I am called Siegfried.' The young man shifted uneasily. 'My captain is called Emory. He needs medical treatment and we will make contact with our allies and then we will go. You should do all you can to help us.'

'Why's that then? Last time I looked we were at war with you.'

'You have a strange courage,' Siegfried didn't know how to deal with Joyce. Was she taking the bravado too far for her own good? Joyce was aware of Esther shooting warning looks from the other end of the table; keen to get Joyce to tone down the way she spoke to these men. But Joyce found it hard to reign herself in. She felt she had nothing to lose.

'But you would do well to hide it from my captain.'

Joyce was on the back foot now. She shook her head in confusion. Why?

'He is hurt, as I said. He is also far more capable of violence than I am. You would be wise to stop your mouth running away with you.'

The back door of the farmhouse opened, and Emory entered. He gave a cursory shake of his head towards the younger man as if to check that everything was alright.

'It is clear outside. It is just these two.'

'So treat your injuries, whatever they are; make contact with your people and get out of our lives.' As the words hit home, Joyce saw Siegfried offer a small grimace.

Perhaps she'd gone too far.

Emory strode over to her and yanked her head back by the hair. Joyce let out a gasp.

'You will speak when I ask you something. Not until then. Do you understand me?'

Joyce nodded.

Emory released his grip and smiled, perhaps enjoying his power over her. Joyce didn't like men like him.

'Now, you will help me with my injury.'

As if to back up this request, Siegfried produced the first aid kit from the cupboard and placed it on the kitchen table in front of Joyce. Now it was time for Joyce to test the skills she had learnt volunteering for shifts at Hoxley Manor.

'It's best if we do this in the bathroom.'

'You will not try any tricks. Otherwise the other woman will suffer. Do you understand?'

'I understand.' Joyce kept Emory's gaze.

Emory indicated for Siegfried to untie her and Joyce felt the shirt go limp around her wrists. She flexed her hands, getting the circulation back into them. Emory nodded for her to stand. Joyce moved away from the table, taking the first aid kit with her. Emory followed her up the cramped staircase.

The bathroom was cramped with both of them in it. She turned her head as Emory struggled to take off his shirt. It wasn't prudishness that made her look away, rather a desire not to engage in any sort of familiarity with this vile man. She could smell body odour and dampness. How long had he been sleeping rough? Joyce couldn't remember when she had seen the firefight in the sky that had brought their plane down, but she thought it had been several days ago.

He sat on the toilet seat and proffered his right arm towards her. The forearm was relatively unharmed, but from near the elbow joint the skin was peeling and blistered, turning brown and then black as it neared the shoulder. The bicep had a circle of shiny blood in the centre and Joyce supposed that it might be a puncture wound. She couldn't see anything sticking out of it, and mentally heard Doctor Channing saying that such a wound was a clean wound. It was difficult to know how much of the upper arm was dirt, skin stained with aviation oil or actual burn damage. Joyce knew that her first job would be to wash it to find out.

'This might hurt.' Joyce ran water into the sink.

'It had better not.' Emory's left hand held the pistol against his thigh, the barrel rubbing against the fabric of his trousers in agitation and nervousness.

'I will try my best. But I've got to clean this.'

Tentatively, Joyce soaked a flannel in the basin. Was it too hot? Too cold? She knew she had to get it the correct temperature. She ran some more cold into the sink, in case.

Joyce pressed the flannel against Emory's upper arm, avoiding the actual wound. He winced. He pushed the barrel of the gun hard against his leg.

'Sorry.'

Emory nodded, accepting that she hadn't applied undue pressure on purpose.

As carefully as she could, Joyce washed the arm, dabbing at the more damaged parts of the skin. She pressed the flannel near to the wound and Emory clenched his teeth to cope with the pain.

'I'm going to have to do that bit.'

'All right.'

As Joyce cleaned the biggest wound, the water in the basin tinged red as she squeezed out the flannel.

'How did you do it?'

'When we were shot down. The fuel. It got onto me as it caught fire. There was no way to get it off. I patted at it; tried

145

to put it out. But I couldn't really do it until I was on the ground.'

Joyce nodded. Now wasn't the time to tell him that her John had been in the RAF.

A rush of adrenaline turned her stomach. She couldn't wait until this was over so she could get to Leeds and find out that it had all been a mistake. Yes, that's what she had to focus on. She'd hold onto that thought and in the meantime, she would do all she could to get these airmen to leave Pasture Farm.

'How is it?' Emory asked. For the first time since she'd met him, she saw a hint of vulnerability in his eyes.

'Honest answer?'

Emory nodded, his face turning serious.

'It needed dressing sooner. I think it may be infected. See the redness here? It hurts you every time I touch it, doesn't it?'

'You must treat it.'

'I don't have the medicines.'

'Then you will find some alcohol or something and wash it with that!' Emory was breathing heavily. Joyce didn't know whether he was angry at the diagnosis or angry at her lack of medical supplies. Perhaps he was angry at everything.

'I'll have to go downstairs.'

'Hurry. And be quick.'

Joyce ran downstairs. Esther was still tied to her chair and Siegfried was standing near her. Both of them looked round at her sudden reappearance.

'I need some carrot whiskey. For the wound.'

'In there.' Esther nodded towards the cupboard under the stairs.

Joyce ran to it and flung the door open. A bottle of carrot whiskey was near the front, nestled next to a mop and bucket. Joyce went to take it, but then she spotted a small tin drum of cleaning fluid. She'd seen Finch use it to clean his tractor parts at the kitchen table before mealtimes, much to Esther's annoyance. It was dangerous stuff, and Finch, not the most safety conscious of men, always wore gloves.

But the cleaning fluid was orange.

The same colour as the carrot whiskey.

Joyce risked a glance back towards the kitchen.

'Have you found some?' Siegfried called.

'Just looking,' Joyce replied, playing for time. Could she tip some cleaning fluid into the whiskey bottle without them hearing? Could she then use it to overpower Emory and enable her to grab his gun?

Siegfried moved towards her.

No, no, no. There might not be time.

'I'll find it in a moment.' Joyce could glimpse Esther out of the corner of her eye. Esther looked terrified. It was one thing Joyce risking her own life. What did she have to lose? But it wasn't fair to risk Esther's.

Joyce took the bottle of carrot whiskey and closed the cupboard. She went back upstairs and cleaned Emory's wound as best as she could, before drying it on a clean towel. Then she dressed it using the gauze and bandages from the medical kit. She was shocked to see how much she needed to cover the area, but her patchwork of lint squares eventually did the job; a makeshift eiderdown of first aid. Joyce taped a bandage to the gauze, got Emory to lift his arm, and wrapped it round and round until it was secure. Emory was wincing in pain. It hurt him to raise his right arm. She'd remember that it hurt him. It might be useful.

Finally, Joyce finished with two large safety pins to keep everything in place.

'Better?' She asked.

Emory nodded, offering no concession of a smile. Joyce supposed she had done as he had asked, that's all. As far as this man was concerned, she was viewed as 'the enemy'. Joyce viewed him the same way. The boy had some compassion, but this man was like the Nazis in the public service films they saw in the screenings at Hoxley Manor.

Joyce handed Emory his shirt. She made a big thing of cleaning the sink and tidying up her supplies so she didn't have to help him on with it. He fastened the buttons, straining to get them across his belly. The shirt didn't fit him. Why didn't it fit?

Stolen clothes.

Of course! John had had to ditch his RAF uniform when he was in France. These men had done the same. But where had Emory and Siegfried's clothes come from? She hoped they were stolen from a washing line.

By the time, Joyce and Emory got downstairs, the kitchen window showed a grey-blue sky as evening started to fall. The frame of the window was etched in condensation. Joyce realised that Esther had been freed from her bindings and was heating up some soup. Siegfried sat at the table, looking exhausted and distant. Emory rummaged through the drawers in the Welsh Dresser and found some of Finch's cigars. Joyce knew that these were dated from before the war had started. She was never sure what special occasion Finch was saving them for . . .

He picked up Esther's matches and lit one, inhaling deeply. He coughed slightly but looked pleased, relaxed, as smoke filled the kitchen. He offered the box of cigars.

'Come on.' Emory billowed smoke, 'It's nearly Christmas Day.'

He seemed to find this amusing and coughed as he laughed. Joyce didn't feel like laughing. If they didn't leave, this looked like being the worst Christmas of her life.

Chapter 9

As the grey streaks in the sky slowly turned to black and people around the country thought about their preparations for Christmas day, Joyce helped Esther to wash up the soup bowls at the sink. They had been untied on the understanding that any resistance would be met with considerable force. Joyce had promised to behave, even though she wasn't sure if she could keep that promise. The two men had left them momentarily. Emory had locked the back door and taken the key in his trouser pocket. They were in the parlour and Joyce could hear their mumbled conversation but couldn't see what they were doing. They talked German when they were together. Every now and then, Siegfried would glance around the door to see what the women were doing.

Esther hadn't spoken since they'd been alone. She seemed transfixed by scrubbing at the bowl in her hand, a repetitive and perhaps reassuring action. Joyce took the bowl from her, smiled and dried it.

'We'll get through this,' Joyce whispered.

Esther nodded, but it was obvious she didn't believe her.

'We've got through so much before,' Joyce added.

'How can you be like this?' Esther voice was cracking. 'What with getting the telegram and everything? I should be the one pulling you – pulling you through it. Not the other way around.'

'I don't know.'

Joyce placed the bowl on the counter. She didn't feel anything. Not yet. Maybe it was all on hold and the dam would break later. For now, she wouldn't give those men the satisfaction of seeing her vulnerability. It would all be under lock and key until they were gone. They didn't deserve to see her thinking about the fate of her beloved John. But did she believe they could get through this?

The farm had never seemed such a remote place and they had never seemed so alone.

But they wouldn't be alone!

Connie was coming tomorrow.

The thought panicked Joyce. They couldn't let her come here.

'We've got to warn Connie.'

'Oh my god, yes.' Esther's eyes darted around as she thought of a solution.

Joyce knew that the last thing Connie would want was to be confronted by the men who had left her in hospital. But how could they warn her? They couldn't get to the telephone and it was doubtful that one of them could run the length of the yard to the gate without being shot in the back.

'What are you women talking about?' Siegfried ambled into the kitchen, breaking up Joyce's thoughts.

'Nothing,' Esther looked up.

'What are you doing in there?' Joyce indicated the parlour.

'What did my commander say about asking questions?'

'It's just I might be able to help.' Joyce looked him straight in the eye. Siegfried shifted uneasily. Joyce enjoyed that she could cause this reaction. After a moment's thought and a quick glance back towards the parlour, Siegfried spoke.

'We are converting the radio to transmit. We need some other components.'

'Like what?'

'You want to help us?' Suspicion tinged his voice.

Joyce nodded. 'Sooner you transmit, sooner you get out of our house. Why wouldn't I want to help?' She was surprised at herself now. She suspected that such an attitude would have earned her punishment from the older man, like before, but the younger one seemed kinder. Could he be their key to ending this nightmare?

Siegfried left the room. Joyce heard the men speaking in German, presumably discussing her offer. Emory raised his voice; he didn't seem happy at his junior officer taking advice. After a moment, both of them came back. Emory's shirt sleeves were rolled up and he had a piece of electrical wire in his hand. He mopped the perspiration from his brow with the back of his left hand. Joyce noted that he was keeping his right hand lowly slung. It was clearly still hurting him.

'You will get us the things we need?'

'If we've got them, yes. Finch has got all sorts of junk out in his shed.'

'Finch?'

'The man who runs this place.' She'd mentioned his name before, but they hadn't remembered. Why should they?

The Germans conferred with each other, both raising their voices. After a moment they came back with their plan of action. 'We shoot her if you betray us.' Emory crossed towards the sink and pushed Esther into a chair. She gasped in shock as she sank into it, narrowly avoiding crashing to the floor.

Joyce nodded. 'I'll take you to the shed.'

Seeing the fear in Esther's eyes made her realise the severity of the situation. She decided to be obedient and non-confrontational, for now.

Emory gave the pistol to Siegfried and told him to watch Esther. If he wasn't back in twenty minutes, he should shoot her. Emory followed Joyce out of the farmhouse into the yard. The night was upon them and a barn owl hooted somewhere from a nearby tree. Joyce passed the dark, empty stables, each one with its top gate open like a row of blackened teeth. They reached the shed across the yard. A tractor wheel was lying by the entrance; weeds pushing through the concrete of the yard and snaking through its bolt holes. Finch had promised to dispose of that tractor wheel at least two summers ago. Like most of his promises for home improvement it had been forgotten about. The door to the shed was a peeling white shop door with nine small panes of glass in the upper part, each one with a series of circles in the glass that made it difficult to see through. But even if the glass had been clear, it would have been hard to see inside as the door was filthy with the dirt of farm life. Joyce pushed it open and switched on the light, a single dull bulb connected to the ceiling by a tenuous, over-long cable and some cobwebs. Inside it was an untidy maelstrom of junk: nuts, bolts, washers, tools, electrical cord, fittings, pieces of wood, empty bottles, paint tins, rubber hosing and many components that Finch would term 'whatsits'. On the far wall was a poster of Vera Lynn, faded and torn. The surface of the workbench could barely be seen and Joyce moved a stack of slightly damp invoices. Had Finch ever paid them? She took down a small metal box from one of the shelves and prised open the lid.

'This is his electrical tin.' Joyce stood aside so that Emory could search through for what he wanted. As Joyce waited, she glanced absently around.

And then she saw it.

The Purdey shotgun propped in the far corner.

Joyce felt her heart racing. In a split second, she had lost the will to be compliant and the tenacious and assertive woman returned.

Could she get to it? Was it loaded?

Emory rustled through the tin, selecting various components as if they were fine chocolates from a selection box.

There was enough noise to cover her edging towards the gun. But could she crack it open to see if it was loaded? No, that would make too much noise.

Maybe she could grab the shotgun and pretend it was loaded? Or just use it to batter him?

She thought of Esther. The thoughts of rebellion subsided as quickly as they'd come. As always, she had to make sure that Esther was safe first. Joyce edged around Emory so that when he turned her body blocked his view of the gun.

She smiled at him as he noticed her. Emory remained blank faced and handed her several small components. Then he pulled out a drawer from the workbench, wrenching it so far that it nearly came out altogether. He sorted through its contents with his hands and removed two metal brackets shaped like small lolly sticks. He put one in the edge of his mouth, dangling it as if he was James Cagney smoking a fag, and tried to bend the other one against the workbench. The metal curved as he applied some pressure and when he'd bent it about twenty degrees from horizontal, he nodded, pleased with his work.

'For the Morse transmitter,' he announced, pleased with himself. He placed the two paddles of metal into his suit jacket. Scooping up some wire and a soldering iron, he checked that Joyce still had the components that he'd given her. They left the shed, but not before Joyce had given one final lingering look to the shotgun. She was pleased that Finch had gone on his pig expedition now. That gun might yet save their lives . . .

In the parlour of Pasture Farm, the front of the radio was laying on the sideboard. The body had been opened out, with wires spilling out like spaghetti. Esther watched the clock nervously. Emory and Joyce had gone outside twelve minutes ago. He'd told Siegfried to shoot her if they weren't back in twenty. Siegfried seemed unconcerned about the seconds ticking away from Esther's life. Would he do it? He seemed more stable than the older man, less likely to lose his temper and act rashly. He sat on the chair by the bureau, one arm resting on it, his head slumped from tiredness. Strands of hair fell over his face and she wasn't sure if he was awake or asleep. One hand still gripped the pistol, but it was pointed towards the floor.

Thirteen minutes elapsed.

Esther shifted uncomfortably. The motion made Siegfried look up, his eyes bleary and tired. Maybe he had been asleep. He glanced at the clock.

'I'm sure they'll be back soon.' Esther was talking to appease her own anxiety.

Siegfried nodded. He didn't look particularly concerned. He rubbed his eyes with his free hand, digging his fingers into the corners in an attempt to wake himself up.

'How old are you?'

'Why?' Siegfried looked at her with reddened eyes.

'I just wondered. I've got a son. He's a bit younger than you, I'd say.' She smiled thinking of Martin and wondering how he was getting on with Iris at the other farm.

'Is your son in this war?'

'Not yet.' Esther had palpable relief in her voice.

'My mother wishes I was not involved either. But here I am.'

Esther couldn't resist glancing at the clock on the mantelpiece.

Fifteen minutes had elapsed.

Siegfried must have noticed her nervous look.

'Don't worry. I will not shoot you.'

Esther heard a gasp escape her lips; a subconscious outpouring of relief. She put a hand to her mouth. Then they heard the back door open. Siegfried looked round the corner from the parlour door to check it was Emory and Joyce and saw they were laden with junk and paraphernalia from Finch's shed. Emory locked the door behind him and pocketed the key and Esther breathed another sigh of relief.

There had been four minutes to go.

Emory entered the room, without looking at either his comrade or his prisoner. Instead, he gently tipped out the contents of his hands onto the sideboard next to the radio. Immediately he went to work, comparing components for size and suitability with the ones already in the set. Siegfried rubbed his eyes again and turned his eyes towards the floor.

Esther watched as Emory took a length of electrical wire and stripped the insulation from the ends. He wound one end around an existing component in the radio and the other he connected to two metal plates that he'd taken from his suit pocket.

'I need the bathroom,' Joyce announced.

'Go then,' Emory didn't look away from his work. 'You cannot get out so do not try.'

'I won't.' Joyce placed the things she had been carrying on the sideboard and left the room.

Joyce went upstairs. Her legs felt heavy and tired. She knew that she was fighting exhaustion. She reached the landing and instead of going into the bathroom, went into her bedroom. She opened the bedside table and reread the telegram. She couldn't stop herself.

A house fire in Leeds.

John had been asleep inside.

She would prove it was a mistake as soon as this ordeal

was over. Her mind wandered and she remembered how John had surprised her on her birthday, flying into the field in a Tiger Moth. And then he'd taken her up for a flight in it. Joyce smiled, and remembered afterwards when they came back to the farmhouse, her legs feeling like jelly. She'd gone upstairs to this room to change her clothes, and John had crept upstairs when Finch and Esther weren't looking. He'd closed the door and put his arms around her, startling her.

'You can't be up here!'

'But we're married.'

'But nothing! Esther will have my guts for garters if she finds out.'

John kissed her and she'd kissed him back before pulling away, mindful that they could be disturbed at any moment. He ran his hand along the contour of her waist, rising up to her arms, neatly hooking her Aertex shirt off from her shoulders. Joyce let it fall to the floor. He kissed her neck, working his way up to her ear. Joyce gasped.

'We can't.'

'We could be quiet.'

'I suppose we could.' Joyce kissed him. He pulled her bra straps down over her shoulders.

'Really quiet.' He smiled his boyish grin at her. Joyce had got up and closed the bedroom door.

Afterwards, she knew they hadn't been that quiet by the smirk on Finch's face. Luckily Esther had been out, otherwise they'd have got a rocket.

And now, as Joyce stared at the telegram with its devastating message, she wished that day could happen all over again. In fact, she wished she could replay them all. Especially the endless ones in the house in Coventry, when she and John would be waiting for Doris to go out or for Charlie and Gwen to go to bed, so they could have a few precious moments together. Joyce refused to believe that John was gone; the love of her life. She would prove the telegram was wrong and then she'd march to the War Office and find whoever had typed it and give them a piece of her mind.

'Hurry up!'

Emory's voice from downstairs. Joyce hurriedly placed the telegram back into the drawer, straightened her hair and rushed out the door.

When she returned to the parlour, she found that Esther had made a pot of tea. Emory drank his while he worked. Siegfried remined slumped in his chair, his tea untouched. Esther poured one for Joyce and as she drank it she felt comforted by its warmth as it travelled down her neck, giving relief to the discomfort of the headache that was brewing.

'Hold this.' Emory proffered a component. When he realised that Siegfried was asleep in his chair, he turned quickly to Joyce. 'You.'

Joyce held a small metal clip in place as Emory soldered it into place. He indicated with an impatient nod for her to let go as he pushed the solder in place. His dirty finger-nails bleached white at the ends as he gripped the metal tightly. Satisfied with his work, he carefully let go. It held in place. He placed the two small metal paddles flat on the sideboard and pressed the top one up and down lightly with his finger.

Click, click, click.

Emory's mouth stretched into a wide grin. He drained the rest of his tea and turned the radio on. Static filled the parlour and Siegfried woke from his slumber.

'It's working,' Emory announced. 'Get the code book.'

Siegfried leapt into action and moved quickly out of the room, returning a few seconds later with his canvas bag. He rummaged inside and found a small leather bound book. He handed it to Emory, who flicked through.

Emory propped the page open and tapped out the sequences of dots and dashes that he saw. Joyce wished that she could remember more of the Morse code that John had told her about. But then she figured that she wouldn't understand the message anyway as it was in code form, relying on being deciphered by whoever was sympathetic to the Germans.

Click, click, click, click.

Click, click, click, click.

It was apparent that Emory seemed to be sending a short message and sending it repeatedly. He kept this process up for nearly twenty minutes until Siegfried was yawning and all the tea had been drunk.

Emory spoke in German to his comrade. The younger man nodded and took Joyce and Esther out of the room. Joyce wondered what was going on.

'You go to sleep now.' Siegfried indicated the stairs.

'Okay.' Joyce went up.

Dutifully and respectfully, he waited on the landing as each woman went to the bathroom. When they emerged he ushered them into Joyce's room. Both of them would sleep there as there was a lock on the door.

Siegfried searched the room, looking in the wardrobe and under the dressing table, before nodding that he was satisfied.

'You sleep. No noise.' Siegfried left, locking them in. The single, small window afforded a view of the side garden of Pasture Farm. There was no footpath visible and few people ever went up the side of the house. The chances of being able to signal to someone to get help were remote.

Esther and Joyce were exhausted. They undressed and Joyce lent Esther some of her pyjamas. The two women squeezed onto Joyce's single bed, back to back, both lost in their own tormented thoughts.

After what may have been three minutes or more, Joyce whispered to Esther.

'It'll be all right.'

There was no answer. Either Esther couldn't offer a reply or she was already asleep.

Lady Hoxley's face looked pinched and drawn. Channing assumed that she'd taken the news about Joyce's husband hard. He knew that she cared about the women working on her lands and that she'd developed a respect for the pragmatic Joyce. On more than one occasion, Channing had faked attentive interest when Ellen had told him what a splendid worker Joyce was. Yes, Joyce was a credit to the war effort.

For his part, Channing found Joyce to be interfering and a nuisance. But he wasn't about to share that point of view.

Channing sat in the drawing room of Hoxley Manor reading

a newspaper and nursing a fine port from the cellar. The drawing room was in a state of disrepair, with cracked coving around the ceiling and patches of damp on the wallpaper nearest the windows. But with a grand piano in one corner and an entire wall devoted to fine books, the room still looked impressive.

'Please come and sit down, Ellen.'

'I'll try one more time.' Ellen pushed an elegant finger into the dial of the telephone and dialled the operator.

'Hello, I'd like the War Office, please.'

'No one is going to be there, Ellen.'

Ellen covered the mouthpiece. 'They have a skeleton staff. The war isn't taking a holiday just because it's Christmas.'

Hearing the irritation in her voice, Channing shrugged and went back to the newspaper. He sipped his port as he watched Ellen pace a few steps one way, a few steps back again, the curly wire of the telephone stretching and contracting as she did so. After a few minutes, Ellen replaced the receiver.

'Try again in the morning, eh?' Channing patted the sofa next to him. Ellen picked up her own glass of port and walked over to him.

'Poor Joyce. I wanted to get some more details for her about her husband. I thought the War Office might put me in the right direction; tell me who I should speak to.'

'Try after Christmas.' Channing was trying to be as supportive as possible. Secretly he wished Ellen would let things go once in a while. The way she seemed to get involved in these girls' lives was irritating and it seemed a massive drain on her time.

And it stopped her giving him all the attention.

Ellen smoothed the back of her skirt and sat beside him. He took her hand and kissed the back of it, before testing the water with another kiss onto her wrist. Ellen smiled, enjoying his gesture of affection.

But then her eyes opened wide in alarm. She was staring right past him now; at something outside the room.

'Look!'

Channing twisted round in his seat so quickly that he dropped the newspaper to the floor. The glass of port stayed in his hand, although a drop splashed out onto his trousers.

'What?'

A flashlight was shining on and off into the drawing room from someone out in the darkness of the lawn beyond the window. The vague outline of a short, heavy set figure in a long coat became apparent with each illumination.

'Who the devil is out there?' Ellen moved to the window. Channing stopped her.

'Stay back, Ellen. I'll go.' Channing scooped a poker from the fireplace and headed out of the room.

'Be careful!' Ellen shouted after him. Then, ignoring his instructions, she ran to the window to see if she could see anything. The torch had gone dark, so all Ellen could see was her own reflection staring back at her.

Then she had an idea. With much of the house requisitioned as a military hospital, there were American army personnel on site most of the time. Ellen ran out of the drawing room to find a soldier.

Channing moved cautiously onto the lawn at the back of the house. He couldn't make out any shapes as his eyes hadn't adjusted to the inky blackness. He glanced up at the coal black sky, the moon offering slight illumination on the grass. He moved along the balustrade.

'Who's there? Show yourself.'

Then he spotted a shape. It was a small, heavy set man standing on the steps leading away from the house to the sunken garden. Channing knew he'd moved to that position so it would be harder for him to be observed from the house.

Channing knew who it was. He felt adrenaline knotting his stomach. This man shouldn't be here. This was all wrong.

'What the bloody hell are you doing?'

'I had to get a message to you.'

'Not here. Get out of here, you idiot.'

'I had to get it to you.' The heavy-set man stressed each word as if he was explaining it to someone hard of hearing.

For added emphasis, he took a menacing step towards Channing. Even in the gloom, Channing could see that he was reaching a hand into the inside pocket of his jacket and knew there would be a gun or a knife there. Channing raised his hands slightly in a way that made it clear he was apologising for overreacting.

'What is it then?'

'Two airmen. They've made contact. The code was a new one, and we didn't understand the location.'

'But they're in the area?'

'Yes. So we don't know exactly where they are, but we're working on translating to find out. It's a matter of priority.'

Channing glanced back to the house. It all seemed quiet. 'So what do you need from me?'

It wasn't his area and was confused as to why the man had risked so much to come here. He could have jeopardised both of their lives.

'We don't need you to do anything yet. But when we get a location, we may need you to go and get them.'

Channing was grateful for the darkness. It meant that the other man couldn't see the colour drain from his face. But he rubbed his mouth to disguise any telling expression that his face may be giving away. He didn't want to be rescuing any German airmen. That could compromise his position. He had a good thing going here.

Yes, that could mess things up for him.

But before Channing could reply, he heard a commotion at the French windows. Three American soldiers, armed with machine guns, were emerging from the house, with a thin, statuesque woman pointing into the darkness. Ellen Hoxley.

Damn it, what had she done?

Channing turned back to tell his companion to run, but the man had already vanished into the sunken garden.

The soldiers ran over to where the doctor was standing.

'Are you okay, Doctor Channing?' The Sergeant had a sleepy Texan drawl. He'd obviously been dozing, if not fully asleep.

'I'm fine.' Channing endeavoured to make his voice sound like he was a little shaken by the events. 'There was no one here by the time I'd got out.'

Channing smiled his most convincing trustworthy smile.

He was relieved when Ellen ran up to him and steered him back to the house before any more questions could be asked. He allowed her to take the poker from his hand.

Behind them, the soldiers fanned out; with two of them going in the wrong direction.

Channing tried his best to cover the anxious emotions that were bubbling to the surface. He hoped the man would get away. Otherwise they might interrogate him and find out everything. No, he couldn't worry about that. If the man was caught, he wouldn't talk. His concern shifted to his own role. What would he have to do? Where would these airmen need fetching from? Could he do as he'd been instructed while still maintaining his cover? The questions churned over and over, each chasing the tail of the previous one.

'Come inside. Let the soldiers search.'

Channing was grateful to hear someone else's voice.

'Yes, that's best. Thank you, Ellen. Although whoever it was is long gone now.' He let Ellen lead the way towards the inviting light of Hoxley Manor. But for how long would it be a sanctuary for him?

Chapter 10

Two days to Christmas.

The day started with the inexorable and ponderous rise of the sun behind winter clouds. The light filtered through the thin curtains of Joyce's bedroom, but she and Esther were already awake. It had been difficult to sleep, both huddled on a single bed, both secretly scared about what would happen to them. Neither of them wanted to voice their fears to the other and Joyce felt that all the time she could keep a lid on what she was feeling then their chances of survival would be greater. She imagined that Esther felt the same. They got dressed in silence, then at last, Joyce spoke.

'Be a lovely Christmas present if they've buggered off, wouldn't it?'

Esther nodded, a small smile playing on her lips. 'We can but hope.'

Joyce rapped on the door and called. 'Are you going to let us out?' They listened and waited. 'Come on!'

And after a minute, they heard the familiar creak of a foot on the bottom step. Esther would harangue Finch about the stairs having woodworm and he'd belligerently deny it. She'd said that one day someone would put their foot right through one of the steps. Joyce knew it was too much to hope for today. The footfalls got nearer and by the short gait and rapid ascension, she assumed it would be the young one. And sure enough, when the door was unlocked and opened, Siegfried stood before them. His boiler suit wasn't fully fastened, his eyes were bleary, and his hair was cascading over his forehead. Joyce realised that they'd woken him.

'What time is it?' His voice was sleepy.

'Six o'clock.' Joyce showed her wristwatch for proof.

'It is too early.'

'When you're a land girl, this is a lie-in.'

There was that plucky, fighting spirit again. She couldn't help herself and knew that she would eventually go too far and get herself in trouble. 'Look, let us go to the loo, and then lock us up again if you need more sleep.'

Siegfried considered for a moment and then shook his head.

'No, we need to transmit again. You can make us something to eat. Go and get ready,' He turned and set off downstairs. Esther and Joyce raised an eyebrow to each other. Still, as long as they were the cooks, they had a reason to be kept alive, didn't they?

Soon the house was filled with the smell of cooking bacon. Joyce knew that Esther was keeping the bacon for Christmas day to have with the chicken. She hadn't planned on sharing it with two German airmen.

As Esther and Joyce made the meal, they spoke about the weather, what the others would be doing now, general chit-chat to take their minds off the guests who were fiddling with the radio transmitter in the other room. The constant tapping of Morse code filled any silence. Soon, Joyce called them through to the table.

It was seven o'clock.

Emory and Siegfried ate their breakfast and slurped their tea. Siegfried was happy to make general conversation with Joyce, but Emory had his head stuck in the small leather code book, ignoring most of the things that the women said. Why was he studying the book so intently? Surely, he'd sent the message several times now. What was the problem?

She knew that no one had replied. But then she assumed that there was no way of Emory taking an incoming message. All he could do was transmit and hope. She wished she knew what they were sending in their message. Were they asking for directions? Help? Someone to come and rescue them? Whatever it was, judging by Emory's worried face something wasn't going right.

She topped up their tea. Emory raised the mug without thanking her. At least, Siegfried nodded when she filled him up.

Emory got up suddenly. The shock of the movement and the harsh grating sound of the chair going back on the terra-cotta tiles startled Joyce. He took his book and his tea through to the parlour to resume work.

After a few moments, Esther got up and began to put the plates and mugs into the sink. Joyce guessed she would busy herself with the domestic chores to keep her mind off things. She should be in the fields, working today. But there was no way these men would let her have free reign by going outside.

Joyce looked at Siegfried. Unaware of her gaze, he craned his hand into his upper pocket on his boiler suit and removed some tobacco and rolling papers and went to work making a cigarette. He was barely more than a boy. Tall and rangy with hair that was short at the sides, but which was probably on the edge of flouting regulations at the front. Still, all the time he kept it swept to one side, he was fine.

'What would you be doing in Germany at Christmas?' Joyce thought it would pass time to make conversation. And she might find out something useful. Esther stopped momentarily to listen, intrigued herself.

'Family things,' Siegfried shrugged, perhaps unsure of how much to share with these enemy women. 'We would go to church. My mother and grandmother. We'd thank God for our lives.'

Siegfried smiled, comforted by the memories of his family.

'What about your dad?'

'He is not with us.' Siegfried spoke carefully as if the emotions were still difficult for him.

'When did he die?'

'What?' Siegfried looked confused. 'No, he is not dead. He ran off with someone else.'

'I'm sorry.'

Siegfried waved it away as he finished making his cigarette. 'We would have a big meal when we return from church. Although not as big since the war started.'

He got up from his chair and reached over to his knapsack. He removed some matches and sparked his cigarette to life. Fugs of blue-grey smoke soon filled the kitchen. Esther winced as it went up her nose.

'We were going to have a big meal on Christmas day.' Joyce watched his reaction.

'Yes?'

'Yes, but some bugger stole our chicken.'

Esther looked tense. Had Joyce gone too far?

Then Siegfried smiled, as he sucked in air past the cigarette. Joyce smiled, relieved that he'd allowed her to joke. There was empathy there. Perhaps Siegfried was a young man who wanted this over as much as Joyce did. It could be good to get this boy on her side, to form a bond with him. It could be useful.

Richard Channing emerged from his room in a dark grey hound's-tooth patterned suit and straightened his tie. He'd chosen a crimson pattern in a nod towards Christmas even though he despised the whole affair. But Ellen enjoyed it, so he felt he should make an effort and today would be the lunch at the village hall. Two days before Christmas. The sound of a Christmas record wafted through the house from a distant room. Channing stopped to admire the Christmas tree in the lobby of the main entrance hall before glancing up and down the corridors. From the hospital ward he could hear a man shouting out in pain. It provided a darkly comic juxtaposition to the jolly Christmas music that was playing. Channing resisted the urge to check on his patients. He knew the nurses on duty would alert him if he was needed. Besides Doctor Gorman was on shift today and despite his inexperience should be able to handle most problems.

Channing walked slowly down the hallway, enjoying the

sound that his brogues made on the parquet flooring, towards the source of the Christmas music.

As he got closer, he could tell it was Bing Crosby's 'White Christmas'.

Channing hated that song, having heard it too many times to remotely enjoy it anymore. Every Christmas event, every party, every drinks soiree seemed to have played it since it was released a couple of years ago.

Christ, it seemed like longer.

But when Channing opened the door to the drawing room and saw Ellen's happy expression, he gave a warm smile as if she were playing his favourite song in the world.

'I thought I'd get us in the Christmas spirit.' Ellen flashed her eyes as if she was doing something shockingly decadent. But then Channing supposed that for her, this was a decadent and self-indulgent departure. Here was a woman who spent half of her time fundraising for the war effort and half of her time worrying she wasn't doing enough for the war effort. It wasn't enough for her that she had leased out some of Hoxley Manor to the Americans for their military hospital, she felt troubled by the half she still lived in. Channing supposed that the act of having money and power in these troubled times was enough to make her feel guilty. And nothing would assuage that guilt.

Channing tried to push aside thoughts of amateur psychology and crossed to the sofa where Ellen was sitting. She was making a paper chain and invited him to take some sections.

'I'd love to.' Channing wanted to appease her and so took

the strips of paper. The war effort had meant that paper couldn't be used for non-essential things like wrapping Christmas presents or making decorations, and Channing noticed that these chain links had fragments of recipes on them.

'One of my mother's old cookbooks.' Ellen preempted a question that Channing hadn't planned on asking.

'How long have you been up?' Channing had noticed that a large spool of finished paper chain was on the floor by the side of them, looking as if a snake had coiled in on itself.

'I don't know.' She looked at the clock for guidance, but it didn't give her an answer. 'Would you like a sherry? As it's nearly Christmas day, I think we're allowed. As long as it doesn't make us tipsy for the service.'

The service. Ah, yes.

Henry Jameson would conduct a special service for the old folk attending the lunch today. And Channing and Lady Hoxley would be expected to attend.

'I'd love a sherry. Thank you.' Channing watched as Ellen moved across to the drinks trolley, her slim hips sashaying back and forth in her simple eggshell blue dress. He wanted her. How long would he have to wait until they could consummate their love for each other? Ellen was understandably cautious after losing her husband and Channing didn't want to rush her, but still.

Bing Crosby was still singing.

He knew that their relationship was an open secret in the village with him finding groups of old women suddenly going silent when he appeared unexpectedly. Everyone knew and yet Channing was forced to maintain this charade. He wasn't allowed to hold her hand in public. Kissing would be out of the question. The most contact he could hope for was to place a guiding hand on the base of her elbow when they were out and about.

Still that was all right for now. Channing's relationship was a useful diversion, nothing more. He was here for work.

Bing Crosby had reached the end of the song. Channing let out a little hurrah inside his head. But as Ellen brought his sherry over, she repositioned the needle at the edge of the record and the song started over.

Suddenly he understood how Sisyphus felt.

The telephone rang. Ellen carefully placed her drink on a side table, cleared her throat and lifted the receiver.

'Hello? Helmstead Six Two Three.'

At first the person on the other end didn't speak and Channing detected Ellen's confusion.

Then the caller said something.

And the line went dead.

'Hello? Hello? Who is this?'

Ellen replaced the receiver and returned to the sofa. She seemed confused by the whole business.

'Who was it?' Channing was instantly on edge, struggling to keep a lid on his emotions.

'A man, but I think he was disguising his voice.'

'Really?' Channing tried to disguise his discomfort. 'And what did he say, Ellen?'

'Well, it didn't make sense. He said New Market. What does that mean? There's no horse racing today, is there?'

Channing was lost in his own thoughts; Ellen's words

flowing over him like static from a radio. The time had come. The code word had been used.

'Richard?'

She was staring at him.

'What is it?'

'Nothing, I was thinking that's a dashed odd thing to say, isn't it?' He took a big slug of sherry, feeling it coating his gums. 'Anyway, we should get back to the paper chain, shouldn't we?'

Ellen picked up the chain and resumed threading the new links onto it. Channing helped her for a while, but after half an hour he stood up as if he'd forgotten something. He knew he had matters to attend to.

'Oh no!'

'What is it?'

'I've just remembered I was supposed to help Doctor Gorman with a patient. I won't be long, I promise.'

'Very well.' Ellen sounded disheartened. He knew that she couldn't stop him from seeing a patient, not with her keen sense of public duty. The action may even deepen her respect for him. Look – good old Doctor Channing puts his patients first! He caught a wry grin appearing on his face and sent it packing before Ellen could spot it.

'I'll meet you at the church.' Channing felt some small relief at leaving Ellen and Bing Crosby to it.

At Pasture Farm, as the Germans busied themselves with the radio, Joyce and Esther sat in the kitchen. Esther asked what they should cook for lunch.

'Do you think we should bother?' Joyce asked, indicating

177

their guests, who they could see working in the parlour, shirt sleeves rolled up. The constant sound of Morse code being sent was beginning to aggravate Joyce; its rhythm a backdrop to her thoughts. It seemed like it had always been there, that tap-tap-tap noise.

'I think they'll expect food, won't they?'

'I suppose. What have we got?' Joyce asked. Esther went to the larder and opened the door. She passed Joyce the items that could appear on today's lunch menu: five carrots, a large parsnip and three large potatoes. Joyce placed the items on the kitchen table and both women looked at the unappealing pile, trying to pluck a memory of a recipe that might use them. Joyce shrugged. She had nothing apart from vegetable soup.

That would have to do.

'I'll help you,' Joyce offered. She thought that it would take her mind off their predicament, off thoughts of John, and relieve the tense band of pressure that was sitting on the base of her neck.

The women went to work as the Morse code provided a backdrop to their actions.

Tap, tap, tap, tap.

After a few minutes of peeling the vegetables together, Joyce caught Esther's eye and whispered something in the hope that the Germans wouldn't hear.

'What time is Connie due?'

Esther shook her head. She wasn't sure. 'It was a vague arrangement.'

'So she might not come?' Joyce couldn't hide the hope and excitement in her voice. Connie wouldn't get hurt that way.

And they wouldn't risk being hurt either in trying to get a message to her.

'She said she would, but I don't know when.' Esther dashed Joyce's hopes.

'Then we need to put her off, don't we?'

'How do we do that?' Esther looked perturbed. 'We can't very well walk out of here and saunter over to the vicarage.'

'We can telephone the vicarage.'

'They won't let us.'

'They might.' Joyce put down the peeler. She walked towards the parlour, with Esther watching nervously from the butler's sink.

'What are you doing?'

But Joyce didn't have time to reply. The Germans looked up as she approached them.

'What do you want?' Emory eyed her.

'We've got people coming. And I thought it might be a good idea if we stopped them. What do you think?' She looked directly at Siegfried, who was crouched on his haunches trying to strip the insulation off a small wire with a penknife.

'How can you stop them?' Emory scrutinised her face. Joyce realised and anticipated that they would think it was a trick. She had to be careful.

'I could telephone my friend, Connie. Tell her not to come.'

'I can't let you talk to anyone.'

'Well you can't very well do it, can you?'

Emory smiled and turned to face her, wiping his hands on a tea towel that they'd seconded for their work.

'You must think I am stupid.'

179

'I won't say anything out of turn. I mean, if I did, you'd shoot me dead, wouldn't you?'

Emory nodded. Siegfried looked more concerned. He touched Emory's shoulder to get his attention.

'We don't want more people here, Captain.' Siegfried looked imploringly. Joyce could tell that the stress of keeping two prisoners was enough of a burden for him. For both of them.

Emory moved quickly towards Joyce.

What was he going to do? Was he going to strike her? But the motion was designed to spook her, nothing more. He walked straight past her. She watched as he marched into the kitchen. He strode up to where Esther was peeling the vegetables by the sink, took his pistol out of his jacket and pressed it against Esther's temple.

'You make the telephone call. If you try to be a hero, I will shoot her.'

Esther whimpered and Joyce knew that he was deadly serious. She picked up the telephone receiver. Siegfried was standing by her side, close, listening. He angled the receiver so that he could hear too. Then he nodded for her to dial the number.

Joyce called the operator. It was strange to hear another person's voice after the claustrophobia of being alone with these two men for what seemed like weeks. Joyce wanted to blurt out everything, but she knew she couldn't. Esther looked imploringly at her, her chin puckered like orange peel as she struggled not to lose it and cry her eyes out.

'Hello, caller. What number do you require?'

Joyce gave the number of the vicarage and asked to be

connected. The operator obliged and soon Joyce could hear the telephone ringing. Eventually a woman's voice answered.

'Hullo?' It was Connie.

'Hello.' Joyce felt her throat seizing up, making her voice higher. Emory scowled at her, willing her not to make a mistake. Esther looked moist-eyed. Joyce could feel Siegfried's breath on the back of her neck. He was close enough that he could listen.

Joyce was aware that she needed to say something. But it was Connie who filled the void.

'I'm so sorry to hear about John.'

'Yeah, well I don't think it's true. He'll be alright, daft old thing. It's a mistake.'

Saying it aloud, under these circumstances, brought a lump to her throat. Now it was Joyce's turn to try not to cry. She closed her eyes to blot out the light. Doing that often helped her not to cry when she didn't want to. And it worked today.

'Thing is, I'd rather not have company.'

Emory nodded his approval.

'You can't be on your own, Joyce.'

'I've got Esther. I'll be fine.'

'Nonsense, I can walk over, and we can talk about your John and everything. Or not talk about him, if that's what suits you.' Connie had a steely quality to her voice and Joyce knew it meant that Connie wasn't about to give in. She'd used that tone on Finch when he was trying to axe their morning tea break – it said that she wanted her own way and she was going to get it.

She had to do something to stop Connie.

But what?

'And if you're worried about lunch. Don't. I'll have something at the village hall with the old folks and then come over.'

Connie had thought of everything, hadn't she?

Time was running out. How could Joyce stop her?

Maybe she couldn't.

Siegfried nodded urgently at Joyce to say something. Emory gripped Esther's arm harder. The void of silence stretched further. If she was too insistent in trying to put her off, Connie might realise something was wrong. She'd smell a rat.

That was it!

She had to make Connie realise that something was wrong but without giving anything away to her captors.

Could she do it? Could she think of something?

Joyce glanced back at Esther. The two women's eyes met. Esther could sense that Joyce was about to do something reckless and potentially devastatingly stupid. But Joyce had to do it. She had to make Connie realise that something was wrong here and that she shouldn't come. And she had to do it without saying it outright or screaming for help. It had to be a coded message, something that only Connie would know was wrong.

Then it came to her.

Joyce realised what she could say, but she still paused for a moment as she weighed up the consequences of saying it. The lives in her hands: Esther at gunpoint and Connie who could be about to walk into the wolf's enclosure if she got it wrong.

'So I'll come round late afternoon then, all right?'

'Yes.'

Joyce knew it was now or never. She knew what she had to say.

'Give my regards to your Vince, won't you? Bye.'

Esther's mouth became a firm line and she licked her lip with nervousness; not enough of a reaction for Siegfried to notice, but Joyce spotted it. Joyce returned the receiver to the cradle. She smiled at the two airmen.

'She's still coming?' Emory was annoyed. 'Why couldn't you stop her?'

'How? You heard her!'

'We have to be ready!' Emory pushed past Joyce and headed for the parlour. Esther sank into a chair, her legs unable to support her. Joyce went to her and comforted her as the men returned to their work.

Tap, tap, tap.

When she was sure that the men would be engrossed again and wouldn't be listening, Joyce whispered in Esther's ear.

'Do you think that was enough?'

'Enough to get us all killed,' Esther snapped, slightly too loudly.

Joyce knew she'd done what she had to do. She'd said the name Vince instead of Henry when talking about Connie's husband. Vince had been one of Connie's violent ex-boyfriends. She felt sure that Connie would mull over this apparent mistake and then realise it was a signal that Joyce and Esther needed help; a signal that something was wrong.

She'd get the soldiers from Hoxley Manor.

It would turn out fine.

Everything would be alright.

As Connie watched from the serving counter, the images of old women and young children, the odd injured serviceman in uniform, the local doctor with his wandering hands all washed over her. The sounds of their revelry and eating as they enjoyed the meal laid on by the church were a blur of background noise. Connie was thinking about her friend, Joyce. In some ways, she'd sounded surprisingly together for a woman who'd suffered a terrible loss.

Henry returned to the counter with a near-empty serving tray, a few fragments of roast potato clung to the side.

'You should have some food.' Henry looked concerned for his wife.

'Not hungry,' Connie was thinking about how Joyce must be feeling at the moment. She'd be raw, in shock, perhaps not even accepting what had happened. And she must be confused as well. Why else would she make the mix-up over Connie's husband's name?

''Ere, why did she think you were Vince?'

'How should I know?' Henry had a hint of annoyance in his voice. He was doing his best to hide it, but Connie knew it was there. It wasn't surprising seeing how Connie had been badgering him with this question for several hours now. It wasn't only the repetition that irked him, but the fact that each time it was asked, it made Henry think about Vince. And Connie guessed that Henry never wanted to think about Vince again, since the man had turned up at the vicarage and done his best to destroy their relationship. Each time the name was mentioned, it probably brought it all back to him. She didn't really want to think about Vince either.

'Maybe she's woolly-headed, with the upset of what's happened to her,' Connie attempted to answer her own question, to stop Henry worrying.

'Quite. She's got enough to worry about at the moment, I shouldn't wonder,' Henry was handed a plate of steaming carrots by Mrs Gulliver and he dutifully headed off to serve them to the expectant crowd. Someone had appropriated the piano and was playing a song as the rest of the people ate.

Mrs Gulliver looked briefly at Connie and eyed her up and down. It was the usual judgemental assessment. Connie was used to it and braced herself for the old woman's unpleasantness.

'How's your head?'

That was unexpected. Mrs Gulliver seemed concerned.

'All right. I've still got a bit of a headache mind.'

'What were those Germans like, then?'

Ah that was why she was being nice. She wanted to know all the details about what had happened.

'I don't really remember.'

'I heard someone say they were giants of men,' Mrs Gulliver stated with the absolute authority of someone who knew. 'Some of them have more teeth too than they should have by all accounts.'

'I don't know.' Now it was Connie who wanted to move off to end this cross-examination. She found a small plate of Brussel sprouts. It had already done the rounds, but Connie thought it'd be a good ruse to get her away from Mrs Gulliver. She moved from the counter to put the sprouts back into circulation. And as she got involved in talking to the people

185

at the tables and then coerced into singing songs for them, Connie nearly forgot all about the fact that Joyce had said the wrong name on the telephone.

Richard Channing had contemplated taking his car, but then he remembered that his petrol ration had run out for the month and that he would be running on fumes. The last thing he wanted was to break down where he was going. So instead, he found a push bike that had been left against a wall by the hospital entrance. He assumed it belonged to one of the service men or perhaps a visitor. As he rode away, he congratulated himself in taking a bicycle, as it would make it harder to identify a person whizzing past. He pulled his trilby hat low, just in case. If you passed someone in a car, they might remember. And that meant they might ask questions later.

What was that Doctor Channing doing out near Panmere Lake the other day?

Channing peddled fast but it still took him forty minutes to reach the lake. It had the code name, Market. The word 'New' on the telephone had meant to come immediately. He stowed his push bike near a fence and hopped over a stile. With the leaf mulch crisp under foot, Channing set off into the wood. His breath formed willowy clouds as he neared the large tree on the south-west side of the lake. The meeting point.

Channing sighed and glanced around. At first, he thought he was alone, but then he heard a twig snap and a large man in a badly-tailored, vanilla-coloured raincoat appeared. He wore a flat cap, and a couple of dead rabbits were hanging over his wrist, each one suspended by a gnarled piece of twine.

To anyone watching, it looked like Channing had just bumped into a poacher, nothing more.

'I don't enjoy being called away.' Channing wasn't going to bother with any pleasantries. He wanted to get this over with as fast as possible and before there was any risk of his being seen.

'We've got the location.' The big man wheezed.

'Where are they?'

'Place called Pasture Farm.'

Channing heard a bitter snorting laugh emerge from his mouth before he had time to stop it. 'No,' he walked away. 'There's no way I can go there.'

'Why not?'

'They know me. I work with some of the girls at the hospital. Isn't there anyone else?'

'No, you're the only one. We need you to do this.'

Was that a threat? Was it a taunt?

Channing knew that there had been rumblings about people not trusting him within the group. Maybe this was their way of testing him; of proving his loyalty to the cause. Yes, that must be what they were doing.

'This could compromise me.'

'You'll do it.' The big man scratched his neck, leaving small red lines on the skin. 'You're the only doctor that I know. And that gives you a cast-iron reason for visiting, doesn't it?'

'How do you square that?' Channing hadn't met this man before, but he'd seen him at the meetings. Those squalid meetings in basements of pale, gimlet-eyed men who thought they could change the world. They'd meet below the butcher's shop, where they'd discuss the rise of fascism and how the economic model could work well for Britain. He knew that on some level it made sense. Channing had heard the plausible explanations that employing business leaders instead of politicians to relevant areas would naturally increase productivity. He'd heard it so many times he was bored by the arguments. No politician he knew would ever voluntarily give up his seat on the gravy train of politics for a business leader. Channing supposed that's why some of the group advocated force. At the meetings, some of the men would give readings. Others would be more strident and talk about smashing the current system. Those people thought that a weakened Britain would be easier to convert to fascism and they thought that they should strike while the iron was hot. Some of the members would suggest more violent courses of action. Channing knew that he'd managed to stay on the fringes until now, doing as little as possible, while ingratiating himself into the group. But even on the side lines, he knew he was no innocent spectator. He'd crossed the line several times, committing atrocities that still haunted him during those quiet, bleak early hours when he couldn't sleep.

'It's perfect you being a doctor.' The large man smiled, seemingly amused by Channing's question. 'One of the women has lost her husband. You could pay a neighbourly call to check on her.'

How could this man know about Joyce Fisher?

Did they have someone in the War Office?

No, that couldn't be right.

And then it hit him. What if the telegram hadn't been real? What if it had been faked by the group to give them just such an excuse? Maybe the whole thing was a charade to allow Channing to go there without any questions.

Channing had to ask.

'Did you send a faked telegram?'

The man sneered and gave no answer. And although he was no wiser, Channing felt a knot in his stomach. If the telegram was a lie, designed to manoeuvre him into going to the farm, then that would be a low blow even for these people. But they were motivated by talking about such things as working for the greater good. And Channing guessed that the greater good meant that they could justify doing anything to achieve their goals; even if it meant lying to a woman about her husband.

And then a thought struck him with welcome clarity amid the rush of jumbled theories and presumptions.

No, they couldn't have faked the telegram unless they knew that the airmen were already at Pasture Farm. And they hadn't been there long enough for that, had they?

Channing cursed himself for jumping to conclusions without thinking things through. He had to stay on his toes. He couldn't afford to make such elementary mistakes. This was only about a stupid telegram, but another time it might be much more serious.

Channing knew he had to ask other questions, ones more pertinent to what they wanted him to do; questions which related to his own survival.

Yes, that was the most important thing, wasn't it?

'So I go to check on Mrs Fisher and what then? I accidentally smuggle two German airmen out in my car?'

'More or less.'

'What?'

'When you're checking on Mrs Fisher, you discover the airmen. Big surprise. You make up something about them needing to give themselves up and you persuade them to come with you to the hospital; to turn themselves in. Your war is over Fritz and all that. They'll go along with the ruse. You bundle them into your car and drive off.'

'Right.'

'And then – whoops – they jump you. Or rather that's what you'll tell everyone afterwards. They'll escape from your car to the safety of our network. You tell everyone you were overpowered and lost them. You'll still be the big hero.'

Channing nodded. He could see a way that he might get away with this. A way that meant he didn't have to be exposed as working for these people. His cosy life with Ellen Hoxley and the hospital could be maintained.

Yes, that was the most important thing.

He mustn't be discovered.

And he knew he'd been damn lucky so far. There had been several times when he thought the jig was up. The worst time and the closest shave had been when Ellen had suspected a saboteur and thought it was him. He'd had to work hard to pin the blame on another one of the group. Harper hadn't been innocent, but he didn't deserve to carry the whole can. And that had backfired on him. His stomach churned as he remembered how Harper had threatened Ellen with a cut-throat razor in the stables. She'd stumbled upon him sending a Morse code message. And Channing had arrived, the valiant hero, and shot Harper dead.

He'd killed to cover his secret.

He'd been the hero then, hadn't he?

But Channing didn't like to think about that.

Channing had saved Ellen and she was none the wiser as to exactly what had happened. In fact, it may have helped her fall in love with him that little bit more. And who was he to complain about that particular silver lining?

And then there was that brash American who'd spoken about secret military plans that Channing had overheard. The group of American soldiers had been ambushed by German fighter planes. It had been obvious that someone had got a message to the Germans telling them where the Americans would be. The surviving soldier had suspected the wrong person of betrayal and by the time he had realised who'd really betrayed him and his men, he hadn't been in a fit state to confront the real culprit. The American lay dying in a hospital bed when he realised what Channing had done. And that had forced Channing to act.

He hadn't wanted to do it.

Why did they always force him to do things?

Calmly, Channing had taken a pillow and smothered the man, listening as the breath he was clinging onto finally left his body.

Even thinking about that made Channing feel sick.

No, he couldn't dwell on the bad things he'd done. They'd

been forced upon him, hadn't they? If everyone could leave him alone, none of those things would have happened.

Then he remembered something else about that incident in the hospital with the American.

The woman helping him at the bedside had been Joyce Fisher. She hadn't known what he'd done to the American, of course, but she had been suspicious at the man's hasty demise. She'd asked questions about how the soldier could have suddenly taken a turn for the worse like that after being in a stable condition. Channing had chivvied her along as she filled in the time of death paperwork. He'd chivvied her so she couldn't think too much about what she was doing. And he figured that the less he gave credence to her concerns the better.

Channing forced himself to concentrate on what was happening now.

The large man in the raincoat rummaged in his pockets. From the look of it, the pocket contained a lot of things; what was the man going to produce?

'As long as I'm not compromised, I'll do it.' A chill wind was whipping through the trees, cutting straight through Channing's long coat.

'You'll go to Pasture Farm tomorrow morning.' The man pulled a small pistol from his pocket. 'And you'll take this, in case anything goes wrong.'

'Nothing will go wrong.' Channing mustered a steely determined look in his eyes. These people had to believe in him. They had to have faith and trust him.

The big man pushed the gun into Channing's hand.

'You'd better get going.'

'Right,' Channing looked at the gun. 'Happy Christmas.'

He had no choice in the matter and as he slowly walked back to the bicycle his mind was alive with the permutations of what could go wrong. He was a logical man, a believer in science. He consoled himself with thinking it all through; working out probabilities and outcomes. Nothing could be allowed to endanger his setup; his cosy life. Nothing could blow his cover. Channing would make sure that nothing went wrong.

He gripped the pistol and slid it into his pocket.

The uninspiring saucepan of vegetable soup sat in the centre of the table, with three placemats underneath it to stop it scorching the wood.

Joyce and Esther watched as Siegfried and Emory drank it from their bowls. Their own bowls remained largely untouched. The worry they both felt about whether Connie would show up had curbed their appetites.

The Germans had been transmitting all morning and the work seemed to have made them hungry. As they ate, Emory scowled but said nothing. Siegfried nodded from time to time or uttered a pleasantry.

Esther seemed relieved that they liked the food, or at least didn't hate it. The meal was warm and filling and sometimes that was all that mattered.

While the men ate, Joyce would fill up their glasses with more carrot whiskey. She hoped that they wouldn't see beyond her apparent generosity. She hoped they wouldn't realise that she was trying to get them drunk.

If she could make Emory fall asleep, she might be able to get the gun off him.

And then what would she do? A shrill, nagging voice in her head pestered her for an answer.

Could she shoot them if she had to?

Could she do that?

Joyce didn't know. She looked at the boyish face of Siegfried, a boy who shouldn't be here in this dreadful war. She looked at the rugged face of Emory. What sort of man would he be without the war? Would he be at home in Berlin or somewhere with his children running around? Would he be a dutiful husband who provided for his family? And yet, here they were, dressed in clothes they'd stolen, waving a gun around and terrifying two innocent women.

Could she shoot them? The voice was insistent; self-doubt and self-loathing going to work on her temples. If war had made these men do dreadful things, what would it make Joyce do? She had already lost everything.

Could she shoot them?

Joyce didn't know.

But one thing was for sure. She knew that she wouldn't let any harm come to Esther or herself. And if that meant stopping these men, then she'd do her best. There would be no option, would there?

As Esther cleared the plates away, Joyce went to top up the men's glasses.

'No more.' Emory placed his flattened hand over the top of the glass. He eyed Joyce with a weary look. Did he suspect that she was trying to get him drunk? No, it was his exhaustion from the situation. They were all tired and running on empty; all hoping that this nightmare would be over. Joyce went to fill up Siegfried's glass and he nodded his consent, until Emory removed the glass from in front of the young man.

'Not for him either. We have to stay focussed.' Emory stood up and pulled up his trousers where they'd constricted around his waist. Joyce noticed that they were too small for him.

'I'm going to check outside. Keep an eye on the women.' Emory placed the pistol on the table next to Siegfried. He moved to the back door, unlocked it and went outside. As Joyce and Esther washed up, they could see Emory pacing in the yard, looking around. What was he planning?

The young man was similarly pensive, idly moving the pistol on the table in front of him, lost in his own world. Was this a good moment to try to get him on her side? There might not be another opportunity.

She put down the dish she'd been drying. 'Tell me if he comes back,' she whispered to Esther, and before Esther had time to question what she was doing, Joyce went back to the table and sat next to Siegfried. He looked startled by this action and looked more alert; suspicious.

'It's all right.'

'What do you want, Joyce?'

'Just to say, my husband was in the RAF. He crashed behind enemy lines. Just like you.'

'Oh? What happened?'

'His Lancaster bomber was on a raid and on the way back they got shot down. Some of them didn't make it, but John managed to parachute to the ground. He got taken in by a farmer and found his way back to me.' Joyce looked wistful.

There was no way that John was dead, not after all he'd been through. All they'd been through.

A house fire in Leeds.

John was asleep inside.

No, that was rubbish. Of course, it was rubbish.

'I want to get back to my home too.' Siegfried's face was more open and unguarded than she had seen before. The dark circles under his eyes and the haunted look on his face showed that he was running out of enthusiasm for what he was doing.

'I know you do. You've got people missing you, haven't you? Be wonderful if this could just end, wouldn't it?'

'Yes, it would.'

'Listen, we're land girls, we grow vegetables. But the thing is, we work with Germans, Italians, all sorts. And they're all prisoners of war.'

'And they're treated pretty well by all accounts.'

The words came from Esther. Joyce was surprised and pleased that she was helping with what she was trying to do. Yes, together they could convince him to turn himself in. Together they could make him convince Emory to end this nightmare.

'They joke and seem happy, honestly. They know they're relatively safe. Their families know they're safe. All of them are waiting for the war to end so they can go home. That could be you.'

She let her words hang in the air; and watched as the warmly comforting temptation played on the young man's features. Siegfried nodded, his brow furrowed as he considered her words.

'But Emory will not surrender. Not when he knows that there are people who will help us get back to Germany.'

Who were these people? The traitors among them. Sometimes there would be a march in London or Manchester, one of the bigger cities, calling for an end to the war, but Joyce had trouble deciphering the motives of such people. Were they conscientious objectors or people sick of the loss and struggle of war? Or were they agitators who were seeking a more unpleasant resolution to the fighting – one where Britain would become a fascist state? Joyce supposed that such marches were made up from all three camps. And while she understood some peoples' weariness to the endless war they were enduring, she knew it wasn't her way to complain. No, she would do her duty and that's what kept her going.

That's always what kept her going.

And it's all she had left.

'Do you think your messages have got through to those people?' Joyce asked. Esther hovered by the sink, wringing the edge of her apron with nervous hands. She'd become transfixed by the conversation and had forgotten to keep an eye on the window.

'I hope the message has reached them. We have been transmitting it over and over. We have no way of receiving a message back, so we don't know.'

Joyce thought about the time the train had been derailed and she'd been quoted in the *Daily Mail*. There had been an explosive device on the line, placed there by saboteurs campaigning against the British. She knew these people were out there.

'The Home Guard are looking for you. I could take you to the town near here. It's called Helmstead. I could make sure you're looked after.'

'They would not shoot me?'

'No, they wouldn't. I could make sure you're all right.'

Siegfried considered this for a moment. Joyce noticed that the gun was still on the table, the young man's fingers idly dancing over the barrel as he contemplated her words.

'What do you think?'

'I'm not sure. I think—'

Joyce never found out what he was about to say as the back door opened suddenly and Emory came in, rubbing his hands from the cold. Joyce and Siegfried froze at the table; both sitting up straight. Joyce struggled to hide the guilty look on her face, but she realised that Emory was looking at Esther, who was studiously avoiding eye contact with him. Joyce knew that Emory had twigged that something was up.

'What's going on?'

'The women say that we will be treated well if we give ourselves up.' Siegfried moved towards his commander.

'Yes, I can take you into the town and—'

Joyce never finished the sentence. Emory lunged across the table and slapped her hard around the face with the back of his hand, the force of the blow sending her tumbling off her chair. As she fell to the tiled floor, Joyce was vaguely aware of Siegfried rising from his chair to stop his commander from doing any more damage. She could hear Esther screaming, but the sound was muffled in her ears as consciousness started to leave her. But something stopped her passing out. Maybe it was the cold of the tiles that jolted her awake or an innate protection reflex; but Joyce pulled herself to her feet, fighting the pin pricks of light that were filling her vision. The room spun around her, the dresser moving fast towards her and then zooming back to where it had been. She steadied herself on the edge of the table.

Emory was shaking Esther to shut her up, but the screams kept coming. Siegfried had his attention on his commander, his hands gripping Emory's arms as he tried to pull him away from Esther. Her hysteria wasn't going to stop unless they stopped.

'No, leave her!' Siegfried pleaded.

Joyce could feel the numbness in her cheek being replaced with a pulsing, insistent pain. Had he broken her cheekbone? She didn't have time to give it more than a passing thought.

The room swam around her again as she tried to focus her eyes. She looked at the thing on the table that could end this nightmare. The pistol had been left, temporarily forgotten.

Joyce moved towards it.

Time slowed to a snail's pace. Emory was shaking Esther, desperately trying to pull his arm back far enough to strike her into silence. Siegfried was trying to stop him. Joyce reached out a shaking hand. The barrel of the pistol was facing her, and she couldn't reach the handle from where she was. So she grabbed the end of the barrel and pulled it quickly towards her.

Emory spotted what she was doing and struggled to free himself from the entanglement with Siegfried and Esther. But

Siegfried assumed he was trying to better position himself for another angled attack on the woman. He gripped his commander more tightly.

'Let me go, you fool!' Emory screamed. The fear in his eyes made the young man realise what was happening. He followed his commander's gaze. But as Siegfried relaxed his grip, they both knew that Joyce had got the gun.

Joyce turned it quickly round in her hand, almost fumbling it and dropping it. But she managed to point it in Emory's vague direction as she gripped the handle, her finger on the trigger.

But she had under a second to enjoy this turn of events. Emory launched himself at her, sending her tumbling to the floor. She cracked her elbow on the table as she went down. Her finger pressed on the trigger and she felt the heat of the barrel as the bullet came out and skimmed the edge of her trouser leg. It zinged across the floor, imbedding itself in the bottom of the sink cupboard, sending splinters into the air in a small cloud of dust. Joyce hit the back of her head on the ground, sending stars into her eyes. She could feel Emory's weight on top of her and smell the staleness of his clothes. He pulled back a meaty fist and went to strike her, but Joyce managed to wriggle to one side, unbalancing him. She clawed at his face with her free hand, the other trapped underneath him. The gun had been lost from her grip in the fall and was now under the table.

She could see Esther trying to reach her, but Siegfried was holding her off. The look on the young man's face spoke of betrayal as if Joyce's words had been designed only to deceive him. He wasn't going to help her.

Joyce struggled with Emory on the floor, feeling her strength draining as she fought him. He pushed himself up, one hand holding her against the floor and tried to manoeuvre his other hand so he could land a punch. Joyce was holding the top of his arms but her prone position meant that she couldn't get any power to push him off. She remembered his injury and how it hurt him to use his right arm and dug her fingers into where she remembered the wound was. Emory yelped and batted her hand away angrily. There was fury and pain etched on his face. He pinned her to the floor with his forearm across her neck and pulled his other hand into a fist. She couldn't move. She couldn't avoid it. There was a grim inevitability to what was going to happen. Joyce braced herself for the punch.

But then someone knocked at the door.

Chapter 11

'L a la la-laaa la la la laaala.'
Mrs Arbuthnott was swaying and singing in time to the music. Her face was flushed as she cajoled some other villagers to join in. Soon the whole room was singing along.

But Henry was looking weary; his charming bonhomie and eagerness blunted by hours of smiling dutifully and making small talk in a hot room.

Connie eyed him with sympathy. She felt similarly exhausted. He'd been sitting at the small upright piano and she'd been standing singing by it for nearly an hour. They'd finished their third rendition of '(There'll be Bluebirds Over) The White Cliffs of Dover' and Connie was heartily sick of the song. She also felt a catch in her throat, a nagging reminder that she hadn't warmed up her voice properly. Doctor Channing had hoped she'd take it easy. But there was fat chance of that.

She and Henry hadn't played together for a few months. Life and the war had got in the way, as had the waning interest of their erstwhile, self-appointed manager, Frederick Finch. Recognising they weren't going to be the cash cow that he hoped, Finch had ambled off to other more lucrative ideas on which to waste his time, but the crowd of old folk in the village hall were lapping it up.

'Can you play 'White Christmas' for us, Reverend?' An old woman in a green coat asked. It was Mrs Fisk, one of Henry's admiring coterie of pensioners. She hadn't taken her coat off or indeed unbuttoned it during the whole meal. And as the temperature in the hall was uncomfortably warm with such a large number of people, this was no mean feat. Perhaps she was trying to hide a stain on her blouse. Connie realised that's what *she* would do. Mrs Fisk was made of stern and upstanding stuff. She sat with her friends and Henry fans, Mrs Arbuthnott and Mrs Hewson. All three women talked in hushed tones about how wonderful the vicar was. All three of them would sing along with Connie as she sang. All three women would look down their noses at Connie. They thought, like a lot of people in Helmstead, that Henry could have done better. They thought that Connie was fast and flighty.

But Connie hoped that she'd shown them how committed she was by how happy Henry seemed in their marriage. For her part, she loved him, with his floppy fringe and his puppy-dog enthusiasm. She loved how she could still embarrass him with an off-colour joke or lewd comment and his face would flush and his hands would fiddle unnecessarily with his hymn book or whatever he was holding. It was a good pastime that warmed her heart.

'Please play it,' Mrs Hewson chimed in. 'It's my favourite Bing Crosby.' She, like the others in the coterie, was looking straight at Henry for his consent. None of them bothered looking at Connie. This meant that Connie felt safe in the knowledge that she could curl her lip in contempt. She wasn't their flaming dancing monkey. Shouldn't she and Henry have the opportunity of a Christmas break too? But instead, here they were waiting hand and foot on the old people of Helmstead and ensuring that they had a good day full of cheer and companionship. Henry caught the curl of her lip out of the corner of his eye. He smiled apologetically at his wife.

'We'll make this the last one then, shall we?' A compromise to appease all parties.

'Yeah, this is all you're getting!' Connie's words came out slightly too forcibly. Mrs Fisk recoiled slightly as if she'd seen something unpleasant.

As Henry played the introduction to the song, Connie got ready to sing. Her voice should hold out for one more song. As she launched into the words, she watched the pensioners swaying in their seats. They'd forgotten that they were in a pokey village hall during a war, with the cold remains of a Christmas dinner in front of them. Instead they'd been trans-ported to the dances they used to go to; the times when they were younger, and music had shaped their nights out at sweaty dance halls. The romance of music moved them, and Connie found that she in turn was warmed by their rosy, happy expressions. One old couple held hands as they listened, the woman nodding in time to the music; the husband transfixed by Henry's playing. The day had taken them all out of the war for a few hours' relief from their worries and anxieties.

Connie felt pleased that she'd stayed, and as she finished the last verse, she noticed that two new people had arrived.

Self-consciously, Richard Channing and Lady Hoxley were making their way in, full of comforting smiles and hellos. But was Channing wincing as Connie sung 'White Christmas'? Flaming cheek. She had a good mind to put him straight. Everyone told her she had the voice of an angel. But as the song finished, Channing clapped earnestly along with everyone else. The new arrivals were attracting a lot of attention and Connie was amused that people had straightened themselves up and adopted a more serious demeanour as the Lady of the Manor had appeared.

Lady Hoxley squeezed past some chairs to make her way to the piano.

'It seems like it's been a marvellous success, Reverend,'

Henry nodded and extended a hand to take Connie's, to draw her into the conversation. Connie wasn't sure of what to say and said something inappropriate.

'You wouldn't believe how much these people can eat!'

Ellen Hoxley nodded as if she'd said something fascinating and non-contentious and gave an anodyne answer. 'It's the highlight of a lot of these peoples' year.'

'How are you feeling, Mrs Jameson?' Channing had a stern look on his face. Connie realised that he wasn't impressed that he'd caught her exerting herself.

'Much better thanks. It's done me the world of good to get out of the vicarage and come down here. Mind you, I didn't know I'd be singing for me lunch though!'

Channing laughed good-naturedly.

'Connie's going to take it easy after this,' Henry volunteered. 'Aren't you, darling?'

'Yeah, I'm not doing the washing up or nothing.'

'Quite right. You can say that's doctor's orders.'

'See, Henry? I told you Doctor Channing was a proper doctor that knew his medicine,' Connie laughed.

As Henry offered Channing and Lady Hoxley a glass of wine, Connie watched as the old couple who'd been holding hands left the hall. They were still hand in hand as they bid their farewells and then they were framed briefly as silhouettes in the doorway as they left. She hoped and prayed that she and Henry would still share that sort of love when they were that age. She felt blessed to have found her soulmate. She was lucky.

Unlike Joyce.

She wouldn't have that luxury.

Channing and Lady Hoxley sipped their wine, with the good grace of guests who knew it was below par but who drank it anyway. They were talking animatedly to Henry about what he had accomplished with the Christmas meal. Connie caught snatches of the conversation, but her thoughts were with Joyce.

Connie felt the responsibility of checking that her friend was all right. Well, there was no way she would be all right, but it would be good to help her deal with her grief, wouldn't it? That's what friends did.

Connie watched Henry as he extolled the virtues of all the people who had been helping him: the verger who has opened the hall and set up the tables and chairs; the townswomen who had collated the rations of people in Helmstead; the ARP Warden who had badgered local farmers for donations. Henry was a good man. He was a man who had changed her life for the better, and a man whom she loved unconditionally. She couldn't imagine how Joyce was feeling. As she collected the sheet music from the piano and put it in Henry's leather bag that was sitting on his piano stool, she decided that she would head off to see Joyce straight away.

'Anyway, I'm pleased that you're on the mend, Mrs Jameson.' Lady Hoxley made a move that made it clear she was about to leave.

'Yes, thanks.' And then Connie thought of the question she needed to ask. 'Is there any word on the German airmen, Lady Hoxley?'

Channing shifted uneasily. Connie assumed that this was because the news wasn't good. Or because there was no news. Maybe they hadn't found them.

'The Home Guard is still searching. I believe they found the remains of a camp that the men had set up near Gorley Woods. Near to where you were attacked.' Lady Hoxley smiled tersely.

'I'm going to see how Joyce is getting on this afternoon. I can't let her rattle around Pasture Farm thinking about her John.'

'That's commendable,' Lady Hoxley smiled her consent. 'I plan to telephone the police in Leeds to see if they have any more details about what happened. It seems odd that John would perish in a fire and yet there are no reports about what happened to his brother.'

Channing looked distinctly uncomfortable and Connie was momentarily distracted by his apparent unease. Maybe he too was troubled by the fate of John's brother. His eyes darted quickly around as if deciding what to say next.

'I don't think you should be rushing around, Mrs Jameson. Not so soon after having a blow to the head.'

'But I'm fine now.'

'And I'm a doctor, Mrs Jameson.'

'Surely a little walk over to Pasture Farm won't harm the girl, Richard?' Lady Hoxley looked questioningly at him. 'The air would do her good. And besides she's been singing and helping here.'

'I would strongly advise her not to go, Ellen.'

'I know!' Lady Hoxley was struck by an idea, 'If you're worried about her walking over there, why not take her in your car? You could keep an eye on her and ensure she's not in any medical danger.'

Lady Hoxley looked pleased with herself.

Channing looked as if he'd accidentally torn up a winning football pools ticket.

'Well, I don't want to be no trouble.'

But Channing wasn't going to give in that easily.

'As I say, I don't think it's a sensible idea for her to go to the farm.' He stared directly at Connie, as if to implore her to see sense and do the right thing; to do what he wanted.

'Well, maybe we could bring Joyce to the vicarage then?' Lady Hoxley looked from Henry to Connie. Connie realised that she wasn't going to give up until she got her own way and would do everything she could to find a way for Connie to see her friend. Connie liked this kind side of Lady Hoxley.

'Fine, I'll take her to the farmhouse.' Channing's harsh tone surprised all of them. Henry and Connie exchanged a look, thinking this must be overspill from a previous argument or some other problem between the pair. Perhaps the morning hadn't gone so well for them . . .

'There we are then.' Whatever she was feeling inside, Lady Hoxley's public mask didn't slip for a moment. Whatever annoyance she felt with Richard for snapping at her wasn't going to be acknowledged in a village hall in front of everyone.

Connie nodded her thanks.

'I don't have much petrol. But I suppose I'll have enough to take you there. Goodbye, Reverend.'

Channing shook Henry's hand, placed his trilby on his head and walked out into the crisp late afternoon air. Lady Hoxley said her goodbyes and wished everyone a happy Christmas.

'I'll send Richard to the vicarage to pick you up.' She gave Connie a tight smile, then she too left the village hall. Henry moved to give direction to some of the volunteers who were clearing up, but he turned to speak to his wife as soon as Channing and Lady Hoxley had gone.

'Are you sure you'll be all right?'

'I'll be fine. I'll stay at the farmhouse tonight and come back tomorrow sometime. That way I won't get tired and no one will have to come back for me today.' Connie was relieved that she was going to see Joyce. She'd worried about her since she heard the news about John and that concern had escalated following the telephone conversation.

'Will you be all right clearing up all this?'

'It'll be fine. Please pass my deepest condolences to Joyce, won't you?'

Connie pecked him on the cheek and made her way outside to where clusters of pensioners were saying protracted goodbyes, enjoying making the warm-hearted companionship of their lunch last that little bit longer. As her eyes adjusted to the unnaturally bright afternoon light, she watched as Channing and Lady Hoxley moved off towards the town square, their outlines silhouetted as they walked. There was a physical distance between her elegant frame and his tailored shape. And Connie wondered if Lady Hoxley was waiting for the right moment to lay into him about his earlier behaviour. Connie knew that's what she would do if she had a beef with Henry. Or maybe posh people didn't behave the same way . . .

'I don't know what's gotten into you today, Richard.'

As soon as they were out of earshot of the people outside the village hall, Lady Hoxley's carapace of calm had cracked. 'Surely there's no danger for Mrs Jameson to be moving around. After all, she's been helping to run the pensioners' lunch and she's been singing songs at the piano. All of that looked quite exerting.'

Richard Channing nodded. He would appease Lady Hoxley with some medical jargon later, obscuring his own true thoughts about the matter. It was a simple problem that he was facing, and he had to face it alone. The logistics were troubling him. Tomorrow morning, he was due to go to Pasture Farm to collect the German airmen. The last thing he wanted was for another person to be added to the equation; another hostage for the airmen to navigate. It was hard enough that he'd have to deal with Joyce Fisher and Esther Reeves, without someone as spirited and unpredictable as Connie Carter being there too.

Why couldn't Connie do as he advised?

People were always messing up his plans. That's why he had to do the things he didn't want to do.

Channing also had some marginal concern towards his patient. Of course, he didn't want harm to befall her or indeed any of the women stuck in the middle of this nightmare. But the majority of his concern was concentrated on saving his own skin. He'd already gone over and over in his head all the things that he could think may happen when he went to the farm tomorrow. Adding the volatile Connie Carter to the mix wasn't helping the ulcers that were gnawing in his stomach.

He hoped he wouldn't be forced to hurt anyone. Not again. No, as long as no one forced him to do anything bad, it would be all right.

Within the hour, as Connie sat in the vicarage listening to the radio, a well-maintained four-door Ford 7W Ten pulled up outside the window. It was a dark green 1937 model, but it hadn't been driven much judging by the good condition of the bodywork. An attractive vertical grille was sandwiched between two bulbous lights that stood off the mud shields on stalks like bug eyes. Connie didn't know when Channing had acquired the vehicle, but she hadn't seen him in it before. He slunk out of the car as if he'd rather have stayed inside and Connie detected a weary expression on his face. She met him by the front door wearing her crimson two-piece suit; a Sunday best outfit to which she had added a fox fur stole in an attempt to appease any medical concerns about her 'catching a chill'. But Channing didn't seem bothered about medical matters. He gave her a cursory smile and silently opened the passenger door for her.

Connie climbed in and then Channing got in his side. He smoothed down his trousers and sighed. Connie had seen this behaviour before in men. They usually did such actions when they had something on their mind; something that needed saying. Hating awkward silences, Connie thought she'd help winkle it out in her own inimitable way.

'What's wrong, doctor?'

'Nothing.' The word that came out of his mouth was in direct contrast to the unease in his eyes and the slight sheen of sweat on his forehead. 'I don't think you should go that's all.'

'I'll be fine.'

'It's not you. It's Joyce. You see when people suffer bereavement, they sometimes need time to adjust. Their recovery is improved if they don't have people coming in and out all the time. They do better if they're left to their own thoughts.'

Connie was no medic, but this sounded utter rubbish; hastily constructed jargon to fob her off. She inhaled and her derision displayed itself as a snort.

Channing bristled, his eyebrows tensing in barely-suppressed anger.

'She'd still be going over it, again and again though. Whereas if I'm there and Esther's there, we can talk about it when she's ready and, I don't know, make cups of tea for her when she wants them.'

Then Connie added her own bit of wisdom, 'Henry says

that bereaved people can never have enough tea. And he knows; he's done enough funerals.'

Channing rubbed his face in his hands, before focusing on the windscreen.

'Very well, but don't say I didn't warn you.'

Connie thought this was an odd and slightly unsettling thing for him to say, but she didn't probe the matter. Instead, she watched as he started the Ford and they pulled away. They drove to Pasture Farm in silence.

When he pulled up in his car outside the vicarage, he hoped that Connie might have fallen asleep. As he mulled over the minimum amount of time he could give it before driving off, Connie opened the front door and waved cheerfully at him. As she walked over to the car, Channing mustered the strength to get out and open the door for her. As she got in, he shut the door. Knowing he was obscured by the angle of her seat, it was the only moment he could allow himself to show what he felt. His face showing a flash of anger.

Why were they forcing him to do this?

As he started the engine, he thought about damage limitation. What would be the best thing to do?

His first thought almost made him utter a small laugh, but he fought the urge to express it. Yes, his first thought was to drive them off the road. If they both had a car crash then he'd never have to go to Pasture Farm. And by the time he was patched up, the German problem might have resolved itself. Or someone else from the network might have picked them up. Yes, that would preserve Channing's cover.

That would be one solution.

But he dismissed this fanciful and desperate idea. It was a risky strategy as he may hurt himself more than he bargained for in the crash.

But it might stop Connie Carter.

No, he had to put that option out of his mind and think of something more sensible; something with fewer random factors involved in the outcome.

The car clattered along one of the country roads leading out of the town. The frost and rain of the last week had left large furrows either side of a central ridge and Channing's car was finding it tough going. They jolted from side to side as he made his way slowly forwards; the weight of the gun in his pocket brushing against his leg as they went over each bump.

Channing's mind was working feverishly to solve his problem. Connie was looking uneasy.

'*Very well, but don't say I didn't warn you.*'

The words echoed in his memory.

Why had he said that to her?

He berated himself for that ridiculous, veiled threat. What was he thinking? It was stupid and it could give the game away.

By the time they got to the end of the bumpy road and found a road with a passable level of tarmac, Channing had decided what to do.

Yes, he had a plan.

He'd drop Connie at the gates of Pasture Farm, drive off and let nature take its course. She'd be walking into the lion's den, but he'd done everything he could to deter her, hadn't he?

'But don't say I didn't warn you.'

Would it make her realise that he knew what was waiting for her? No, he couldn't afford to over-analyse things. He'd been talking about the healing process for Joyce and how Connie's presence could harm that, that's all, hadn't he?

Just drop her off and forget about her.

Yes, that's what he'd do.

But there was one thing he hadn't planned for.

As they pulled away on the road from Gorley Wood to Pasture Farm, Connie spied a lorry parked at the side of the road. It was blackened and burnt out, but the livery of Edgar Varish and Sons, Fertilisers was still legible on the tailgate. She recognised it from when it would make deliveries to Pasture Farm.

'That's Alfred's lorry.'

And as they pulled level to it, Connie waved her hand at Channing. 'Could you stop please, Doctor Channing?'

'What?'

'Please stop! I know the man what owns it!'

Barely masking his annoyance at this unexpected delay, Channing put his foot on the brake and eased the car to a halt on the other side of the road.

'I'll see what's happened.' Connie pulled open her door and got out. 'I won't be a moment.'

Channing watched her cross the front of the car and head over the small road to the lorry. From this angle, he could see that there wasn't much left of it. The metal framework on the back was still intact but blackened and charred. Most of the engine had been lost in the fire. The cab was blackened but the livery was still readable on the door.

Idly, Channing wondered what had happened to it. The fire didn't look that recent, maybe it had happened a couple of days ago. As Connie checked the cab and walked around the vehicle, she glanced back and Channing and shrugged.

Did she expect to find the man she knew inside? She seemed to have a grim fascination in finding out, but Channing was sure that a body would have been removed by now. After a moment, Connie seemed to reach the same conclusion, but she remained standing at the front of the cab, a look of bafflement on her face as if working out what might have happened to Alfred Barnes.

And Channing had a new idea suddenly.

He removed the brake and moved the car slowly forward off the verge on his side of the road and positioned it centrally in the lane. Connie looked over. He hoped that she would think he was getting the car in position to move off when she was ready. He eyed her in the wing mirror as she walked away from the truck.

He could reverse now and knock her down.

That would stop her getting in the way and complicating things tomorrow, wouldn't it?

Leave her for dead.

He could tell everyone that he last saw her at the gate of Pasture Farm. That's where he'd delivered her to see her friend Joyce. No, he didn't know why she had wandered down the road to Gorley Wood. No, he didn't know what had happened to her.

A tense smile spread on the doctor's face as he played this scenario out in his head.

But could he get away with it? The impact would dent the rear of his Ford, linking him to the crime. That would be hard to explain. Unless he was lucky enough to hit her without denting it – in which case he might be all right.

But it was a big risk.

The seconds spent deliberating robbed Channing of the impetus and opportunity to complete the crime. He couldn't act in such a reckless, spur-of-the-moment way. Not again.

His luck at getting away with murder wouldn't last surely?

Connie reached the passenger side of the car and got in, not realising how close she had come to being flattened.

'There's no sign of Alfred.'

'I daresay he got out before it exploded. Did you know him well?'

He asked the question, not because he was particularly interested in the answer, but because he wanted the normality of conversation to fill his head rather than his exhausting thoughts of murder. The human brain wasn't made for such thoughts and the accompanying continued rush of adrenaline that came with them. He felt as if he'd had far too much coffee, the veins in his temples pulsing. As he drove along the country lane, the burnt-out truck receding in his wing mirrors, he enjoyed the feeling of normality as Connie's chatter washed over him.

Think normal thoughts.

'Alfred would come to the farm, see? He'd supply us with fertiliser. But Finch always played tricks on the poor man. He put brandy in his tea once. And Alfred Barnes is a proper teetotaller, so that wasn't appreciated! You can imagine!'

Connie looked pensive. 'I suppose I should say he *was* a proper teetotaller, shouldn't I? On account of him being dead, eh?'

'You don't know that he's dead.' The winter sun dappled through the trees onto his windscreen. 'I can find out from the hospital staff what happened, if you like? They might know.'

'Yeah, thanks.'

Soon they came to Pasture Farm and Channing pulled to a halt outside the gate.

'I won't go any further. I don't want to interrupt if Joyce is settled.'

Connie nodded and thanked him for the lift.

'I'll come back for you tomorrow if you like?' Channing was surprised that he'd said the words, but even as they landed, he realised it made perfect sense.

Yes, you clever man. There was the subconscious helping him out in his time of need.

If she agreed, then his return to the farm would now have a perfectly legitimate motive. He would come to collect Connie and just happen to meet the two German airmen. He'd seemingly overpower them and force them to get in the car; before bringing them to safety.

It sounded perfect.

And it eased the pulsing in his temples to think of it. He had an alibi; a reason for being at the farm; that he felt comfortable with.

'Well, if it's no trouble. Thanks.'

'No trouble.'

Channing watched her out of the corner of his eye as she

got out of the car and went to the gate, pulling up the latch. There was no doubt about it, she was a beautiful woman, but one with the coarse nature of an alley cat. He liked her spirit and her mettle.

As he drove away, he wondered if he'd have to kill her tomorrow.

Connie was pleased to be away from Doctor Channing. He was a strange fish. She didn't like his arrogance or his abrupt changes of mood. She'd met too many men who had a violent streak not to suspect that Channing was capable of similar things.

She walked along the yard and around to the back door of Pasture Farm. She could see condensation on the kitchen window and idly thought that they must have finished lunch by now. That was fine. She'd eaten anyway at the village hall.

She reached out to knock.

Chapter 12

Everyone froze at the knock on the door. All eyes glanced towards it. Emory Mayer brought his hand down towards Joyce's face, but instead of hitting her, he gently pressed his hand over her mouth to stop her calling out. Siegfried held Esther by the top of her arms as she stopped struggling. The four of them listened. In the glass of the door they could make out a shape; nothing more.

'We'd better answer it.' Esther's voice was a tremulous whisper, betraying the fear that gripped her. Joyce couldn't speak and was finding it hard to breathe with Emory's hand over her face. He was also pressed against her on the floor, forcing the air from her lungs. Emory shifted his weight, putting a meaty hand out onto the tiles to push himself up. He shot a look of contempt at Joyce as he got off her; a warning to be silent. She knew that this was unfinished business. Emory crossed to Siegfried and they spoke quickly and quietly in German.

There was another knock at the door.

Joyce squinted to try to make out any shape in the glass, but whoever was there was standing too far away from the door.

After the brief, whispered discussion, Siegfried came over to Joyce and helped her up from the floor. Her elbow was bruised, and her cheek was swollen. She realised that a small amount of blood was trickling from her right nostril. Emory threw a tea towel at her.

'You need to get them to go away,' Siegfried whispered. 'Get rid of them.'

'We will kill your friend if you try any tricks,' Emory added. He picked up the pistol and pressed it against Esther's temple. She squealed in panic. Wordlessly, he clasped a hand to Esther's mouth and guided her gently back from the sink and through to the parlour.

'Answer it,' Emory whispered to Joyce.

Esther's eyes were wide with panic. Emory closed the door to the parlour. Shakily, Joyce moved towards the back door, but realised she couldn't open it – it was locked.

'Won't be a minute!' She stalled for time. 'I'll just get the key.' She patted at her cheek and nose with the tea towel and tried to straighten her hair as best as she could.

Siegfried moved quickly to the parlour where he spoke to Emory. She heard a few whispered words in German and then Siegfried returned with the key. He threw it to Joyce and then made his way to the staircase, hiding himself in the recess at the bottom. She could still see him as he nodded for her to open the back door. Then he disappeared from view.

Joyce glanced at the table; four places visible to anyone who cared to look. Esther may have cleared the plates, but the glasses, napkins and side plates were still there.

But there was no time to change that.

Joyce felt her stomach fall into her boots. She wished she could run away, but there was no alternative way out. With a heavy heart, she put the key in the lock and opened it. She affixed her best false smile as she let the cold air and her old friend in.

Connie looked shocked at the sight of her. Joyce could feel that her nose was bleeding.

'Joyce?'

'I'm all right. You shouldn't be here, should you? There's no need for you to come out here today.'

'What sort of friend would I be if I stayed away?' Connie smiled. Joyce noticed her smile falter as she noticed the signs of the struggle in the kitchen. A knife and fork and napkin lay on the floor by the sink; along with an overturned chair.

'What's happened here?'

'Nothing. Look you should go.'

'Joyce?' Connie wasn't having it.

Joyce realised that she had to make something up to explain it, 'I fell off my chair, that's all. I'd had too much carrot whiskey. You should go.'

A drop of blood dribbled from Joyce's nose. Connie's face showed that she didn't believe this story for an instant. Joyce struggled not to crumple into tears.

'Please . . .'

'No.' Connie's voice was soft, but resolute.

And at last, the two friends looked at each other with a silent understanding. Joyce knew that Connie realised something was badly wrong here.

Connie reached the door and gave it a knock. As she did so, she heard something – cutlery maybe – clatter to the tiled floor inside.

And did someone groan? No, that must be her imagination. Don't be daft, Connie.

She waited for an answer and wished she'd brought some sort of gift with her. She should have smuggled a bottle of Mrs Hewson's dandelion wine along with her. It was rancid stuff, but it did the job. And beggars couldn't be choosers when there was a war on.

Connie moved closer to the glass and stood on tip toes to see through. Like the kitchen window, it was heavy with condensation from the oven and she couldn't see anything inside.

But then the door opened.

Joyce stood in front of her. It wasn't a warm welcome. In fact, Joyce looked like she wished it wasn't Connie stood there. But that was fair enough. Connie wouldn't stay long if they didn't want her to. She just wanted to show her support, that was all.

Joyce looked more dishevelled than she'd expected. Her clothes looked crumpled and her hair was a mess. Connie moved inside the kitchen and looked at Joyce properly in the light. Her friend looked haunted, pale and bruised. Why was she bruised? Yes, her cheek was swollen.

There were four places at the table. What was going on? Everyone was away, weren't they? It should only be Esther and Joyce in the house. Maybe Martin and Iris had come back from Shallow Brook Farm and—

Then she saw the blood trickling from Joyce's nose.

'What's happened here?'

'Nothing. Look you should go.'

'Joyce?' Connie knew that nothing didn't cause damage to people's faces.

'I fell off my chair, that's all. I'd had too much carrot whiskey.'

Connie looked at her friend. She could see in her face that it was a lie. But why was she covering up? She had every right to be honest in this time of grief; every right to take owner-ship of anything she had done during her trauma. Even it was knocking over a chair in anger or frustration.

'You should go.'

A drop of blood dribbled from Joyce's nose. Connie didn't believe this story for an instant.

'Please . . .' Joyce was biting her lip; struggling not to cry. Connie could see the panic and fear in Joyce's eyes; the implicit, unspoken underlining of Joyce's words, the universal sign of someone straining their eyes to be as wide as possible as they talk to you. It was a silent warning. She was telling her to run away, to save herself from something awful.

'No.' Connie wasn't going anywhere; not when her friend needed her. It wouldn't have been right to leave her. Mind you, none of this seemed right.

Later, Connie would realise that she might have been able to walk away at that moment. If she'd have turned on her heel, nodded to Joyce's request and gone, she'd have left the farm-house none-the-wiser as to what was happening. She could have avoided all the conflict to come if she'd taken Joyce's words at face value. But Connie was a good friend, so she didn't go immediately. Instead, she asked one more question.

'Tell me what's happening.'

And that question meant that the time to walk away was over. From that moment on, Connie would be trapped in the same waking nightmare as her friend.

She'd taken a fork in the road.

Some days change your life forever.

'Tell me what's happening.' Connie seemed to look deep into her soul; as if she already knew everything there was to know.

Joyce tried to stop her face from crumbling. She'd tried to look neutral, to give nothing away. Not like when she used to play cards at home with her mum and Gwen and Charlie. Then her face was an open mirror to the cards in her hand. She didn't want Connie to see the worry and the fear. She wanted her friend to get out and go back to Henry, her loving husband. Connie had already come off worse from meeting these two airmen, and Joyce didn't want her to experience any more pain at their hands. But Joyce couldn't stop her face from giving it away. She couldn't stop her voice from trembling slightly and betraying her. She wished she could have acted better at that moment.

Out the corner of her eye, she saw Siegfried rising from the stairs. Connie hadn't noticed as the young man slowly and stealthily made his way behind her. The chance to get Connie to leave was gone. Joyce wished there had been another way.

There was nothing else for it. Joyce had to warn her friend. That was the least that she could do.

'Connie, you've got to get out!' Joyce screamed the words,

making Connie startle slightly. But then Connie noticed from her peripheral vision the young man in the overalls coming towards her. Did she recognise him from when she'd been knocked off her bicycle? Connie moved quickly towards the back door and got a hand to the doorknob, before Siegfried caught her.

Connie raised a hand to block Siegfried as he tried to grab her, but he had his arms locked around her before she could fully raise it. Emory appeared from the parlour, holding a frightened Esther at gunpoint. Connie snarled in anger. She struggled as if she was a landed eel, but Siegfried had pinned her arms. Connie's struggles were futile. She tried to bring her head down on his to head butt him away, but he was too low against her body. Joyce stood helplessly, powerless for now, knowing that Esther might be shot and Connie hurt if she intervened.

'Get off me!' Connie shouted.

'Stay still!' Siegfried shouted back.

Connie tried to twist and tried to knee him in the face, but again she was at the wrong angle to make it land and for a moment it looked like they were engaged in a strange and ludicrous dance.

Finally, his weight managed to pull her over and they landed on a heap on the floor, with Siegfried still gripping her and Connie landing on her bottom. He took a step back, breathless, and viewed the fiery eyes of Connie Carter as she stared balefully up at him.

'Stay down there if you don't want to get hurt!' Siegfried snapped.

'What the hell's going on?'

'You are our prisoners.' Emory pushed Esther towards the farmhouse table, where she pulled out a chair and sat compliantly. She knew the routine.

'If we do what they say, we won't get hurt, lovey.' Esther looked pleadingly at her. Connie glanced at the two strange men. Did she believe Esther's reassurances? Joyce looked like she'd already been hurt.

'You're the airmen. You're the bastards what knocked me out.'

'We can do worse things than that if you don't cooperate,' Emory flexed one his hands, tensing it into a fist. Joyce noticed that Siegfried looked uncomfortable; once again perhaps showing signs of compassion that the older man lacked.

'What is your name?' The older German moved slowly closer.

'Connie. Connie Carter.' Then she corrected herself. 'I mean Jameson. Connie Jameson. I'm married. What's your flaming name?'

'If you want to see your husband again, you will help us? Do you understand?'

'Yeah.' Connie's belligerent expression was firmly in place on her face. Joyce realised that Emory was wary of this new prisoner. She knew from bitter, recent experience that Emory was at his most dangerous when he felt threatened. As a good friend, she knew she had to tell Connie to ride this one out. She had to be less confrontational; for now at least.

But Connie's expression wasn't softening or showing signs of being more compliant. Instead, her mouth was open in what looked like disgust and disbelief. What was she playing at? What was she doing?

Connie was transfixed by the blue and white spotted hand-kerchief that poked out of Emory's breast pocket on the suit that didn't fit him. She knew that the suit belonged to Alfred Barnes of Varish and Sons, the fertiliser salesman.

As Siegfried went to help her up, she pushed him away. His overalls had a small badge sewn into the pocket – the Varish and Sons logo. These two men must have had something to do with Alfred's lorry being torched. What had these monsters done?

'Did you kill Alfred?'

The question caught them off-guard.

'Who?' The older German shrugged.

'The man whose suit you're wearing. Those overalls are his too, aren't they?' Connie put her hand to her face, realising what they had done. It was made even worse by the fact that they didn't even know Alfred's name. He had just been a random man who had got in their way; a life that they'd ended because he was in the wrong place at the wrong time.

'You will sit down and be quiet!' Emory's rage made Esther flinch. Eyeing him with contempt, Connie pulled out a chair and sat at the kitchen table. Joyce sat down too. Siegfried locked the back door and moved off to have a talk with Emory; the two men staying in the doorway of the parlour so they could keep an eye on their captives. After a moment, they came back, and Emory spoke.

'You will all go upstairs.' Emory's eyes narrowed.

'What?' Esther looked confused, unnerved.

'To the bedroom. Now!'

'Why?'

'Do not ask questions!'

Connie got up from her seat. Tentatively, Esther and Joyce did the same. Emory waved the gun to chivvy them along.

Dutifully, the women moved up the narrow staircase, with Emory a few steps behind them. He motioned with the gun for them to go into Joyce's bedroom. Connie and Esther went inside, but as Joyce went to follow, he grabbed her arm.

'Hey, leave off her!' Connie rounded on him.

'Shut up! You will not get another warning.' Emory closed the door.

Connie heard the key turn in the lock and listened to the sounds of Joyce being dragged across the landing. It sounded like they were going to the bathroom. Connie heard the bathroom door slam. What was happening?

'Let me out of here!' Connie banged on the door.

Esther sat on the bed, a lost expression on her face. Connie noticed her lack of resistance.

'Here, it'll be all right, you'll see.' Connie hoped that she could believe what she was saying was true.

Joyce was pushed into the bathroom with enough force to make her tumble towards the bath. Emory came in behind her and closed the door.

'What do you want?' Was he going to continue the beating that he tried to give her in the kitchen? Or – Heaven forbid – was he planning something worse?

'You will dress my wound.' Emory tucked the gun into the waistband of his suit. He pulled off the jacket and threw it over the edge of the bath before rolling up his sleeve.

Joyce felt palpable relief.

'Yes, of course. I'll need to get some more bandages, from the first aid kit.'

'Where did you put it?'

'It's back under the sink in the kitchen.'

Emory considered this for a moment before giving a curt nod. Joyce emerged from the bathroom and moved down the creaking staircase. Siegfried greeted her at the bottom with a curious look.

'I need more bandages. From the kitchen.'

'All right.' Siegfried made way for her.

Joyce went towards the sink, feeling him watching her. As she bent down to open the cupboards underneath, she was aware that his attention had switched back to the stairs. He shouted something in German up to Emory and waited for a reply. Joyce took the bandage that she needed from Esther's tin and closed the cupboard. She stood up and noticed the breadknife on the draining board.

It was too sharp thanks to Finch's insistence on grinding it on his sharpening wheel.

Siegfried was still talking, still distracted.

Joyce picked up the breadknife. It would be a useful weapon to keep to hand in case things escalated. But she needed to bide her time. She couldn't defeat both of them on her own. She knew she needed to get it upstairs to her room.

If only she had her gumboots on; the blade could be slid down the boot and hidden easily from view. But here she was dressed in a blouse and trousers with flat shoes.

Maybe she could slide it down her trouser leg, suspended from the waistband. Yes, that could work if she went upstairs carefully.

But then she thought about tending Emory's wound. That would mean she'd be crouching in the bathroom and the blade would clatter out. And unless she was ready to use it, that would be disastrous. If she got into a fight, she needed Connie and Esther to be free from the locked bedroom to even the odds.

'What are you doing?'

It was Siegfried with suspicion in his voice.

Joyce ducked down, opened the cupboard under the sink and slipped the breadknife inside. It would have to wait until she was better prepared.

'Just got the wrong bandage.' Joyce was covering for the delay. She was impressed with how easy a lie could come when she was under pressure. She stood up with a smile, closing the cupboard, the bandage in her outstretched hand; the knife stashed inside the cupboard.

'Come on then, get on with it.' Siegfried waved her past.

Joyce ran back upstairs and went into the bathroom. Emory eyed her with contempt. Carefully she pulled his sleeve up away from the bandage that was already in place. There was some staining and as she peeled away the fabric, she could see that something was wrong.

'Does it hurt?'

'Of course, it hurts.' Then he took a more sanguine tone. 'It feels like it is burning, you know?'

'It's infected.' Joyce knew enough from her volunteer shifts at the hospital to recognise the signs. 'You need to get it treated.'

'You can treat it?' It was a question not a statement; the first sign of vulnerability.

'Not really. I mean I could wash it again with alcohol and put a new dressing on. But you need a doctor to look at this.'

'Do that. Do those things. Do what you can.' Emory sighed. 'The doctor part will have to wait until I am away from here.'

Joyce washed his arm in the sink; watching as he winced in pain. Emory gritted his teeth, breathing fast in an effort to suppress the discomfort. The skin on his upper arm was the crimson red of Connie's suit, with blotches of orange. Joyce did the best job she could, before binding it tightly; but she wondered what would happen if he didn't get it treated. He winced as she applied a safety pin to the dressing and the wound was obviously more painful for him than it had been previously.

After she had finished the work, Emory took her across the landing and locked her in the bedroom with the other women.

'Are you all right?' Connie asked.

'Yes, just had to dress his wound. I'm so sorry you got dragged into this.'

'I realise now you was trying to warn me, weren't you? Getting Henry's name wrong on the telephone. That was a warning, wasn't it?'

233

Joyce nodded.

'I just thought you were confused.'

'Sorry. I wish I could have made it clearer.'

They listened as Emory stomped downstairs. After a few minutes, Joyce could hear the distinctive tap-tap of the Morse code transmitter in the parlour, the sound of which seemed to carry around the small farmhouse. The worsening state of Emory's condition had obviously galvanised him to get help. Joyce hoped that someone would answer his call soon so they could be free of this nightmare.

She looked at the tired face of Esther and the concerned face of Connie. Would they all be kept in this room until it was over? An early evening breeze rattled against the windows.

Joyce could feel another frost coming.

Chapter 13

Esther dozed fitfully on the bed.

Connie and Joyce sat on the floor at the end of it. Joyce played with the tassels on the eiderdown and watched as the sky in the window frame darkened. She'd waited until Esther went to sleep before discussing what they were going to do. Esther was exhausted and needed to sleep. Connie seemed lost in her own thoughts. From time to time, Connie and Joyce would glance at each other; an unspoken solidarity and strength in the face of the odds facing them.

'So what do you think they'll do?' Connie voice was a whisper. She didn't want to wake Esther or be overheard by their captors. Neither of them could be certain that the occasional creaks on the landing were just the sounds of an old building settling on a cold day.

'They're sending messages using the wireless,' Joyce replied, keeping her voice equally low. 'They think someone will come for them.'

'Who's going to come?'

'Just like there are evasion lines in France for our airmen, there's something similar here. Although I don't think it's as well organised as the French one. I don't know.'

Joyce couldn't help but think about John as she spoke about evasion lines and France. They'd brought her husband back to her. No, she couldn't think about that now.

A house fire in Leeds.

John was asleep inside.

She had to shut out those stupid lies. She had to focus on escaping from this situation. She had to focus on saving Esther and Connie.

'How long will they have to wait then?' Connie asked.

'I don't know.' Joyce shrugged. 'They can't get incoming messages on the wireless. So they may have been sending the messages to no one.'

'So we could be holed up in this room for days?'

'No.' Joyce had an air of defiance in her voice. 'It's Christmas Eve tomorrow. Finch and Iris, Frank and Martin will all be back. Whatever happens, things will be bound to change when they do. And the home guard will resume searching too.'

'But will they come here?'

'Horace came the other day to tell us what was going on. He was surprised to hear there were two airmen out there.'

'Why was he surprised? I told Doctor Channing that a few days ago.' Connie found that strange. 'You'd think he'd have got the message out to the people doing the search, wouldn't you?'

'Maybe he was busy.'

'Too busy to do something important like that? Seems odd.'

Joyce shrugged in agreement. Yes, it was strange that the

message from Channing hadn't been disseminated to all members of the Home Guard. But then she couldn't be sure that some of them had been told and forgotten, thanks to the fog of old age and the preoccupation of the impending Christmas celebrations.

'Still, they know now. And I'm sure they'll come round here again to check on us.'

The level of confidence was high in her voice, but the truth was that she wasn't sure. The fact was that the Home Guard might not come back again. What if the search was called off? Or what if they were following leads that led them far away from here? And if they did come back, would they make it in time?

'We can't wait.' Connie had reached the same conclusion. 'We've got to have a plan to get out of here, Joyce.'

Joyce nodded. She leant forward and spoke even more softly and told Connie about the breadknife downstairs and her plan to smuggle it upstairs. She told her that she needed to be wearing her gumboots to smuggle it up here. Connie had an idea.

'The chickens – the layers – we'll need to collect the eggs and check on them. If we can both get out there, we'd be wearing our boots. And then one of us could smuggle the knife up here, couldn't they?'

'Then we'd have a weapon at least.' Joyce closed her eyes, thinking it through.

It sounded a good plan. Or the start of one at least. She felt slightly re-energized by having Connie here. Esther seemed lost; a woman retreating inside herself until the danger was gone. At least Connie would give her someone to discuss her plans with, someone who could veto the more dangerous or risky ones; someone with whom she could share the responsibility of escape. She had a partner; a friend who would be looking out for her.

'We're assuming they'll care about the chickens though!' Joyce was playing devil's advocate.

'They will if there's no other food in the house.' It was Esther's voice. She'd startled both of them as they had assumed she was asleep. She swung her feet off the bed and yawned, glancing at the darkening window. Esther closed the curtains and then sat on the end of the bed so she could join in the hushed conversation with Connie and Joyce.

'So we get the knife up here. And then I suppose we threaten them to leave. Is that what we do?' The truth was that her head had been so muddled that she'd been too exhausted to think far beyond that. It wasn't much of a plan.

Connie shook her head. 'Trouble is that they've got a pistol, haven't they? If only we had a gun – that could even the odds.'

Then Joyce told them what she'd seen in the tool shed.

'Finch bought a shotgun, remember? When he went to buy that flaming pig, he came back with a shotgun. It's in his tool shed!'

'Then we use the knife to distract them while one of us runs to the tool shed. Then we use the shotgun to get rid of them!' Connie's eyes were blazing as the idea took hold.

Joyce liked the euphemism of Connie's last words. That could mean anything from driving them away from the farm or shooting them. Joyce thought she'd be happy to see them gone, by whatever means was necessary.

'When do you think we should try to get the gun?' Esther stretched her neck to relieve a knot in it.

'We could do it when we collect the eggs first thing tomorrow morning. And we use the egg collection tonight to get the knife up here into the room.'

The three women agreed; it sounded a workable, if perilous, plan. But what plan wouldn't be perilous? The egg run tonight – they'd get the knife. The egg run tomorrow – they'd get the gun.

'Now we've got to hope they like the idea of an egg for breakfast.' Connie was smiling. Joyce laughed and found that the laugh threatened to morph into heaving-shouldered crying as her body tried to let out all the anxiety and stress of the last few days. She let it come. Connie and Esther hugged her as the sobbing subsided. Joyce kept insisting that she was all right, but then she'd find herself crying some more. Esther told her to let it all out. It was for the best. She couldn't keep it bottled up.

An hour and a half later, Emory and Siegfried stood in the bedroom doorway looking at the three women in front of them. Joyce and Esther had catnapped while Connie kept an ear out for their captors. And when Connie heard the men coming up the stairs, she woke her friends.

'You will come downstairs.' Emory moved to one side.

'Why?' Connie stood up.

'Because we tell you to.'

'We need you there in case anyone comes to the door this evening,' Siegfried explained. 'And we'd appreciate it if you would cook us something to eat please.'

Emory glowered at his companion. Joyce assumed he didn't see the need for politeness. He obviously preferred the more heavy-handed approach, as she'd seen.

'We don't really have much food in.' Joyce was laying the first stage of the plan.

'Then improvise.' Emory turned to go.

'We could collect some eggs from the chickens. Make an omelette.'

'Very well,' Emory left the room and Siegfried waited for the women to gather themselves. They all trouped downstairs.

When they reached the kitchen and Joyce started to put on her boots, Emory had an idea.

'Why don't you kill a chicken?' To Emory it was the most obvious thing in the world. Joyce didn't have an answer to that. These men were hardly likely to respect the law of the land and observe the rules of rationing.

'We could. But we still need to collect the eggs.'

The men conferred with each other. Finally, Emory nodded and pointed at Joyce.

'You come and do it. The others will stay.'

'It's a big pen,' Connie piped up. 'It's a two-person job.'

'Let her help me, it'll be quicker with two of us.' Joyce tried to modulate her voice, so it was a throwaway statement, and not the most important thing in the world.

'No,' Emory wasn't having it. 'You will do it on your own.'

This was going wrong.

This would scupper the first part of the plan. How was Joyce going to get the knife from under the sink if she was alone with these men? She needed someone else with her to act as a distraction. She couldn't slide the breadknife down her gum boot without being spotted otherwise. But what could she say without it raising Emory's suspicions? As Joyce pondered what to do, help came from an unexpected source. Siegfried spoke in German to his commander, before repeating it in English for the benefit of the women.

'We keep Esther hostage in case there is any trick.'

'Fine,' Joyce suddenly felt awkward that she'd agreed Esther's fate as flippantly as it was deciding who wouldn't have a second biscuit at teatime.

'Yes, that's fine,' Esther put on a brave face. 'The important thing is that it's done. Otherwise we'll have nothing to eat the rest of the time you're here, will we?'

She sounded like a landlady speaking to her guests rather than a hostage speaking to her captors. But for Joyce a different message was being conveyed. Esther was saying that she was happy for Joyce to go. She was saying that their plan was the most important thing. For them to escape, they had to execute the plan.

Joyce and Connie moved to leave, with Joyce wearing her gumboots. Connie was still wearing her high-heels and her crimson suit. It wasn't suitable attire for mucking out the chickens, but they didn't exactly have a choice in the matter. The men weren't likely to give them time to change.

Siegfried took the gun from Emory and watched Esther as

Emory left. 'See you in a moment.' Emory made his way through the door.

'Wait a minute.' Joyce needed to complete the next stage.

'What is it?' Emory was annoyed at the delay.

'I need something for the eggs. Something to put them in.'

As Joyce moved to the sink, Connie smiled at Emory with an awkwardness as if they were too strangers who had made too much eye contact while waiting for a bus. She knew how to get someone's interest and that's just what she intended to do.

Emory was distracted by Connie as Joyce opened the cupboard under the sink. Emory glanced back at Joyce. Connie knew she had to try harder to hold his attention.

'Do you think I could have a look outside on the step for some boots? I'm going to mess these lovely red shoes right up,' Connie indicated the length of her heels in a bid to distract him. She knew that the turn of a heel could sometimes stop Henry from writing his sermons and she hoped it might have a similar effect now. And indeed, Emory looked momentarily interested in her shapely legs, before he returned his interest to Joyce.

'Well, can I have a look?'

'What?'

'For some boots?'

'Go on.' Emory unlocked the back door and opened it for Connie. She made a big play of looking around by the mat and the boot scraper. Dolores's boots were there. Connie picked one up.

'These are too big for me. That Dolores has got feet like skis. But I don't know what choice I've got really, do you?'

Emory shook his head, focusing his full attention on her. 'You keep your shoes. I won't have any messing around.'

'There will be plenty of mess around if I keep these shoes on,' Connie replied, buying Joyce more time.

Joyce slid the breadknife from the cupboard; making sure she didn't make a sound as she hid it down her gumboot. She stood up, before remembering that she'd said she was looking for an egg basket. That was the cover story! Don't blow it now. She scooped up a small wicker basket from the cupboard and closed it. She smiled at Emory and Connie, holding up the basket as if it was a trophy.

Mission accomplished.

The two women followed Emory out to the yard. Joyce hoped that her hidden weapon didn't ride up out of the top of her boot as she walked, so she ensured she took measured steps as she walked towards the chicken coop. This pen was a good deal larger than the one in which Finch had kept the birds destined for the table. The coop contained thirty-five chickens and the structure was showing signs of wear and tear despite having been built only four years ago. But then Finch had been the man who had built it. The roof had warped by a few degrees, meaning that heavy rainfall would leave a small pond of water above their heads. Joyce always wondered if it would give way when she was inside, soaking her to the bone. Some of the wooden uprights had been painted with green paint, but some were still bare wood; a job half done. Most of them were stained dark with water damage.

Connie tottered into the enclosure and collected the eggs, placing them in Joyce's basket. Emory watched them keenly, remaining at the entrance to the coop, as their figures receded along the long, narrow building. The whole place smelt of damp and chicken feed. The hens were clucking excitedly as the visitors investigated the egg traps. Emory sauntered over to the chicken nearest to him. He scooped it up and tried to clasp it between his good arm and his body, but the bird was flapping its wings in agitation. Finally he managed to subdue it.

Joyce glanced back and saw him leave the enclosure. She could see his shadow against the window, caught in the light of the farmhouse. He performed a quick and brutal action with his hand and the hen in his arms stopped moving. Joyce busied herself with the eggs and noticed that her trouser leg had ridden up slightly, exposing the handle of the knife. Quickly she pulled it down again.

With enough eggs to look convincing, the two women walked towards the entrance and met Emory coming in. The dead chicken was clutched in his left-hand; blood specks were on his knuckles and his cheek. He threw it towards Connie, who managed to catch it before it splatted against her best suit.

''Ere mind out!'

'Prepare this to eat,' Emory ordered, before marching back to the farmhouse. Connie brushed herself down and holding the chicken she followed him. Joyce checked again that the knife was still concealed and moved after her.

It was late by the time they'd prepared, cooked and eaten the chicken. The women had little appetite but ate to keep up appearances. Instead they watched as the Germans stripped the bones. Joyce noticed that Emory was in discomfort, continually wanting to scratch at his injured arm. For most of the time he let it dangle by his side. She assumed that it hurt to raise it up to table height. He was also fighting to stem the sweat that was coming from his forehead, continually dabbing at it with a tea towel. His eyes looked red and rheumy. How long could he last without medical attention?

After dinner, Siegfried thanked them for the meal. He said that they hoped to be gone tomorrow. Joyce said, as pleasantly as she could manage, that she hoped that too. Siegfried smiled, appreciating her attempt at dark humour. He escorted them upstairs and waited outside the bathroom for each of them before securing them in Joyce's bedroom. She heard the key in the lock and then listened as Siegfried ambled downstairs.

When she was sure that the coast was clear, Joyce pulled up her trouser to reveal the handle of the knife. Carefully she took it out of her sock. Connie and Esther smiled with relief.

Now they had a weapon.

In the parlour, the smog of cigar smoke greeted Siegfried. He fought to stop himself from coughing, instead using his hands to clear the air. The offending cigar, taken from Finch's collection, was burning in an ashtray next to the prone form of Emory Mayer. He had the back of his hand positioned over his forehead like a Victorian heroine in distress, as he lay on the sofa. Siegfried was worried about his commander.

'Captain?'

There was no response, just a listless murmur from the older man.

'Captain? I have locked the women up in their room. What do you want me to do now?'

'Sit down,' Emory's voice was weak. 'Sit down and talk to me.'

'You must be strong for a little longer, Captain,' Siegfried hoped the words would encourage him, and was surprised when Emory lashed out a meaty hand and grabbed him around the back of the neck, pulling him towards him. Siegfried could see the strain playing on Emory's face as he did this. It wasn't easy for him.

'Don't tell me what to do.'

'Sorry. I meant that I'm sure we won't have long to wait until they come for us.'

'What if they don't?'

'They will.'

'What if we've been sending the message and no one has heard it? What then, eh?'

'We must believe that someone has heard it, sir.'

'I wish I had your optimism.' Emory let go of the boy. 'But what if no one comes?'

Siegfried took a deep breath. He knew what he hoped would happen. And he knew that Emory wouldn't agree. Did his commander really want him to voice what that was? He knew he had to say it for his own sanity.

'Maybe then we give ourselves up?'

Emory smiled in a manner that said that would never happen.

'No, we wait until lunchtime tomorrow, then we leave,' Emory struggled to focus his tired, burning eyes on Siegfried. 'It is Christmas soon. People will be distracted with their preparations. We should be able to get a long way before they find us.'

'All right. And what do we do about the women?'

Emory pondered this for a moment. The longer the silence went on, the more fearful Siegfried became of the answer. And when Emory eventually spoke, Siegfried felt his stomach knot in anxiety.

'They could lead the soldiers to us if we let them live.'

'But Captain—'

'We shoot them all.'

Siegfried was shocked, and he struggled not to show too much on his face. He knew that Emory would get angry if he showed compassion to the enemy. Like it or not, this would be the way things would be.

'If no one comes for us by lunchtime tomorrow, I will shoot the women and we will leave. Now, get some sleep.' For his part, Emory already sounded drowsy.

'Yes, Captain.' But Siegfried doubted that he'd be able to get much sleep that night.

There was only space on the bed for two of them, so Joyce elected to sleep in the chair. They didn't bother getting undressed. Connie thought they should be ready for an early start, ready for any opportunity that presented itself. They'd played cards for a time. Pontoon was a game that Joyce had played back home, and it was one of her favourites. But none of them could concentrate. Joyce put the cards on the floor and they worked on their plan instead. They'd placed the bread-knife in the bedside drawer for when it was needed tomorrow. Going over the plan was reassuring and Joyce felt comforted by it. The more they talked, the more she hoped they'd spot any potential loophole. They discussed the plan of events again and again. Joyce outlined what she thought would happen.

'Two of us will go to the chickens, and I expect one of the Germans will come with us to keep an eye on things.'

'Yes, Esther and I will go into the coop.' Connie agreed.

'If we get a choice.'

'Yes, if we get a choice.'

'And when Connie and me are in the coop, I'll pretend to hurt myself. I'll fall over and make a lot of noise.' Esther flailed her arms in an approximation of a woman in distress. Joyce quietly hoped her acting would be better than that tomorrow. Connie continued the plan.

'Then while the German is distracted with Esther, I'll run to the tool shed to get the shotgun.'

'Meanwhile, I'll be in the bedroom and I'll call the other German upstairs and threaten him with the knife.'

'That's it Joyce!'

'It sounds like it could work.' Esther sounded full of hope for the first time since the men had blighted their lives. For her part, Joyce saw a flaw.

'I'm sure it will work. But only if we time it really well.'

'What synchronise watches and all that palaver?'

'What are you thinking?' Esther looked keen to iron out this loophole.

'Ten minutes after the two of you go out to the coop, I'll

get the knife and call the other German up to the bedroom.' Joyce scanned their faces for their reaction.

'Ten minutes?' Connie let that sink in. 'It's not long is it?'

'It's more than enough. You don't want to have to finish the egg collection before the time's up. Ten minutes should be fine. But it starts the moment you walk out that door. We all have to check our watches at that moment. I'll be watching from the window here. All right?'

Esther and Connie nodded.

With the three of them mulling the plan over in their heads, they turned the light off and tried to sleep. Joyce could see the silvery outlines of Connie and Esther on the bed, tinged in the moonlight coming through the top of the curtain rail. She watched them shift around. No one was asleep. Everyone was just resting; on edge. Finally, Connie sat up in bed and Joyce saw her large brown eyes catching the light.

'I never had time to ask how you were.' Her voice was barely a whisper.

'I'm all right. Well as all right as I can be.' The truth was that Joyce felt numb. She still refused to believe that John was gone. She was hanging on to the fact that it had been a dreadful mistake or a mix-up of some sort. She knew she wouldn't be the first person to think that. Thousands of wives and mothers had gone through the same denial when they got those typed words from the War Office. But somehow she just knew that he'd be all right. All she had to do was escape from the clutches of these two men and she could find John.

'You should talk.' Connie looked imploring at her.

'I'm too tired.'

'We all are, but none of us can sleep, so we might as well do something.' Esther chipped in.

'It's not the right time.' Joyce didn't want to get into it now. Part of her didn't know what to say and part of her was worried that if she outlined her theory about it being a mistake that Connie or Esther would puncture her hopes. And she couldn't cope with that now. What if they saw something she had missed in the confusion and exhaustion of the last few days? What if they read the telegram and spotted something that she hadn't in the dozens of times she'd read it? No one could sever the lifeline she was desperately grasping onto. If they thought she was wrong, she'd have nothing left. No way of finding the resolve and strength to survive this situation; no way of surviving what they needed to do tomorrow morning.

'I'll talk when this is over.'

Connie and Esther shot her sympathetic looks.

'Make sure you do. And by the way, if we get out of this, I'm going to treat you both to a slap-up meal with all the trimmings. I don't care if it costs me a month's wages.' Connie grinned at the thought of this future celebration.

'I'd thought about us having a meal too.' Joyce smiled. She looked wistfully at the pair of them; her friends through so many good and bad times. 'Difference is, I imagined having a lunch when we were much older. The war will be over and long gone and we'll get back together and meet somewhere near here. Maybe even in The Bottle and Glass for a pub lunch.'

Connie considered this offer.

'The landlord may even have cleaned the pipes by then.'

'And we'll look back on all this and we'll wonder what it

was like because you know, I bet we won't be able to remember. Not all of it. Not really. Not all the smells and sounds, and what it felt like to get up at the crack of dawn after being on a mattress where the springs dig into our backs. We won't remember how our legs ached and our hands split; or the blisters on our feet from those flaming rough socks; or the perspiration trickling from our headscarves down our necks. It'll all be a hazy memory. All of it long gone.'

'We'll remember this Christmas though, that's for sure, lovey. No matter how many Christmases we see, this will always be one we remember.'

Connie was lost in thought, perhaps considering what Joyce and Esther had said.

'I hope the war's over soon. I've had enough of it. One thing's for sure, I don't want my baby born during it.'

The comment hung in the air.

What did Connie say?

'Your baby?' Esther looked as if she had misheard.

'She means if she was to have a baby, she wouldn't want it born with all this going on.' Joyce surmised, before turning to Connie. 'Don't you?'

They both looked at Connie. She smiled awkwardly.

'Me and my big mouth, eh?' Connie looked Joyce in the eye. 'I'm having a baby with Henry. And I'll be a good mum, you'll see.'

'I bet you will be.' Joyce recognised that Connie felt uneasy sharing this news. It had just slipped out and she assumed that Connie was worried about sharing something joyous when Joyce was at rock bottom.

Joyce felt tears welling up in her eyes. This wasn't news she'd expected to hear. She didn't even know that Connie and Henry had been trying for a baby. How wonderful! A new baby; hope during a time of darkness. It felt like a glorious celebratory moment; a moment that those men couldn't take away. They'd locked them up, but they could still fill their hearts with a moment of joy.

Joyce reached out a hand and touched the back of Connie's hand. 'I'm really pleased.'

As Connie explained to Esther that she thought she was about three months gone, Joyce felt the warmth of the news slipping away. She was distracted, thinking about the locked door, the men downstairs. She thought about what they had to do tomorrow. Joyce resolved to give Connie a big, proper celebration when this was all over.

Professor Lance Patrick was a man with vociferous opinions, a loud dress sense, and an uncanny ability to spray food from his mouth around the table while he was talking. His wife, Prunella Patrick, had dull opinions, dull clothes and an over-fondness for wine. Together they were the dinner guests from hell.

And that's where Richard Channing felt he had ended up. Was this his punishment for the bad things he'd done?

Lady Hoxley had invited guests for supper to celebrate Christmas. As Professor Patrick, an archaeologist, expounded on his latest theory about Hitler's next move, Channing smiled in terse politeness. He had little time for them but found it hard to extricate himself from the meal. He sat in irritated silence, serving Prunella with more wine each time her glass went dry. He had to do this so regularly that he had to fill a second decanter with red wine. These people could seriously dent the dwindling cellar at Hoxley Manor if they were regular guests. Where was Prunella putting so much wine? Channing didn't give any credence to the decidedly unscientific theory that she might have hollow legs, but she certainly didn't seem inebriated by how much she was drinking. Also unusually she didn't seem to get any louder or more opinionated from the effects of the wine. As a scientific man, Channing almost found it interesting.

Almost.

Lady Hoxley sat at the other end of the table, a picture of the graceful hostess. From time to time, her eyes would meet Richard's, but she was too polished and polite to let slip her feelings in public. Instead she laughed good-naturedly as the Professor attempted a joke and obfuscated her answers when Prunella asked how much something cost.

By ten-thirty, as the meal was ending, Lady Hoxley arranged for one of the American soldiers at the hospital to take the Professor and his wife home. The Patricks said their goodbyes, promising to host a return meal soon. Channing said that would be most agreeable. In his head, he knew that he must never allow that to happen. Finally, the couple sauntered off down the driveway to where an American Army jeep was waiting. Prunella seemed excited by the chance to ride in a jeep. Patrick was more concerned about her falling out. Channing didn't wait to wave them goodbye. He walked back inside, enjoying the crisp cool air as it cleared his head and rattled down the hallway. Lady Hoxley closed the doors. She'd given the servants the evening off as it was nearly Christmas and had cooked the, admittedly simple, meal herself.

Channing and Lady Hoxley faced each other in the corridor.

'That went well. Considering.' Richard raised his eyebrow.

'Considering what?'

'Considering who our guests were.'

'Quite.' Ellen conceded a smile. 'Will you have a night cap?' She asked.

'I'm tired. Maybe we can have one tomorrow night on Christmas eve, that would be nice, wouldn't it?'

Lady Hoxley nodded, smiling agreeably. Channing pecked her on the cheek, the smell of her subtle perfume hitting him. It was a smell that made him feel safe, protected. She was a strong capable woman and she would make sure everything was all right.

As he walked away, she turned and called after him.

'Oh, Richard.'

'Yes, Ellen?'

'I forgot to say, I heard back from the people in Leeds.'

Channing looked momentarily blank until he nodded as he remembered. 'I had left messages asking for more details about the house fire that claimed John Fisher. Do you remember?'

'Yes of course. And what did they say?'

'I think I should come with you tomorrow to Pasture Farm.'

Channing smiled in an accommodating manner. But his head was screaming at him to stop her at any cost. She couldn't come to the farm with him. What would happen to her? She would be another variable in a situation that was already out of control.

There had been enough random factors coming into play.

As Channing was wrestling his own worries, he didn't think about the reason why Ellen might want to come to the farm. What was the reason?

What had she found out about the house fire in Leeds?

Channing went to his room. He locked the door, paced around in frustration for a few minutes and then sat on his bed, trying to clear his head. The four glasses of wine at dinner were blurring his thoughts. He had to think rationally. He had to think this through.

Tomorrow would be difficult, and he had to be ready for any eventuality. Firstly, he didn't know what had happened to Connie after he dropped her off at the farm. The airmen might have killed her for all he knew. He assumed that she hadn't escaped, otherwise they would have heard about it. So she was still at the farm, either dead or alive. Maybe all the people at Pasture Farm were dead. Channing had no way of knowing; he had no way of knowing what he was walking into tomorrow.

And the last thing he needed was Ellen coming along.

He checked his pistol and then placed it in his medical bag.

But as his temples pounded with adrenaline and fear, Channing had an idea. He got up, combed his hair, unlocked his door and disappeared into the corridor. There was a way to stop her.

The medical wing was cloaked in semi-darkness; the home-made Christmas bunting hanging in the wards and a skeleton staff of nurses on duty. Channing made his way to the medicine storeroom, unlocked it and went inside. Within a few seconds, he'd found the item he required and slipped it into his trouser pocket. He made his way back to the main part of the house, smiling and wishing the nursing staff a happy Christmas as he went. Good old Doctor Channing.

Soon he was outside the door to Ellen's living room. The light was still on, illuminating the corridor with a thin sliver of amber at the bottom of the door. At least that blasted record wasn't playing. He cleared his throat and knocked. After a few moments, Ellen came to the door, surprised to see him. Channing gave his most convincingly charismatic smile.

'I thought we should have that drink. It's nearly Christmas after all.'

'Of course.' Ellen checked that the corridor was clear and let him in. She moved over to her bureau, on which sat a letter on a sheet of headed paper and an envelope. The ink was still wet, shiny black in the light from the fire. Ellen was waiting for it to dry before she folded the letter into the envelope.

The envelope had the name 'Mrs Fisher' written on it.

'What are you doing?' Channing asked.

'I thought I'd write a letter to Mrs Fisher. Joyce. It will stop me forgetting anything when I speak to her tomorrow.'

'I see.' Channing crossed to the drinks' cabinet. A decanter of gin was about a third full. Channing swilled it around in the decanter. 'Gin and tonic?'

'Perfect.' Ellen placed the letter into the envelope and sealed it. If he'd been looking in her direction, Channing might have noticed the small perturbed frown on her brow. But he was too busy with his own thoughts to notice.

With her occupied, Channing poured the gin into two crystal tumblers. He took the vial from his trouser pocket and coughed as he snapped it open. He poured half of the liquid into one of the glasses. He added the tonic and mixed the spiked glass with a spoon. By the time Ellen had finished her letter, Channing was standing over her with the drinks in his hand. He gave her the spiked one and toasted their health.

'Here's to us.'

'To us!'

They chinked glasses and both took sips before moving to the sofa. Channing sat next to Ellen, watching her keenly. It was hard to get the dosage of Potassium Bromide right and he often had to use trial and error on the wards, but Channing hoped he'd given her a big enough dose to knock her out for a good few hours. The strong taste of the gin and tonic should obscure it. He knew that the drug had a cumulative effect, so if she was awake in the morning when he left, he resolved to give her another dose. That second dose would work with the stuff already in her bloodstream to make her sleep until lunchtime. She'd miss the appointment at Pasture Farm. Channing congratulated himself in dealing with one of the random events that threatened to spoil things.

'I can put that letter in my medical bag if you like,' Channing was eyeing the letter on the bureau. 'Then we won't forget it tomorrow.'

'All right. That's a good idea.' She gave him the letter and sat down again. He smiled with satisfaction as she took another sip of her drink.

'What about the Professor and his wife then?'

'Oh don't! Still, I feel we've done our duty in seeing them. Although I fear that they will view this as a Christmas tradition and want us to come to their house next year.'

She finished her drink. Channing watched for any drowsiness, but it hadn't absorbed into her bloodstream, yet.

'Shall we have another?' Ellen announced.

'Capital idea,' Channing replied, going to fix the drinks.

Chapter 14

Christmas Eve

Joyce slept sporadically, unable to get comfortable or warm enough on the chair. Her neck felt like it had been twisted and all her attempts to straighten it out resulted in sharp pains. It was just before seven in the morning. Esther and Connie were still on the bed and possibly asleep. Joyce could hear the sounds of someone making tea downstairs. Maybe that was what had woken her up from her most recent nap. She sat there, stretching her neck in silence, thinking about the plan.

Esther and Joyce would go to the chicken coop.

The ten minute countdown would start as they left the house.

At ten minutes, Esther would fake an injury and Connie would use the distraction to get the shotgun.

Meanwhile at the same time, Joyce would threaten the other German with the breadknife.

Ten minutes.

259

Everything would change forever in ten minutes.

Esther murmured in her sleep and then her eyes shot open; a look of confusion on her face as she took in her surroundings. Then she remembered where she was, and the worries and stresses instantly appeared back onto her face. Connie woke a few seconds later.

'Gah, I was hoping this was a bloody nightmare.' Connie stretched.

'No, it's bloody real. But it'll be over soon.' Joyce reassured them both.

'I hope Fred doesn't come back from Leicester too early.' Esther looked fretful about that prospect.

'What time is he due?'

'You know Fred, he's not one for making detailed plans. He just said he'd be back some time on Christmas Eve.'

'Maybe he meant the actual evening part of Christmas Eve?' Connie reasoned.

'Who knows, lovey. Who knows?' Esther shrugged. It was pointless trying to second guess Frederick Finch.

They heard someone coming up the stairs. From the spring in the person's step, they assumed it was the younger man. They were correct. Siegfried unlocked the door.

'Morning, ladies.'

Esther, Connie and Joyce gave an unenthusiastic chorus of hellos back and dutifully filed out in turn to use the bathroom. Siegfried remained on the landing as each one went inside and then made sure they went back into the bedroom when they were finished.

'Do you want some breakfast?' Esther dried her hands.

'That would be nice.' The German looked touched. 'Thank you.'

Soon they were downstairs, and Esther and Connie were busily making scrambled eggs. From the kitchen window, Joyce could make out something sticking out from the postbox near the gate. They hadn't collected the post for a couple of days. Joyce asked if she could go to collect it.

Emory refused. He seemed in an even worse condition than yesterday. His face was blotchy, and he was sweating; his hair plastered across his forehead.

'You stay here.'

'I have to collect it. Otherwise they'll know something is wrong when they come with the post later.' Joyce stood her ground. Emory was wavering. He spoke to Siegfried and, after some a heated discussion in German, Emory reluctantly agreed to let Joyce go.

'You be quick, and you do not try any tricks.'

'We'll be watching.' Siegfried unlocked the back door. Joyce put on her gumboots and went outside and set off.

It was a familiar journey from the farmhouse to the gate at the edge of the farm – a daily pilgrimage to get both messages of hope and letters confirming the worst.

She barely dared to look back. She knew they would be watching. She walked slowly and deliberately across the yard of Pasture Farm as if walking on an invisible tightrope; but enjoying the small freedom it allowed her. She relished the feel of the cold morning air against her skin; revitalising her from the rough night she'd had. But in under a minute, she reached the tin box that Finch had erected on a gnarled pole near the gate.

She had collected the post every day since she had arrived at the farm. Unofficially, it was Joyce's job. Sometimes, the short journey was taken with a spring in her step, sometimes with nervous foreboding such as the time she was waiting for news about John. The seasons changed, cooling and warming in predictable cycles; sometimes, like today, she'd trudge in gum boots across the mud, other times she'd skip across baked ground in her flat summer shoes. Through wind, rain or sunshine, she made this short journey to see what the tin box contained. It was always Joyce's first job after breakfast.

Today the tin box had letters sticking out of it that had arrived the day before. They hadn't seen the postman, so they knew that today's post was still to come.

As she took the bundle from the box, she contemplated continuing forward out of the gate. It was so tempting. Could she walk away? No, she knew that couldn't happen. Even with everything that had happened before, she couldn't leave the others behind. Her duty was here, as it had always been.

Besides they had a plan.

And, if it worked, the plan would ensure that they all got out of here. They all would escape if things went well.

In her hand, among the letters for Finch and Esther was a package. Joyce realised it was addressed to her. It was approximately eight inches by six inches in size, stuck down tightly with an unnecessary amount of tape. It had a Birmingham postmark on it. She didn't recognise the writing at all, and she couldn't think of anyone she knew in Birmingham. Guided by some instinct, Joyce decided to carefully tuck the package into her jumper, carrying the rest of the bundle in her hand so the people in the farmhouse could see them if they were watching.

With a sigh, she walked slowly back across the yard towards the farmhouse; despite every ounce of selfish, self-preservation telling her to run the other way.

Siegfried nodded, seemingly pleased that she had returned without incident.

She had left the bundle of letters on the kitchen table and asked if she could use the bathroom. Siegfried agreed. Joyce went upstairs, smuggling the parcel inside her jumper up to her room. She tossed it onto the bed, closed the door as quietly as she could and then went to the bathroom. She flushed the toilet to give authenticity to the lie, washed her hands and went downstairs.

She ate some scrambled egg and drank three cups of tea. She watched Emory as he pushed the food around his plate with little interest. Dark circles framed his eyes and he seemed to have trouble focussing. After a while, he left the table and slouched into the parlour, pushing the door ajar. Joyce heard the sounds of the Morse code message.

There was desperation as he tapped out the message, again and again.

'We'll need to sort the chickens out again in a while,' Joyce threw this out as casually as she could to Siegfried. He nodded his consent.

'These eggs taste good.'

'That's one of the advantages of living on a farm.' Connie

shrugged. He ate his food with gusto and then used the fork to scoop every last morsel up. The childlike action made him seem even younger than he was. Joyce hoped that she wouldn't have to hurt him. She hoped that she, Connie and Esther could escape the farm without any resistance. If things went to plan, no one had to get hurt and the Germans would end up imprisoned in a prisoner of war camp before Christmas Day.

She decided that she might need another cup of tea to keep her alert. Joyce filled up the pot with hot water and placed it on the farmhouse table. As she stirred it to strengthen the brew, she glanced at the faces of Esther and Connie. They all hid their expectation and fear as best as they could. Joyce could tell that everyone was excited that Siegfried had agreed so easily to them going to the coop again.

The first stage had gone to plan.

Channing had breakfast alone.

Ellen hadn't come down to join him. He assumed that the two spiked drinks had done their work and hoped that she would be asleep until lunchtime. He hoped he hadn't given her too much.

What if she was dead?

No, he couldn't think about that. Not now. He had enough to worry about. She was asleep, that's all.

But what if he'd killed her?

The insistent voice wanted an answer. Channing knew he wouldn't get any peace until he'd answered his own question. If that was the case, he'd have to get rid of her body so that no post-mortem could reveal the drug in her veins. How could he dispose of Lady Hoxley's body?

He didn't really want to think about it; and besides that problem could wait until later. He had to deal with things at the farmhouse first. He had to sort those German airmen out.

But whatever happened, Channing knew that he would do anything to protect himself.

Channing put such thoughts out of his head. There was no point in worrying about things that hadn't happened. He was a man of science, used to dealing with quantifiable facts not suppositions.

He read some poetry and ate some toast.

Then he left the dining room and took the corridor that led to his room. The hospital wing was still quiet but waking up for the day. He could hear patients calling for nurses; the rattle of the medicine trolley and somewhere Vera Lynn was playing. Channing collected his medicine bag, hat and coat from his room and set off. The letter was in the bag. He'd deliver that while he was there.

When he'd almost reached the main entrance to Hoxley Manor, Channing wondered if he should check on Lady Hoxley. The nagging feeling of what had happened to her was eating away at him.

Channing decided that it would be best to leave right away for the farm. He'd check on her later. Besides, if he went to see her now, she might wake and he'd then have the problem of having to take her with him. No, he had to go alone. And he had to go while she was still asleep.

Channing opened his car door and put the medicine bag

on the passenger seat. He started the engine and slowly pulled away from Hoxley Manor. His pulse was going ten to the dozen and he struggled to calm himself. But he knew he had to keep a level head. This would soon be over. He just had to remain calm and logical and treat every eventuality as he had planned.

All that mattered was that he survived and that no one discovered what he was.

Channing reached the road outside Hoxley Manor. He took a deep breath and pulled away.

At Pasture Farm, Esther washed up the breakfast things as Connie and Joyce sat at the table. Everyone was too tense to speak; all lost in their own thoughts and fears about the day ahead. Without conversation, the air was filled with insistent tap-tap-tap of the Morse code transmitter in the next room. Siegfried stayed in the parlour with Emory but ensured that he came out to check on the women from time to time.

'He's not well.'

'I know.' Joyce knew the signs of infection and she knew things would get worse.

'What can you do?'

'Nothing, he needs a doctor. His arm is infected.'

Siegfried looked perturbed and a little lost. 'I need to get him away from here. We need people to come to help us.'

Esther came up with a potential solution. 'We could call Doctor Wally Morgan?'

But Connie shot it down.

'Oh I hate him. He's got the worst bad breath and his hands won't stay where they should, if you know what I mean.'

'But he is a doctor, yes?'

'Yes, but I don't think we should get him here.' Joyce didn't want to endanger anyone else's life; even that of the shambling, drunken local doctor. 'He's not very good and I don't think he'd be much help.'

Siegfried turned to go back to the parlour.

Joyce decided that this might be a good time. Strike while he was distracted about something else.

'Can we sort out the chickens?'

Siegfried turned back, weariness on his young face. He scratched his head; revealing the grubby sleeve of his stolen overalls. 'Sure.' He moved towards the parlour. 'I'll get the key. But only two of you go, yes?'

Joyce nodded.

'Me and Esther will do it,' Connie sounded like she'd just thought of the idea.

Siegfried shrugged. It made no difference to him.

'I need to go to the bathroom too.'

Siegfried didn't respond to Joyce's comment. Perhaps he hadn't heard her or perhaps he was too preoccupied with talking to Emory.

'Just go.' Connie whipped her head in the direction of upstairs. Joyce didn't need telling twice. Quickly and silently she made her way to the foot of the stairs.

She splayed all her fingers and thumbs out to Esther and Connie. Ten minutes.

They all knew that the countdown would start as soon as Connie and Esther stepped outside.

Tick tock.

Joyce mouthed 'good luck' to them and tip-toed upstairs as quickly as she could. The plan was going better than expected. She'd bargained on having been locked in her bedroom and having to get one of the Germans to come upstairs to let her out. This way she could go upstairs with no locked doors in her way. She could come down when she wanted – with the breadknife.

Ten minutes.

Joyce went into her bedroom and pulled the thin curtain back so she could see the yard outside the back door.

As soon as Connie and Esther appeared, she would begin her countdown. She glanced nervously to the bedside cabinet that contained the breadknife.

Channing pulled his car to a halt halfway between Hoxley Manor and Pasture Farm. He'd managed to calm his breathing, but he could still feel that his face was flushed. Taking some deep breaths, he wiped his clammy hands on his trousers and tried to focus on feeling more grounded.

Focus on the plan.

He opened the medical bag and took out the letter that Ellen had written. It was the perfect cover for his visit to the farm. He had to deliver news to Joyce Fisher.

Thank you, Ellen.

Deciding that he needed to know what it said, he ripped it open and scanned it quickly; his eyes betraying no emotion as he took in the message.

Okay, he'd deliver that message to Joyce Fisher.

And then he'd convince the Germans to 'turn themselves

in' and come with him. He'd leave the farm with them in his car and then stage it so it looked like they'd overpowered him and escaped. But in reality, he would have taken them to Panmere Lake to hand them over to the contact he'd met yesterday. Channing decided that he might need to make it look like he'd been hit to make the escape look convincing. He made a mental note to ask one of the Germans to hit him. It would be a necessary discomfort, but he knew where he could be punched without it being too painful.

Nothing could jeopardise his survival.

Siegfried didn't like the look of Emory. The older man's skin was a blotchy patchwork of ivory white and angry crimson. His eyes looked rheumy and were large like pickled eggs. A thin veneer of sweat covered his face and hands. The collar on the shirt was stained darker than the rest of the material. With effort, Emory hauled himself up from the armchair that he'd moved into to be close to the radio transmitter, holding onto the arm for support.

'The women need to tend to the chickens.'

'You go. I don't feel so good.'

'You keep the pistol then, Captain.'

Emory looked confused as if he didn't know where it was, so Siegfried went to the suit jacket that was draped over one of the chairs and removed the pistol from the inside pocket. He handed it to his commander.

'I won't be long.' Siegfried was about to go when Emory stopped him in his tracks.

'I prayed.' Emory blinked at the light as if it was causing

him pain. He waited for the effect of the words to land. Siegfried knew that his commander was a man who put his faith in his own abilities. Seeking help from a higher power seemed like an act of desperation; a last resort. It wasn't a good sign. Emory continued, picking out his words as if each one was hard to find and elusive. 'I prayed that we would be delivered from this place. And that we'd get back to Germany.'

'We will go back home.' Siegfried hoped he sounded confident and full of reassurance.

Emory wobbled and nearly overbalanced, but Siegfried caught his arm to support him. The action made the commander wince and Siegfried realised that he was holding the man's wounded arm. He removed it as if he was scalded and apologised profusely.

'I'm sorry, I didn't realise.'

Emory shook his head dismissively. It didn't matter.

'Go with the women, but don't be long.'

'I won't.' Siegfried saluted his commander and left the room. Emory slumped back into the armchair and half-heartedly continued to tap out his Morse code message.

Some days change your life forever. And Joyce Fisher knew that today was one of those days.

She hadn't planned it to turn out that way, of course, but the trouble was that you rarely had any warning which days would be the ones to change things. You could plan for saying yes to an invitation or moving house or getting married. But other life-changing events could leap out in front of you, like a distracted deer on a country lane, giving you no opportunity to prepare; no opportunity to weigh up the options. Sometimes there was no time to think about consequences. Sometimes there was only time to act and then hope that things turned out all right.

She waited for the sound of the back door opening.

She waited to start the countdown.

Tick tock.

Connie and Esther waited by the back door for Siegfried.

Connie had gone through this very door, with its peeling paint and weather-beaten timbers, a thousand times and most of the time she'd be moaning about the work she had to do or the work she'd done, making some caustic comment to get the girls to laugh, wondering what was for their morning break snack or passing an opinion on someone's new fancy man. But she'd never been this tense before. There had never been so much at stake.

Esther looked petrified. Connie got as close as she could to her, all the while watching for when the parlour door would open and Siegfried would emerge. She knew that Esther had to hold it together, for all their sakes. Esther had to be the one who'd fake a collapse in the chicken coop. She had to be convincing; invested in what she was doing. She couldn't crumble or they would all be dead.

Connie acted out a silent, mimed conversation, fearful that they'd be overheard otherwise.

Are you all right?

Esther nodded.

Connie clenched her fists in a gesture that meant Esther had to be strong.

Esther nodded. She would be.

Connie nodded her head. Was she sure?

Esther nodded.

Connie had no choice but to believe her friend and hope that her assurances would come good. She gave Esther's arm a squeeze above the elbow. Good luck.

There was no time for any more pep-talks. Siegfried emerged from the parlour with the key. The women obediently stood out of the way for him so he could unlock it. Then he took a step back and looked them up and down. He was suspicious. Why was he looking at them like that? Something was wrong.

'You've forgotten it?'

Panic passed over Esther's face, but Connie knew she had to keep it together; otherwise Esther would give the game away for both of them.

'What's that, then?' She spoke with a good dose of Connie insouciance to cover any nervousness in her voice.

'Your basket. For the eggs.'

'Of course!' Connie scurried over to the sink and opened the cupboard door. She took out two small wicker baskets, handing one to a grateful Esther. 'There we go.'

The three of them went outside and walked across the path towards the large chicken coop.

From her bedroom window, Joyce saw them leave, her heart in her mouth and her pulse banging in her temples. She looked at her watch.

Ten minutes.

Tick tock.

It had started. And now there was no going back.

Channing drove on. The morning sun was struggling to peek through fronds of grey cloud, and it dappled across his windscreen. He approached the entrance to the farm and slowed down; the brakes uttering a small squeal of protest as he took the turning a little too fast.

He focused on the next few minutes.

He had to be clear-headed to survive. He had to be prepared for every eventuality.

He pushed open the gate to the farm. The postbox was open and empty to the side of it. There were no signs of life from the farmhouse. What would he find inside?

What had happened to Joyce, Connie and Esther?

What had happened to the airmen?

And if the women at the farm got suspicious, he'd deal with them too. Could he do that, though? Could he shoot three innocent women to protect himself?

Channing knew he would if he had to. Casualties of his war.

He got back in his car and edged it through the gates to where he parked it next to one of the empty stables. Turning the engine off, he braced himself before getting out. He collected his medical bag from the passenger seat and trudged off across the yard with a grim finality.

Siegfried, Connie and Esther had crossed the dirt track towards the large chicken coop and gone inside moments earlier. Channing hadn't seen them, and they hadn't seen him.

Joyce watched from her window. Siegfried, Connie and Esther entered the chicken coop. She checked her watch and tried to steady her breathing. Deciding that it might steady her nerves to sit on the bed, Joyce sat down, feeling the springs give underneath her.

Bang, bang, bang.

At first, she thought it was the bed protesting or even breaking; her mind not anticipating any unexpected sounds.

What was that?

Was it gunfire?

It took her a second or two to realise that the hammering was someone knocking on the back door.

But Siegfried, Connie and Esther hadn't come back from the coop. She'd have seen them.

Joyce's mind raced. Who the hell could it be?

She heard another noise; a man moving heavily and with difficulty from one of the rooms underneath her. Emory was on the move.

Joyce checked her watch.

Nine-and-a-half minutes to go.

What should she do?

'Come down!' Emory hissed, as loud as he dared from the bottom of the stairs. 'Come down!'

Bang, bang on the back door.

What should she do?

It was too early to confront him.

Joyce moved slowly towards the bedroom door. Again, the insistent voice came. 'Come down!'

Should she take the knife?

She hesitated.

'Now!'

There was no time.

She went out onto the landing and looked down at him. He looked diminished, frail and small. But he was holding the pistol and that scared her. He indicated for her to get down here quickly. Joyce ran downstairs and Emory pushed her towards the back door and then hid in the nook of the stairs.

Joyce straightened her hair and went to open the door. Flinging it open, she was surprised at the identity of their unexpected visitor.

Doctor Richard Channing was standing there, clutching his medical bag.

'Good morning, Mrs Fisher.' Channing was behaving as if it was the most normal day on Earth.

'Doctor Channing?' Joyce felt almost too exhausted to attempt any charade; her voice revealing her fatigue.

'I've come with some news.'

'What?'

'I've got some news for you.'

'What are you talking about?'

Joyce wasn't expecting this. She was focussed on the plan and this was delaying things. She desperately wanted to check her watch. But what was Channing going on about?

'You might want to sit down.'

Joyce's mind started to focus.

This could be important. Something about John.

Joyce didn't know what it could be. What else could there be that required her to be sitting down. She knew about John, she'd been told he was dead. What other shock could be in store? What other news could Channing have?

Maybe John was alive.

Yes, maybe that was it. She needed to be sitting down because that would be a shock, wouldn't it?

With a cursory glance towards the stairs, she sat down and Channing pulled out a chair next to her. Emory shifted on the stairs, his shadow moving in the background behind Channing.

'Lady Hoxley contacted the police in Leeds to see if she could get some further details about what happened to your husband.'

Ah, that was it. They'd found out more. Was Channing going to tell her that they'd found that Teddy, John's brother, had been the casualty instead? Yes, that could be it.

'I'm afraid they couldn't identify his body from the fire, but the height and build match that of your husband.' Channing spoke slowly and deliberately; a man used to imparting bad news.

'But it's a mistake, isn't it?' Joyce heard herself say; her voice seemed thin and reedy.

It wasn't her talking, was it?

'I'm afraid it's no mistake. They found his kit bag by the bed. Some of the material had burnt away but the name tag was still clearly visible. Flight Officer John Fisher. Inside were his personal effects, including a letter he was writing to you.'

Joyce couldn't listen. The words washed over her as if they were corrosive chemicals, each one hurting her more. No, it couldn't be happening. She just wanted to scream and smash up the kitchen.

'It's a mistake.' Joyce felt her voice crack.

'I'm afraid that your husband is dead.'

Joyce sobbed, silent, shoulder-heaving tears. She had been holding so much in; fencing in her feelings and anxieties because of the Germans. Now, she couldn't cope. Her wall of denial had been ripped down and now there was no avoiding the ugly, monstrous truth that was staring her in the face.

Her beloved John, the love of her life, had really gone.

No, it was too much to bear.

Joyce bolted from the table, fighting back floods of tears. She ran to the stairs, pushing Emory out of the way. She didn't care that he had a gun; she didn't care that Channing would see him as she barged at him. She wanted to get past and rush up to her room and sink into the eiderdown and sob her heart out. She had lost everything.

In her rush, Joyce didn't see what happened next.

Channing looked at the German.

Emory raised the pistol.

Channing shook his head and waved his hands desperately.

'I'm here to help.'

He spoke as quietly and as quickly as he could manage; the way anyone would talk if someone was pointing a gun at them. The sound of crying was coming from upstairs, but Channing still didn't want to speak too loudly. But Emory advanced towards the kitchen table. Channing backed away and Emory matched each step with one forward. He seemed to enjoy the medic's discomfort. Emory levelled the pistol to the doctor's eyes. Terrified, Channing tried to fumble for his own pistol, but he managed to knock the medicine bag off the table to the floor. It clattered onto the tiles; knocking the clasp open.

Medical supplies – dressings, creams, stethoscope – spilled out.

Emory looked confused by this development and hesitated.

'I got your message.' Channing's voice cracked with fear. 'Do you understand? Please say you understand for pity's sake.'

Emory considered this.

Channing spoke in German, saying that he'd got the message. He said he had come to help them. He said that he'd prefer it if Emory would stop pointing a gun at him.

Finally, Emory nodded; his craggy face showing nearly as much relief as Channing's own face. Emory lowered the pistol and ushered Channing to pick up his bag.

'I speak English. You come into that room.' Emory indicated the parlour. 'I need medicine.'

'All right.' Channing raised his voice for Joyce's benefit upstairs. 'If you force me to do it, I'll help you.'

There was no response from upstairs, but Channing hoped that she'd heard it. He felt he'd covered himself either way. Emory looked at him as if he was mad before stumbling into the parlour. Channing followed, closing the door behind him.

Esther gave the coop door a shove; the wooden frame had stuck against the door thanks to the chilly damp air of the night. She and Connie entered the enclosure, to the usual excitable noises from the chickens. Siegfried followed behind, resigned to waiting for them to do what they needed to do. He lit up one of Finch's cigars while he was waiting and coughed noisily on it. Connie guessed that he wasn't used to smoking.

With the smell of cigar smoke mingling with the hay and chicken smells in her noise, Connie collected some freshly-laid eggs. She watched as Esther took a wire brush and a metal bucket from the far end and used it to scrub at the mesh of the laying areas, glancing back to Connie from time to time.

Connie checked her watch.

Eight minutes to go.

Siegfried seemed unconcerned with what the women were doing, perhaps trusting them not to escape. Maybe he thought things had settled into a workable relationship now. The women would do what they were told as everyone bided their time for this to be over. Connie noticed him absorbed in the ramshackle architecture of the coop, his eyes trailing the large wooden beams that supported the corrugated iron roof. A section of the roof was missing and the ground underneath the opening was sodden with water. Connie couldn't remember where that piece of metal had gone but it had probably been given to the war effort. One thing was certain; she knew she'd asked Finch to repair it on numerous occasions.

Siegfried coughed as his love-hate relationship with the cigar continued.

Esther scrubbed the wires; waiting, waiting.

Connie collected the eggs, as the minutes ticked down.

Joyce paced by the window in her room, watching the coop through tears in her eyes. She couldn't concentrate on it and she couldn't focus on her watch, the face blurred and hard to read. She sniffed and snuffled and tried to clear her eyes. She knew she had to focus but she was finding it so difficult. Time had slowed down; things no longer mattered. And yet they did. She knew that she had to concentrate.

Eight minutes left.

Tick tock.

The breadknife and the parcel were on the eiderdown. Joyce wasn't thinking about either item. Instead, she struggled not to tumble away as her mind sought to escape from her problems and take refuge in the comforting haze of the past. The present was too dreadful. The past was inviting. John leaving her mother's house, sandwiches in hand, turning back with a warm smile; the two of them whispering to each other in bed, hoping that Gwen and Charlie, in the next room, wouldn't overhear; the day that John appeared in a Tiger Moth to sweep her off her feet on her birthday; John returning from France after being shot down; the glorious day when he was demobbed and supposedly safe from danger. And then John had been managing the neighbouring farm and Joyce would sneak over at night so they could sleep together. She loved those stolen nights of companionship and excitement.

The memories tumbled over and over; all the moments, big and small; all the times with John. She could feel herself closing off from the present day.

There were seven minutes to go.

But Joyce didn't notice anymore.

The parlour looked like a workshop; components and tools were dotted about on the sideboard and the floor; spools of insulated wire rested on the arm rest of the chair. Channing could tell that the men had been busy here. Where was the other one by the way?

He put the thought out of his head and concentrated on the job at hand.

Using his medical scissors, Channing carefully cut open the bandage on Emory's arm; the smell of stale alcohol and infection wafting up to greet him. The German seemed taciturn but amenable to Channing redressing it, but Channing was aware that his reaction was being scrutinised as he peeled off the old dressing. He was used to this and therefore well-versed in playing a poker face so as not to alarm patients. They always wanted reassurance. No one wanted to see a doctor looking aghast.

The wound looked dreadful. It was badly infected.

This man needed hospital treatment straight away.

Channing thanked his lucky stars that Emory was in this state. It made the lie of telling Joyce and the others that he would take the airmen to hospital all the more believable. Yes, this helped his cover story.

Everything was working out well for him.

So far, his luck was holding out and the plan was panning out. He'd soon be back at Hoxley Manor with his mission completed and these airmen passed over to the people who'd help get them home.

'What is it like?' Emory indicated the wound.

'It'll be fine.' Channing looked in his medical bag for lint and tape so he didn't have to make eye contact. Lying was easier if you didn't have to look someone in the face.

In the bag, he rummaged the gun out of the way and found the supplies he needed, before shutting the bag. Emory didn't notice the gun. That would be Channing's insurance.

'I have to sterilise the wound and dress it.' Channing busied himself with a bottle of Iodine and a swab of cotton wool.

Emory braced himself. He chewed his lip as Channing prepared. 'Where will you take us?'

'To people who can help you.'

'How can I trust you?'

Channing had no choice but to look him in the eyes now.

'I was told about your message. I'm here and I'm helping you.' Channing's face didn't falter from his previous poker expression. 'Isn't that enough?'

Emory frowned.

Seemingly it wasn't.

Channing didn't care if the German was fully on-side. As long as he could get them away, do what was required, that's all that mattered. But his thoughts turned back to the issue that had been nagging him since he arrived.

Weren't there supposed to be two Germans?

Joyce sat on the floor, hunched next to her bed. The patterns on the threadbare carpet shimmered in front of her; the lines moving in and out of focus. The playing cards from last night were scattered over the floor.

It was a similar pack to those that Joyce had back home. It wasn't the same pack, of course. That had been lost in the fires and the bombing like everything else she'd owned. But it was similar enough to remind her of the times she'd played with John, her mum, Gwen and Charlie; the five of them cosy around the dining table on a Friday night, the wireless playing dance music on the sideboard, bottles of stout dotted around the table, the calming ticking of her mum's clock on the mantel.

Joyce's mum, Doris, was cheating, but she blamed it on her poor memory about whose go it was. No one believed her, but no one liked to say anything. It was played for fun; a companionable activity that enabled everyone to relax after a week of work. Back then, in the early days of the war, Joyce had been a hairdresser and John had worked at the Triumph factory. Gwen was a secretary at the same factory and prided herself on having the fastest shorthand speed of any of the girls in the pool. Charlie worked at the factory too, but Joyce was never sure what he actually did. He worked on a different section to John and he never elaborated on what he did.

Joyce could remember this game of cards vividly. She could remember Gwen being all dressed up to the nines in a white and red patterned dress. She'd knocked off early and Joyce had done her hair in the front parlour. She hoped that she and Charlie could go to a party that evening. Charlie preferred to stay at home playing cards. Joyce remembered the tension. Gwen would fidget and check the clock from time to time.

'It's not too late.' Gwen looked hopeful.

'It is too late. I'm not changing my shirt now.' Charlie was settled.

'You said we'd play a couple of hands and then go to the party.' Gwen was looking daggers at him now. He'd reneged on a promise. Not that he had any memory of making one.

'I never said that. I said we might go. But frankly I'm worn out and I could do with staying in.'

The evening ended abruptly with Gwen throwing down her cards and storming upstairs. Doris, John and Joyce raised eyebrows to each other. Charlie stayed for another hand, but his heart wasn't in it. Joyce knew that Charlie would get a rollicking whatever time he went upstairs and he decided to get it over with, following Gwen upstairs. Doris went to check on the cat, leaving Joyce and John alone.

That night, in their room, John slipped off his braces and prepared to get into his pyjamas. Joyce applied cold cream to her face at the dressing table. They could hear a heated row coming from Gwen and Charlie's room. Then everything went silent as the argument probably ended, as it always did, with them turning their backs on each other and going to sleep. Outside in the street, Joyce could hear a woman and man laughing as they tumbled back from the pub. Someone down the road yelled at a yapping dog to shut up. Joyce looked at the bedside clock to check the time –

The time!

Oh my god!

There was five minutes to go.

Joyce looked at her watch, dragged away from the comfort of the past. She felt disorientated and confused. What was happening? What should she be doing now? It was so hard to think clearly . . .

In the coop, Connie's basket was nearly full with eggs and Esther had cleaned three of the caged areas. Siegfried was rocking from foot to foot, evidently bored of the whole enterprise. He stared at the stub of his cigar, the end still smouldering, as if considering whether to risk another drag on it. Finally, he rubbed it against the wall of the coop, sending red sparks to the ground. Connie knew they wouldn't have long before he was chivvying them back to the farmhouse.

Four minutes.

They had to stall him a bit longer.

Connie felt her pulse quickening. She had to calm down. With Esther at the far end of the coop, Connie was determined to stay as near the entrance as possible. That way she could run out as soon as Siegfried went to Esther when she faked her collapse. Connie had no choice but to busy herself with collecting the eggs in the area where she was standing.

'Are you nearly done?'

'I won't be long,' Connie smiled. 'Here, do you have eggs in Germany?'

'What?' Siegfried looked baffled, before realising that she was joking. 'Of course, we do.'

'Bet they don't taste as good as these ones, eh?'

'I suppose they're different.'

'Go on, you can say it.'

'All right, they're not as good as these ones.'

Connie and Siegfried shared a smile. Esther threw Connie a confused look. Connie hoped she would realise that she was stalling; playing for time; rather than cosying up to the enemy.

Esther stopped scrubbing and stood motionless for a moment. She was biting her lip nervously and glancing anxiously at Connie. Her body language was screaming that something was wrong. What was she playing at? Connie needed her to get a grip before Siegfried noticed. She couldn't have got freaked out by Connie joking with him, could she?

Connie shook her head to try to convey a message.

Calm down.

Esther shot a look of panic back, motioning towards her wrist. And then Connie realised the root of the problem.

Esther didn't have a watch.

She didn't know what the time was.

No, no! What had happened?

Had she had it on earlier or forgotten? Maybe she'd taken it off when she washed her face in the bathroom this morning.

It didn't matter.

Connie had to worry about what was going to happen, not the journey that led to that point.

She glanced at her own watch and then splayed three fingers against her crimson skirt so that Siegfried wouldn't see. For the time being, he was distracted; looking towards the open door, where winter sunlight was pouring in.

Three minutes.

Three minutes.

Joyce was empty; a staring, unthinking, exhausted husk. She had almost forgotten that the knife was in her hand.

Then the parcel, with its unfamiliar handwriting, swam back into view. Who had sent her a parcel? She was certain it wasn't

286

from anyone she knew. What did it matter now? Parcels didn't matter. Nothing mattered now. She already knew what she had to do; what she was expected to do. The details of the plan had come swimming back into view; but Joyce found it difficult to think straight. She found it difficult to care.

She didn't have the strength. She'd been through so much. She wanted to curl up under that eiderdown and let tearful and exhausted sleep wash over her. That's what grieving people did, wasn't it? That's what she should be allowed to do.

Not this.

But time was running out.

She knew that everything was about to change.

And yet, she couldn't find the energy; the motivation to continue; the impetus to even put one foot in front of the other and leave the room.

Joyce struggled to focus.

Come on, think of Esther. And Connie. They needed her.

She couldn't hear any voices downstairs. What were they doing? Her left-hand tensed, feeling the handle of the bread-knife, unyielding and warm with her perspiration.

She thought about Finch, Esther, Connie and all that had happened. A world ripped apart, the war finally landing on the bucolic doorstep of Pasture Farm. Nothing would ever be the same again. She yearned for the time before, when the war was only starting, and it hadn't blighted her life. A time when making different decisions may have led her somewhere, anywhere, other than this bedroom at the farm, on this day.

Joyce gripped the knife, took a deep breath and moved

towards the door. The floorboard near the door creaked, as it always did.

She knew that her war was about to end, one way or another.

But then she froze, finding it impossible to move forward. She had always been the stoic one; hiding her loss and soldiering on; the one who obeyed all the posters and advertisements from the War Office; the one who found a purpose thanks to the war. But she didn't have anything left. The losses had mounted up and she couldn't do it anymore.

She couldn't do this.

Joyce dropped the knife to the floor.

Channing didn't hear the knife fall as it clattered to the bedroom floor. He was busy putting unused bandages and lint back into his medical bag. He nodded to Emory that his work was complete, and the German pulled down his stained business shirt over the newly dressed arm; wincing as he did so.

'What is your plan?'

A note of distrust was still present in the German's voice.

'We simply walk out of here. You make it look like you're forcing me to comply with your wishes.'

'I use the gun?' Emory pulled the gun from the jacket pocket.

Channing nodded. 'It's a simple plan. But in my experience, they are the ones that work. You hold me across the chest and walk behind me with the gun at my side. I'll look a suitably terrified hostage and I'll get you into my car and we'll drive away.'

'This will work?'

'I sincerely hope so. My life is on the line here as much as yours is.' Channing looked at him coldly. This man was a burden; an irritant who could wreck everything.

'Now, I was told there were two of you. Where's the other one?'

One minute.

Connie placed a final egg into her basket and splayed one finger on her dress for Esther to see. Esther nodded, her mouth moving slightly. Connie assumed she was counting down the seconds. What was she doing?

But then Connie felt Siegfried brush against her.

'What is going on?' He had seen Esther's behaviour too.

'What do you mean?'

'You were signalling to her.' Siegfried turned to look at Esther. 'What is going on?'

Connie suspected he had a feeling that something was happening. It was like that feeling you get when you walk into a room where two people have been talking about you.

Esther froze, the old look of terror turning up like an uninvited relative. Connie's mind whirred, as she desperately tried to think of something.

'I was saying I think we're done here.' Connie tried to cover. Then she realised that there may still be forty seconds or so to go – until Joyce was synched to do her part of the plan. How could she stall him?

'In fact, another forty seconds or so and we'll be finished.'

That was a mistake.

Too specific.

'You're not as clever as you think.' Siegfried gripped Connie's face with his hand. He squeezed her cheeks together and forced her head round to look at Esther. Connie couldn't speak. Siegfried addressed Esther.

'What is happening? What are you planning?'

'Nothing.'

'Tell me, or I'll break her neck!'

Connie tried to speak, but Siegfried's hand was pinching her cheeks together. She struggled and Siegfried raised his other hand into a fist. She wasn't going to wriggle out of this.

'No!' Esther screamed.

Connie used the momentary distraction to knee Siegfried as hard as she could. The German screamed and doubled up in agony; spittle falling from his open mouth as he retched.

Connie didn't have time to celebrate. She started for the door; Esther following as quickly as she could.

'Lock him in here while I get the gun! Lock him in!'

Connie was out of the door and running hell for leather towards the shed.

'Stop! You witch!' Siegfried rose painfully to his feet. Esther looked at him, calculating what to do. But she hesitated for too long. She seemed mesmerised as Siegfried used the wire on the cages to drag himself up. His face was red, and his eyes were wet with tears. He gasped for breath as he steadied himself on shaky legs.

Esther snapped out of it.

She ran to the entrance, ran through it and closed the door.

She was about to slide the bolt across when Siegfried pushed hard against the door, sending it smashing open.

'You get out of the way!' Siegfried pushed Esther onto the ground, as he stumbled and ran towards the yard.

But in the parlour, Emory heard the shouting. He gripped the pistol and moved towards the door. A confused Channing followed.

Thirty seconds.

Joyce stared numbly at the knife on the floor. She didn't care if they'd heard it. She couldn't go on.

But then something made her look back towards the bed, towards the package. Joyce picked up the parcel and held it in her hands, confused, numb. And then she tore it open.

When she saw the contents, nestled within the ripped brown paper, Joyce felt like she'd woken from a dream. It wasn't possible. How could this be? Her fatigued mind fumbled to make connections; fumbled to make sense of this impossible package.

Chapter 15

Four days to Christmas, Birmingham.

Trade had been slow. Bethany Wallace watched the men and women rushing by. They had more haste than usual; keen to finish their shopping and beat the queues at the butchers for Christmas day. The drizzle and cold weather of the last two days hadn't helped; and the snow at the start of the month hadn't either. They kept their heads low and their hats pulled down. Few of them were distracted in their tasks by the menus that hung in the window; and fewer still came in over the threshold.

Each time someone neared the door, Bethany would prepare her best smile, a menu ready in her hand. For the most part, it was a smile that was never seen as the people kept walking instead of coming in.

She knew it would be like this. Having run Butler's Tea Rooms for seven years, Bethany had seen the repeated patterns of feast or famine and was sanguine about it. Her brother, Barnaby, was less inclined to shrug it off, worrying about each fallow day that the restaurant suffered. He would be the one pacing around in the upstairs flat as Bethany tried to sleep in the next room.

He would be the one who would drink too much as he worried about their rent and the wholesale prices they had to endure.

Bethany had never married. Instead she had taken it upon herself to look after Barnaby, who had been afflicted with severe asthma all his life. This was the reason that he hadn't had to go to war. It pained her to see the customers who would look down their noses and quiz him as to why he wasn't fighting. Every day someone would ask.

'Why aren't you fighting then, son?'

Once, someone had sprayed the word 'conchie' on the windows outside, deciding erroneously that Barnaby was a conscientious objector. This daily stress only added to Barnaby's anxiety.

This current slack period had lasted a week and a half. Bethany knew it would pick up between Christmas and New Year, and again, better than ever, in January.

'What are we going to do?' Barnaby was worried.

'What we always do. Wait.'

She'd made a list of tasks and jobs that needed doing. During the busy periods, they never had time to do them, but the slack periods were ideal for repairing a shelf, repainting a wall or revising a menu. Barnaby was always annoyed at helping with these jobs, thinking that they distracted him from the business of willing customers inside solely by the power of thought.

A few days ago, Bethany had taken it upon herself to clear their lost property box. It hadn't been done in ages, and some of this stuff went back several years. She threw away the items that she'd find hard to reunite with their owners; the umbrellas, the scarves, the books; the teddy bears; and concentrated on the ones that she might rehome. She had found it an exciting process, trying to find addresses for names; tracking down people. It was like doing detective work and that felt more thrilling than managing a tea room. Bethany wished that she had worked in the police force. She'd often imagine what it would be like writing up case notes for the officers where, of course, she'd solve the crimes; spotting things that the men had missed.

But no, she was running a tea room instead.

And now, the postman, the elderly Joshua Burton, stopped his bicycle outside, tipped his hat to Bethany and brought in the post. Seeing him approach, Bethany wondered if he'd want a cup of tea, but decided that he might view her offer as being on the house. She couldn't afford freebies; not this time of year. The postman gave her a bundle of mail.

'Here's today's for you, Miss Wallace.'

'Thank you, Mr Burton.'

When she looked at her letters, Bethany was disappointed to see that the parcel had come back. It had a Coventry postmark and was sealed within a small hessian sack with a note explaining why it couldn't be delivered. She'd sent it off a few days, perhaps a week, ago when she first worked on the lost property box.

'The house isn't there anymore,' Bethany read the note giving the reason for the return.

'Ah, that's that then.' The postman touched his cap.

'Not necessarily,' Bethany was warming to her idea. 'Maybe I can find out from the War Office where she moved to . . .'

'She's lucky you don't give up.' Joshua considered. 'She's a lucky woman, this Joyce Fisher . . .'

One day before Christmas.

With the countdown forgotten and the knife on the floor, Joyce Fisher stared at the contents of the impossible package. There was a small note on lilac notepaper inside. The headed paper was from Butler's Tea Rooms and it had been signed by someone called Bethany Wallace.

She read the handwritten note.

Dear Mrs Fisher,

I hope this finds you. This item was handed to us a few years ago. It was found dumped in the street outside our restaurant. I would have sent it sooner, but we've only recently had a clear out of our lost property. I apologise for the delay.

But when I sent it to your address that I found stitched inside, it returned to me saying that the house wasn't there anymore. And that's when I had the most fortuitous piece of luck in finding you. I telephoned the War Office and explained my predicament and they let me know that you are a land girl in Warwickshire.

If it is you, please find enclosed the purse you lost nearly four years ago.

Yours sincerely,
Miss Bethany Wallace

Joyce held the purse in her hands, feeling its shape and texture. It was strange, four years ago she would handle it nearly every day, but now it felt odd and outsized in her hand. She'd got used to making do with a smaller one since it had been stolen. She opened it. Any money that had been inside had long gone thanks to that thieving Alice Ashley, or whatever her real name was. Joyce was about to put the purse down when she spotted a sliver of white paper sticking out of one of the pockets. She pulled it up out of its leather enclosure and looked at it.

It wasn't a piece of paper.

Some days change your life forever. And Joyce knew that today was one of those days.

It was a small photograph of the house on Friday Street in Coventry. Joyce's old home. There were people smiling outside the house. Joyce was standing with John, her mother and sister. They were all smiling for the camera as Charlie took the photograph.

At the time it was nothing special; a forgotten moment. But now, it was the only photograph Joyce had left.

The only image of her family.

And they had come back to her.

Joyce traced the tiny image of her mother, proud in a house coat. On that day, she'd been baffled by the need to come outside and have her photograph taken. But Charlie had borrowed a camera from somewhere. Joyce remembered her mother wanting to go back inside, fearing that the neighbours would wonder what they were doing. Look at them with their airs and graces. Joyce had told her not to worry. Stuff what people thought. She'd touched her mother's shoulder to put her at ease and her hand was still there when the photograph was taken. Gwen was looking pissed off, annoyed perhaps at another one of Charlie's get-rich schemes. This time he'd wanted to be a photographer. Weddings would be profitable, he said. And maybe even funerals. Gwen had frowned with contempt, quashing that idea. Then Joyce remembered that Charlie's friend wanted the camera back and that was the end of that scheme.

And there they were; a moment long gone, on a street that was no longer there.

Joyce was surprised as she felt her spirits lift. She couldn't work out the reaction. Maybe it was because she had something; a memento more reliable than her memories. She could look at their faces; see their personalities; remember how they were. Maybe it was because it had come back into her life when she was feeling at her lowest ebb. But whatever the reason, now she had something to touch; a solid reminder of the time before the destruction of Coventry. Whatever she was going through, she could look at that old image and remember a time of love and joy.

Now, she could see her mother's face as clear as on the day it was taken. She knew they were still with her, watching over her. She felt her strength returning.

Tears came, but this time they were happy, hot tears of joy. They'd come back to her.

At a time when she'd needed them the most.

At a time—

God, the time!

With horror, Joyce realised that the deadline had passed! The ten minutes had ticked away and she hadn't noticed. She was two minutes late.

Connie and Esther were out there!

And she was two minutes late.

Joyce clutched the breadknife in her hand and ran out of the bedroom dreading what she would find outside and hoping against hope that they would be all right.

The life-changing photograph was left on the eiderdown.

Connie ran into Finch's shed; scanning the cluttered surroundings for the shotgun. Where was it? At first, she couldn't see it among the junk, broken tools and off-cuts of wood. Talk about needle in a haystack. But then she saw it propped up against the work bench.

She plucked it up into her hands. It was a heavy, single-barrelled Purdey. Outside the sound of fast-moving boots was getting closer. She didn't have much time. Snapping it open, Connie was relieved to see it was loaded, but she couldn't see any other shells. But then she saw a small hessian sack that contained about six more. Stuffing them messily into her pocket, she snapped the gun shut and ran back into the yard, nearly colliding with Siegfried.

He skidded to a halt as she brought the shotgun to bear on him. Esther was running up behind, and in the distance, Connie could see the other German running from the house. Doctor Channing was with him and Joyce was some way behind, coming out of the door.

Where had she been? Why hadn't she stopped the other German like she was supposed to?

'Get back or I'll shoot!' Connie waved the gun threateningly at Siegfried.

Roland Moore

Siegfried hesitated and then grabbed Esther; using her as a human shield.

'No!' Esther looked terrified.

'Let go of her!' Connie waved the gun.

The other German was getting closer and she could see that he had a pistol. Connie didn't have much time. And yet she couldn't get a clear shot at Siegfried because of Esther being in the way. She hadn't fired many guns in her time and there was no certainty that she'd hit him if she had a clear shot anyway. But Esther had to get out of the way.

'Drop the gun!' The other German got nearer.

'Don't listen, Connie!' Joyce shouted.

'Drop it!'

'Connie, please . . .' Esther sobbed.

Time seemed to stop. Connie was aware of the older German getting closer, raising his luger; Siegfried was holding tightly onto the struggling Esther; Joyce was running towards them.

Connie made a decision.

She lowered the shotgun.

Siegfried smiled; relief etched on his face.

'That's a good girl.'

But then Connie fired it at his leg.

It was the only part of him that she had a clear shot at. And at close range she knew she couldn't miss. It exploded in a geyser of red and sinew.

'Ahhhh!' Siegfried screamed and crumpled to the ground, clutching his shattered ankle; writhing in pain.

As he fell, he released his grip and Esther ran away from

him. She ran over to Connie. Connie fumbled for the hessian bag from her pocket, but the shells tumbled out onto the ground.

Emory glanced at the fallen, screaming Siegfried and ignored him. He levelled his pistol at Connie as he got closer. Joyce chased after him, the breadknife in her hand. But she was still ten feet away.

'You betrayed us!' Emory looked furious as he spoke in Channing's vague direction. 'It's a trap.'

'What are you talking about?' Channing shouted.

There was no time for more debate. Emory wasn't interested in discussion. He was interested in survival.

Joyce heard it but didn't have time to process it. She was a few feet away now from the German as Connie picked up a shell, snapped the shotgun open and desperately tried to reload.

She wouldn't manage it in time.

Emory shot Connie.

The gunshot pierced the silent morning air with a high-pitched whistle, hitting Connie. She didn't feel any pain at first. She was aware of feeling like she'd been pushed and she could feel herself falling backwards as her head spun dizzily. Somewhere far, far away, she could hear Esther screaming and she was aware of something wet splashing her face. It was blood. She hit the ground, feeling small stones on the concrete pushing against the back of her head. Her arms flopped lazily down beside her; with the echo of the gunshot ringing in her ears. The shotgun fell onto the ground by her side.

Emory went to line up another shot to finish her off.

But Joyce had reached him. He started to turn, realising he was about to be attacked. Joyce acted quickly. She plunged the breadknife into his back. It sliced easily through the suit jacket and the shirt, embedding itself. Joyce felt the resistance to the blade as it met sinew and muscle underneath. Emory screamed. He turned round and fired off two shots in Joyce's general direction. But his aim was desperate and reckless. The bullets whipped past her head as she ducked forward; using her momentum to push Emory over. The knife snapped off in his back as he hit the yard floor and he screamed even more loudly. But he still had the pistol in his hand and tried to bring it to bear on Joyce. She desperately tried to pin his arms down. She was surprised by the strength that he still possessed. But then he was desperate and wounded and he was fighting for his life. And that made two of them.

Joyce couldn't hold down his hands. Emory strained to bring the gun up towards her face.

Why was Channing standing there? Why didn't he help?

She punched at Emory's injured arm and he released his grip on her. Joyce scrambled away to one side and got to her feet as Emory tried to grab her again. She staggered backwards falling onto her backside, but she was free of him. But then he scrambled to a sitting position and brought the pistol up. The barrel levelled with Joyce's face as they sat opposite each other in the dirt.

This was it.

Point blank range with no escape.

Joyce was certain that she was going to die.

There was no way she could get away in time and no way

could she grapple with him to get the gun. Not before he shot her anyway.

She thought of the photograph; the smiling faces on Friday Street. And in a split second, Joyce knew that if she was about to die then she'd meet her loved ones again; free of pain and free of suffering.

They'd all be together.

Time seemed to stop, and she didn't notice Esther pluck the shotgun from the ground near Connie's motionless body and run over. It was unloaded so Esther flipped it round and holding it by the barrel whacked Emory hard in the face with the butt; snapping his head back and shattering his nose. He fell backwards, knocked out cold; the pistol flying from his hand.

Time restarted.

Joyce could hear the wails coming from Siegfried as he writhed around on the ground in a mess of blood. Esther was standing motionless holding the shotgun by its barrel; the shock of what had happened hitting her. And then Joyce heard a faint whimper coming from Connie, who was lying flat on her back; her best crimson suit torn and ruined.

She was still alive!

Joyce hauled herself to her feet and staggered over to Connie. She held her by the elbows and gently shook Connie so that she'd focus on her.

'Connie? Come on!'

Connie's big brown eyes looked at Joyce. They glazed over. She gave a tight-lipped smile. Joyce assumed that she was going into shock as well.

'How do you feel?'

'I dunno,' Connie couldn't really think straight.

'I'm so sorry I was late.'

'It's done now, innit?' Connie licked her lips, nervous of what she was about to ask. 'How bad am I?'

Joyce feared the worst and was scared to look. She forced herself to glance down. The left shoulder of Connie's suit had a small hole in it and the crimson fabric was darkened with blood.

'He only got your shoulder, I think.' Joyce realised that this was probably a minor wound. 'He only got your shoulder!' Joyce said, excitedly.

But she was unsure what to do.

And then she remembered Doctor Channing.

'Doctor?' Joyce got up.

Channing appeared lost in his own world, standing numbly in the yard as if he too was in shock. Joyce supposed that traumatic events could do that to passers-by. But why hadn't he helped?

'Doctor Channing!'

He snapped out of it and rushed over to Connie, kneeling at her side. He found his voice. 'Mrs Jameson? Can you, can you hear me?'

'Yeah, think so.'

'Fetch my medical bag, Joyce.' Channing pointed to where it had fallen. Joyce walked as quickly as she could. She didn't trust herself to run as her legs felt like jelly and she didn't want to fall. That wouldn't help Connie. She found Channing's bag and turned to find Esther and Channing working together to take off Connie's jacket. Esther had lifted Connie's head slightly and Channing was pulling the sleeve of her jacket off.

'I'm going to sterilise it and then dress it to stop the bleeding. When we get to the hospital, I can get the bullet removed. Is that all right?'

'Sounds all right to me, Doc.' Connie seemed reassured by his words.

Channing stared at the carnage around him; assessing what had happened and how it affected him.

The two Germans were on the ground, one of them possibly dead and the other in a lot of pain. The dead one knew of his involvement, but the younger one had never met him, had he? That was good. The young one couldn't betray him to the authorities. The threat was over. He was dumbstruck by the brave and foolish actions of these women. What had they done?

It didn't matter.

What mattered was how they viewed him now?

Did they suspect him?

That bloody German had mentioned being betrayed. He'd mentioned a trap. But maybe they hadn't heard that. Yes, surely, they wouldn't have heard it in the heat of the fight that was going on, would they? There were gun shots and shouting; they wouldn't have heard. And even if they had, he could talk his way out of it. He could say that they misheard what the German had said. Or he could say that the German was clutching at straws as to what was happening.

Yes, he could get out of this.

When he went to help Connie Carter, Channing was buoyed by the fact that Esther and Joyce were helping him. They didn't hang back or look distrustfully at him. No, they were interested in helping Connie and relaxed around him.

Perhaps they didn't suspect a thing.

Within thirty minutes, Esther had used the telephone in the farmhouse to ask for help. Soon after, some American soldiers from Hoxley Manor arrived in a jeep. They helped lift Connie into the back.

'Here, do you remember when I first came here?' Connie was wrapped in a blanket to keep her warm and seemed in good spirits.

'Yes.' Joyce remembered it well. 'You turned up in one of these jeeps, didn't you? You were singing away to the soldiers that had given you a lift. We couldn't believe it. Talk about making an entrance!'

Connie smiled. She was looking forward to seeing Henry. Joyce was certain that she would be all right. Esther went with her to keep her company. Channing had insisted that they all get themselves checked over at the hospital.

'Thanks, Joyce.' The Americans started the engine on the jeep.

'What for? I was late,' Joyce felt bad that she'd let them down.

'But you saved my life.'

Joyce watched the jeep as it drove slowly away. Connie's face looked back at her as it shrank to a miniature version of itself and finally disappeared. Joyce felt immense relief.

'You should get checked too.' Channing was standing

beside her, watching the disappearing jeep. His voice had made her jump.

Joyce nodded.

'I can drive you over there if you like?' Channing smiled.

Joyce felt a strange, irrational feeling of unease. Why hadn't he helped them when they'd needed him? Don't be silly. This was good old Doctor Channing. He'd helped John back to health. He'd just frozen when everything escalated out of control, that's all. People often froze.

She could trust him, surely?

Yes, she supposed she could.

'Thanks.' Joyce moved towards the farmhouse. 'I'll just get my coat.'

Chapter 16

Channing was driving too fast.

The lane was passing in a blur of skeletal trees and evergreen hedgerow; the engine straining and the wheels squealing at each turn. Joyce assumed he was concerned about Connie and her injury. Perhaps he wanted to do the operation on her; remove the bullet himself. But even so, the speed seemed excessive.

'Can't you slow down, Doctor Channing?'

'I need to get to the hospital.'

'But what's the point if we end up wrapped round a tree? We'll need a hospital ourselves.'

Channing made a small dismissive grunt and relaxed the accelerator. He slowed to a reasonable pace and Joyce felt more at ease as the car slowed, releasing her tight grip on the seat beneath her.

'Happy?'

'Why should I be happy?' Joyce fixed him with a stare. But the doctor kept his eyes on the road, his hands gripping the top of the steering wheel. Had he forgotten the dreadful news he'd personally delivered to her? Sometimes she marvelled at the way men could be insensitive.

'What I mean is that you must be relieved that those Germans are no longer a problem for you?'

Joyce nodded.

'The whole ordeal must have been really unpleasant and terrifying.'

'We did wonder if we'd get out of it alive,'

Channing continued: 'You know, when I got there, I had been trying to convince the older one to turn himself in. I figured that he was in command. Was I right?'

'Yes, he was the captain or whatever.'

'I thought if he would give himself up then the younger one would follow. That was my thinking. And I nearly convinced them you know.'

'What did you say to him?'

'What do you mean?'

Joyce sighed and thought carefully about what she was about to say. The doctor seemed on edge and she didn't want to antagonise him any further; especially when he was in control of a car in which she already felt unsafe. But she needed to tackle him on what Emory had said in the final moments. He'd said he felt betrayed or something similar, hadn't he? What did that mean? She couldn't let it go; as tempting as it was to close her eyes and let sleep wash over her. Joyce focused on steering the conversation so she could find out the truth.

'I mean, you must have made them some promises?'

'Promises?'

'To convince them to turn themselves in.'

'Ah I see,' Channing continued to watch the road. 'Yes, I suppose I did make some promises. General things like the fact he'd be treated fairly as a prisoner of war if he gave himself up. That sort of thing.'

'So is that why he said you'd betrayed him?'

And there it was; the question out in the open.

The words hung in the air between them. The heavy silence that followed seemed to stretch to eternity. Joyce listened to the sound of the engine as she waited for him to speak. But a strange, terse little smile was playing on his lips. She didn't know what he was thinking. Had she hit a nerve? Surely, he'd say something soon.

What did she want him to say? Why had she asked that? It was so annoying; especially as Channing thought Joyce might not have heard the German's words.

Oh, why couldn't she leave things be?

What did she expect him to say?

Channing mulled the possibilities, but as he thought everything through, he couldn't stop a bitter smile registering on his features. After all the stress he'd been through, why did she have to ask him that? He'd been so careful, meticulous in planning for every eventuality.

Why couldn't they all leave him alone?

When they'd left Pasture Farm, he'd driven fast, fulfilling some primal urge to shake off the tension he felt by seeing his surroundings flashing past. But that hadn't helped. And then she'd asked him to slow down.

She had been needling him all the way.

Was she suspicious?

Channing wanted her to shut up. He wanted her to stop harassing him. He was so close to getting away with this. He couldn't let her destroy things now. But it was so hard for him to think straight.

Come on, he was nearly home and dry.

Concentrate.

After a lengthy silence, Channing spoke, finally answering her question about why Emory had thought he'd betrayed them. The easiest way was to agree with the scenario that Joyce had given him. He had promised them safety in a prisoner of war camp, and they had thought he had betrayed them when the shooting started.

'I should imagine so, don't you?'

Channing glanced her way, fixing her with a craggy grin.

Joyce nodded and watched the road. The answer hadn't made her feel any less uncomfortable. Other things were nagging at her. Pieces in a puzzle were falling into place. She hadn't intended for that to happen; it was like her subconscious was piecing things together. She'd let them off the leash and they were following the scent on their own.

She remembered that Lady Hoxley had, for a time, suspected Channing of being a sympathiser for the Germans. But that had all worked out, hadn't it? Channing had even saved Lady Hoxley from a real sympathiser; risking his life in the process. Yes, he'd come into the stables and shot the man dead. So he couldn't have been working for the Germans, could he? But then why did Lady Hoxley suspect him? There must have been something to make her suspicious.

Channing looked back at the road and Joyce tried to relax to allow her exhausted brain to make its connections.

What else was there to consider?

Ah yes . . .

Why hadn't Channing told the Home Guard that they were looking for two airmen? Horace Winstanley had no idea that's how many they were hunting and yet Channing had that key information from Connie and he had promised to pass it on.

So why hadn't he?

She struggled to remember what had happened as she'd run out of the farmhouse kitchen. The exact details of what happened. Had Channing been surprised to find Emory there? She wasn't sure. He hadn't been her focus at the time. But there was something else about Channing when he'd arrived. What was it?

Then she remembered he'd had a medical bag.

Why did he have that with him?

He didn't need it, did he? He was delivering a message to her. And he'd made no attempt to give her any sedative or medicine when he'd broke the news. There was no need for a medical bag. Unless he had it with him on the off-chance that she might need something after he broke the news.

That was one possibility she supposed.

The alternative was that he knew in advance that he might need it; because he knew he might have to treat injured airmen.

Joyce felt the hairs on her neck stand up and her stomach lurched. It wasn't beyond the realm of possibility to think that Channing may have picked up their Morse code message.

She needed time to think; time away from Channing.

'I want you to stop the car please.' Joyce kept her voice as level as voice as she could manage.

'What are you talking about?'

'I need to get out. I feel sick.'

'No, you don't.' Channing voice was flat and emotionless. 'What's going on, Joyce?'

With her exhaustion removing any filter, it all came out, in an ill-advised and dangerous gamble. Joyce heard herself saying the words that she'd been mulling over in her head. But suddenly they were released into the wild.

'Lady Hoxley was right, wasn't she?'

'What?'

'She was right.'

'Right about what? What are you talking about?' Once again, his voice was flat, unruffled. Chillingly cold.

'You want me to spell it out?' Joyce heard her voice crack with imminent tears. 'You're in league with the Germans. A sympathiser, aren't you?'

Channing snorted in derision.

He put his foot down hard on the accelerator and the car squealed around a bend.

'Why couldn't you stop with your questions?'

He muttered the words more to himself than to her.

'I'm right though, aren't I?'

'You want to know? I'll tell you what I am,' Channing

glanced briefly at her, a strange enigmatic smile playing on his face. It chilled her to the bone.

'I'm an agent for the British, for the War Office.'

'What?'

'I'm on your side, you stupid, stupid woman. I was employed to infiltrate a group of fascist sympathisers; gain their trust; become one of them. And that's what I did. That's exactly what I did.'

The road was a blur as Channing went faster and faster. She gripped the seat; her mind struggling to process what he was saying. It was crazy, wasn't it? She followed her gut instinct.

'I don't believe you.' Joyce was shaking.

'Don't be silly.' Although it was the kind of thing you'd say to a child, in Channing's mouth it was loaded with so much contempt it sounded like the ultimate derision.

'You told Lady Channing that lie when you killed the sympathiser in her stables. But if it was true – and you were a British agent – doing that would have blown your cover, wouldn't it? The rest of the group would have known you were a British agent after that. You couldn't have gone back to them.'

'I assume the rest of the group didn't know what I'd done.'

'Everyone knew. Your heroic act was the talk of the whole of Hoxley Manor and most of Helmstead. Word would have got back to them. And they wouldn't have trusted you after that. I'm right, aren't I? You're not a British agent. You're a sympathiser who was covering his tracks by killing that man in the stables.'

Channing said nothing, but his face was a collage of contempt and exhaustion. And then he spoke, raising his voice to be heard about the straining engine.

'I'm a British agent.' Channing insisted desperately. Joyce wondered if he repeated it enough he might believe it.

'I don't believe you.'

Channing looked like he was about to reply, but before he could say a word, a tractor filled their windscreen suddenly. There was no escape. Joyce instinctively tried to open her door to get out. Channing slammed on the brakes, but couldn't stop in time. The Ford plunged head on into the tractor, sending Channing crashing hard against the steering wheel; the windscreen shattering over him. Joyce was luckier, managing to dive down into the passenger well and open the door as she was thrown forward. She tumbled out of the car as it hit the tractor and she rolled hard down a verge by the side of the road. Every branch and rock came up to meet her as she fell. The pain washed over her as she tumbled and eventually crumpled in a heap halfway down the embankment. She was still for a long while, knocked unconscious. But slowly sensation came back, and she moved, as if testing each limb to see if it was still attached.

Murmuring in confusion, Joyce struggled to get to her feet but, unable to cope with the dizziness of the fall, promptly fell backwards. She tried again, slower this time, and managed to crawl onto her knees and then up onto her feet. Her wrist was badly bruised, her ankle was twisted, and she had various cuts to her arms, but apart from that she thought she was in one piece. The car and tractor up at the top of the embankment were bathed in steam from the smashed radiator of the Ford.

She moved slowly down the embankment being careful

not to tumble again. At the bottom she could see the end of the platform at Helmstead station. It was lightly occupied with passengers from an arriving train. A short engine with four carriages was parked in the station. None of the passengers were looking her way. Maybe none of them had heard the crash over the noise of the train. Maybe they were distracted with greeting or saying goodbye to loved ones.

Joyce waved, but lost her balance again. She tumbled forward onto her bad wrist. She winced and struggled to get up.

She glanced behind her.

She was surprised by what she saw.

A man was making his way down after her; his face a bloodied mess. Channing had survived and he was coming to get her.

Channing pulled himself off the steering wheel. Blood was pouring down his face and he was finding it hard to breathe. He knew he'd broken a rib or two in the impact and that the ribs had severed one of his lungs. But he had to block out the pain and the discomfort. He had to stop Joyce.

She could mess everything up.

He fumbled for his medical bag that had fallen into the footwell and opened it up with his blood-slippery hands. He pulled out the pistol, wiping his hand on his trousers to get purchase on it. Channing tried to open the door, but it was crumpled in the impact. Wincing in pain, he pulled himself over to the passenger seat and got out from Joyce's open door.

Staggering from the car, the disorientated but uninjured

farmer who had been driving the tractor glanced accusingly at him. Channing waved the gun in the man's general direction and he obligingly disappeared from view.

'I don't want no trouble.' The farmer retreated.

Glancing down the embankment, Channing could see Joyce about halfway down. She was struggling to stay upright and it looked like she was limping. She was making slow progress.

He had to deal with her.

Later, he'd tell people that she compromised his cover.

Yes, that's what he'd do.

Channing tried to aim his pistol, but he was too far away and his hand was shaking too much. He had no choice but to get closer. So wheezing and groaning, he hurriedly made his way down the embankment after her as fast as he could.

Joyce scrambled down, nearly losing her balance again. Her ankle was becoming more painful to move, but she forced herself onwards. Channing was about halfway down the embankment above her. He had a pistol in his hand. She'd seen it glint in the light.

Could she reach the bottom, cross the rail track and get to the end of the platform before Channing could get a shot at her? The platform was about three hundred yards from the bottom of the embankment. She'd be safe then, amongst the crowds.

She had to try.

Joyce fell onto her bottom, skidding down the last few feet on a bed of shingle. She got to her feet. Channing was gaining on her, realising that time was running out.

318

'Stop! Stay where you are!' It was Channing's voice further up the embankment.

The train was about to pull away. Joyce could see it gaining speed as it left the station. It was a four-carriage train, and Joyce knew that if she didn't cross the tracks before it reached her then it would be a barrier in front of her. It would trap her on the same side as Channing.

The train moved closer and closer. The track was ahead in front of her. Joyce remembered her mother telling her to be careful about crossing train tracks. And here she was about to risk her life doing just that. But it was the only way she could escape.

Joyce ran desperately for the track. The train was closing. Channing knew he had to reach her. He lunged for her, missing the collar of her shirt.

But he managed to grab her arm.

'Get off me!'

'I can't let you go!' He brought the pistol round towards Joyce's side. 'I'm so sorry!'

The train sounded its bell, the driver spotting them at the edge of the track, but unable to stop in time.

Joyce threw a punch at Channing's face. It didn't connect with any solid impact, but it moved the gun off target and made him let go of her arm. She could feel the vibration of the train. It was that close. She could smell the burning coal and hot oil. Joyce had a split second to get in front of the train or it would be too late.

Clang, clang, clang.

With its bell sounding, she leaped over the rails, falling in an untidy heap on the other side. There was a gunshot. Channing made the leap a second later, but the train thundered past. He didn't make it to Joyce's side. She felt a blast of wind from the train, forcing her to close her eyes from the dust it was throwing up.

Eyes tightly shut, Joyce pulled herself backwards, as the rest of the train went past and then, breathless with exertion, she dragged herself to her feet. The train disappeared in the distance. She opened her eyes.

She tried to make out where Channing was.

Where was he?

Where had he gone?

Had he been hit by the train and thrown backwards? She couldn't see any sign of him. Joyce knew he must be there somewhere. There had been no scream; no sound of a body being hit. Of course, such sounds may have been blocked out by the sheer noise of the train going past with its bell clanging.

A man's hand touched her shoulder.

Joyce jumped.

'It's all right, miss, you're safe.' The station master looked down at her, taking in the sight of a dishevelled young woman. 'You took quite a risk there.'

'Where is he?'

'Your boyfriend?' The grey-haired old man looked concerned.

'He's not my boyfriend.'

'That man?' The station master sucked air between his teeth, pondering. 'He may have been thrown some distance up the line or if he was unlucky, his clothes will have got caught, and he'll have been dragged along,' he said. 'He could end up a way away before he falls.'

Joyce nodded.

'So do you think he's dead?'

'I'm sorry, miss. I'd have thought so.'

'No apology necessary,' Joyce exhaled deeply.

It was over.

The station master helped her along the tracks to the station platform. He had a smell of brandy about him and Joyce imagined the station staff had shared a drink to commiserate having to work Christmas Eve. Joyce could see a small group of passengers looking at them as they got nearer. These people had arrived in Helmstead and hadn't bargained on seeing anything so traumatic in this sleepy town.

The station master helped Joyce up onto the platform. She dusted herself down and straightened her hair. The onlookers were gazing at her, full of unanswered questions. Some of the women were smiling sympathetically. Some children were looking confused at what they'd just seen.

Joyce tried to process all their faces, but she was finding it hard to focus. Stars were swimming in her field of vision, and everything seemed distant and too loud. The sky seemed too bright. She knew what was about to happen.

The station master propped his hand underneath her elbow to stop her falling.

'I've got you.'

'I'm all right,' Joyce's voice sounded a long way away.

One younger man came forward, pushing through the cluster of people. He had a look of concern and surprise on his face. He seemed familiar. A slim-built man in his mid-twenties, blessed with good looks, kind eyes and dark brown hair – Joyce knew who he was.

But that wasn't possible, was it?

With too much light in the sky behind him, John Fisher held out a hand to his wife.

Joyce thought of the photograph. All her loved ones on Friday Street. All of them were gone. And now, finally, she knew what had happened and the truth came to her with a feeling of serenity and calm.

Channing had shot her, hadn't he? At the last moment as she jumped across the track, he'd shot her. She'd heard the gun go off.

And this was the end.

Yes, that's what this was. But it was nothing to fear.

Joyce slid to the platform, feeling the cold concrete beneath her fingers. She didn't feel any pain, not anymore. She wasn't aware of where she had been shot. She didn't need to look for a wound. She knew what was happening.

John crouched with her, a kind smile on his face. He was always there and would be forever and he was holding her as the darkness descended.

But there was a smile on Joyce's face as it enveloped her.

Chapter 17

The night before Christmas.

Connie Carter opened her eyes.

The first thing she saw was Henry, looking down at her, a relieved expression on his face. He called for a nurse and then turned his full attention back to his wife. She realised that she was in the hospital wing of Hoxley Manor. Again. It was all familiar; the makeshift hospital. The high ceiling with its ornate coving, plunging down to built-in oak book-shelves; the hospital beds placed in rows in front of them on the parquet flooring. She didn't like being such a regular visitor.

'I'm making a right habit of this.'

'You're going to be all right!' Henry bounced up from his seat excitedly.

'What happened?' Connie tried to speak but found it hard. She saw Esther come into view. 'You helped see off those two German airmen, that's what happened.'

Before Connie could ask any more questions, a nurse arrived with a doctor. She didn't know who the doctor was. It wasn't Channing, but a small, Scottish man in a patterned waistcoat. They checked Connie over and the doctor looked into her eyes with a light before smiling at her.

'You're making an excellent recovery.'

'What about my . . .?' Connie needed to know.

'It's all right.' Henry held her hand, 'Our baby is all right.'

'And we got the bullet out of your shoulder. The wound was clean, and it should all heal perfectly.' The doctor glanced at his clipboard as he spoke.

'That's such good news, lovey,'

'Yes, and we'll expect you back on the farm in a few days.'

The words were followed with a distinctive chuckle and Connie knew that it was Frederick Finch. 'I come back from Leicester and find out you've turned my farm into a war zone!'

She looked towards the end of the bed and saw that Finch was flanked by Iris and Martin as well. They all smiled at her. They had all come to see her.

'We can't leave you for five minutes,' Iris looked happy and content, pleased to be with Martin.

'We've asked if you can come out of hospital for a Christmas dinner tomorrow!' Finch chuckled.

'The doctors said no,' Esther looked sternly at Finch.

'But we're going to spring you out for a couple of hours anyway. If you want to, of course.'

'I do. Be lovely to see you all and have a chuckle.'

And then Connie realised there was someone she hadn't seen, someone she hadn't enquired about yet.

'What happened to Joyce?' She asked. 'Where is she?'

At first no one knew what to say. Finch shuffled awkwardly.

Martin and Iris looked at the floor. Henry smiled consolingly. But it was Esther that stepped forward.

She smiled kindly at Connie.

'I don't suppose you've heard, love . . .'

In the living room of Hoxley Manor, Lady Hoxley poured more tea into her best china cups, before handing them to the men from the War Office. They were called Bartholomew and Matthews; which sounded more like a firm of solicitors than the names of two agents. Bartholomew was the older and more experienced agent, the one who did most of the talking. Matthews was the trainee, who spoke little and watched his superior avidly for clues about how to conduct himself.

Ellen had told them about the last days of Richard Channing and they were all trying to piece together what had happened and what it meant.

For her part, Ellen had woken late on Christmas Eve with no understanding of what would have made her sleep for so long. She hadn't been especially tired. Bartholomew pushed his wire glasses up to the bridge of his nose. He thought that Channing had probably drugged her to keep her out of the way. Matthews took a blood sample. Bartholomew thought that if the sedative had been something like Bromide then it would hang around in the bloodstream. They would send the blood sample for testing, but he suspected it would show some signs of a sedative.

'Have you found his body?'

'Not yet, Lady Hoxley.' Bartholomew took a sip of tea. 'But

I'm sure it'll turn up. Without wanting to be graphic, bodies can be dragged quite a distance.'

'Could he have survived?'

'It's unlikely.'

'But not impossible?'

Bartholomew shook his head. Then he opened Manila envelope. Inside was a photograph of Siegfried Weber. Ellen didn't know who he was, and Bartholomew explained that he was one of the Germans who had been holed up at Pasture Farm.

'He didn't interact with Richard Channing, so he doesn't know if Channing was there to help them. He doesn't know if Channing answered their call for help. The other German could have told us more as he presumably talked to Channing,' Bartholomew sipped more tea.

'But he died?'

'Yes, he'd died at the scene.'

'This is all a dreadful shock. Not about the German but about Richard. You think you know somebody and then they surprise you in such hideous ways' Ellen felt betrayed by him. The whole debacle was forcing her to reassess every moment of their friendship as she searched for clues as to his double-life. 'I suppose the big question I have is, was Richard a sympathiser or a British agent? It's still not entirely clear to me. And it would have a bearing, as matters progress.'

She'd picked her words carefully, but both agents knew that she was referring to the type of funeral or church service that Richard Channing would have if his body was found. Would it be a hero's send-off or the ignominy of a traitor's passing?

Bartholomew chose his words equally as carefully.

'We have no record of him working for us. But he could have been working for a special department.'

'So we still don't know?'

'I'm sorry, but no,' Bartholomew got to his feet. Matthews took his cue and rose as well.

'And presumably you won't necessarily tell me if you find out?'

'Not if it conflicts with any ongoing work. Sorry.'

Ellen tried not to show how vexed she was by this development. That wouldn't do at all. What was she supposed to say to people now? The agents obviously didn't care about the wagging tongues in the village.

Bartholomew tipped his hat to Ellen and made towards the door. Lady Hoxley nodded her thanks to them and saw them out. Then she called for her maid to take the tea things away.

Feeling awkward in the silence of her room, Lady Hoxley put a record on the player. It would comfort her to hear the song one last time before she packed it away.

'White Christmas' played, the tune wafting through Hoxley Manor.

The song could be heard as vague, ethereal whispers in the large ward of the hospital, as if it was almost the memory of the song and not the real thing. Joyce opened her eyes and looked at the coving above her; white and ornate. This was a place where she expected to see angels. But the light diminished and instead of heavenly bodies, she was aware of the Earthly rattle of the medicine trolley in the distance.

A small, Scottish doctor in a patterned waistcoat was explaining that she'd passed out from exhaustion at the station. She'd been out cold for quite a while. And after the ordeal she'd been through, it wasn't surprising.

'But you're going to be fine,' the doctor reassured her.

'How long have I been here?'

'Not long. Nine hours or so,' The doctor nodded as a nurse appeared. She wrote some things on a clipboard as the doctor moved to leave the bedside.

'I thought I'd died.'

'You were lucky to survive. The train missed you by inches by all accounts.' The doctor indicated a small distance between his thumb and forefinger.

'It was funny though . . .' Joyce hadn't intended the words to be heard by the doctor or the nurse, just by herself, 'In those last moments on the platform, I saw my husband. He'd come to tell me it was all right to let go. He was holding out his hand for me. It made me feel calm, happy during what I thought would be my last moments. So now I know if anything does happen to me, that my mum, Gwen and my husband will all be waiting. And that's a comfort, I suppose.'

'That's reassuring to hear, isn't it?' The doctor was leaving. But then he stopped and turned; a look of confusion on his face. 'But that's odd you say that.'

'Why?'

'About your husband waiting. Well, the man who brought you in said he was your husband.'

'No, he's the station master. You must be mistaken.'

'Of course.' The doctor conceded. 'But anyway, he wanted to see you when you woke up. He's been waiting to check you're all right. I'll send him in anyway, shall I?'

The doctor and nurse left. Joyce pulled herself up in bed. She primped her hair, ready to make small talk with the station master. She felt gratitude towards him for helping her and it was good of him to bring her to Hoxley Manor for treatment. It was kind of him to wait, especially so late on Christmas Eve. She would thank him and perhaps invite him to lunch at the farm sometime.

The door opened.

But the man who entered wasn't the station master.

It was John Fisher.

Joyce's mouth gaped open in disbelief; a lump in her throat; tears pricking her eyes.

'John . . .?'

She felt that she might pass out again. This couldn't be happening. It didn't make any sense. What sort of hallucination or trick was this?

'Darling Joyce,' John sat on the bed and took her hand in his. 'You must have been so worried. I came as soon as I could.'

He looked like John. The voice sounded like his. And his hand felt soft and familiar. He felt warm. He didn't feel like a ghost or an angel.

'But it's impossible.' Joyce's voice was breaking, 'The fire. They said you died in a fire. They found your belongings. Your kit bag was next to you. They told me!'

'But it wasn't me.' Tears filled his eyes.

'But— I don't understand.'

'I was attacked a few days before Christmas and my things were stolen. It was the man who robbed me who must have died in that fire. I didn't know anything about it until this morning. Teddy was up and about, and he'd gone to the butcher's and some people were saying – they were giving him condolences because they heard I'd died. He told them not to be so stupid. And he told me. And I found out the Police had found my bag at the scene. I realised they must have put two and two together and made five. So I came back as soon as I could.'

'Oh my god.'

'You must have been so worried.'

Joyce couldn't speak. Instead, she wrapped her arms around her husband and pulled him towards her. They both sobbed and kissed and held each other. It was the happiest moment of Joyce's life. The happiest moment of both of their lives. They knew that love could conquer all.

Neither of them would ever let go.

Chapter 18

Christmas Day, 1944

It was a day that Joyce Fisher never thought she'd see.

Paper chains, borrowed from the event at the village hall festooned the kitchen in Pasture farm, where it was a hive of activity. Steam belched out from an ill-fitting saucepan lid as the potatoes finished cooking and Esther mopped her forehead with the back of her hand. Iris was helping, slicing carrots on a breadboard. The smell of cooking filled the room with every oven on the range in use.

The wireless was playing in the parlour. Finch had got it working after the Germans' tinkering and a man with a severe, clipped voice was wishing the listeners a very merry Christmas. He didn't sound very merry himself.

Martin was supposed to be laying the table, but he was spending more time talking to Iris than putting out cutlery. He was outlining the tentative idea for a date. A bold move.

'There's a dance over in Brinford, day after tomorrow, if you fancy it?' Martin quickly expanded the invitation to cover his awkwardness. 'If any of you fancy it.'

'Oh, sounds nice. I might come along.' Esther was being devilish, offering a smirk to Iris.

Martin's face fell.

'I'm teasing you!'

'Anyone else?' Martin was hoping the answer would be no.

'I think my dancing shoes are at the menders, so count me out. Unless there's a free bar. Then I'll bring my drinking shoes.' Finch chuckled.

Iris saved him from his torture.

'I'd love to come to that. Thank you.'

Martin's face lit up and then he struggled to hide the fact it had lit up. 'That's wonderful.'

'Yes, it will be,' Iris bit a carrot suggestively. Martin's mouth almost fell open with shock. Then Iris realised that she hadn't meant to be so suggestive, so rude. She shook her head, red-faced with embarrassment. He looked embarrassed too and then they relaxed slightly and looked at each other for a long moment, until both of them felt self-conscious. Iris returned to her carrots and Martin returned to his knives and forks.

Joyce came downstairs. She'd put on a cream coloured dress decorated with a red rose pattern; her hair and makeup were done. Her wrist was bandaged and she had some abrasions to her face, but they were only visible if you looked for them. She felt much better for taking time to pamper herself a bit.

'How are you feeling, lovey?'

'Good.' There was a knock at the door. Joyce straightened her hem. 'In fact, I think I feel really good.'

Joyce went to the back door and opened it.

John was standing on the threshold with Connie and Henry.

He'd brought them over in Finch's van. Joyce invited them all in, kissing her husband as he passed the threshold.

'Got to pay the toll.'

'I'll go out and come back in again, if that's the case.'

Everyone welcomed Connie to the table with a chorus of 'how are you' and Finch pushed out a chair for her to sit down. She looked frail and delicate; her skin was whiter than usual in contrast to her ruby red lipstick. Her arm was in a sling and the dressing on her shoulder was visible in the opening of her blouse. But whatever her current physical discomfort, there was no denting her spirit.

'Here, I hope you haven't skimped on lunch. I'm starving,' Connie announced to the room.

'No, we're having rabbit pie, potatoes, carrots and cabbage. And a Christmas cake to follow.' Esther was fighting to see through steam that was rising from the open oven in front of her.

'Sounds better than what they going to serve in the hospital!'

'We got the dried fruit for the cake,' Martin announced.

'From Birmingham,' Iris added.

'Oh, did you go to Butler's Tea Rooms?'

'We did, Joyce. And it was lovely.'

Joyce thought how she should visit the tea room herself. The owner didn't know how much help she'd given Joyce, and by turn, Connie and Esther, in sending that photograph. Joyce needed to go there and say thank you.

But that would wait for another day.

Today, she had Christmas to celebrate!

'Here, Connie, if you're hungry, start with this then,' Finch chuckled, pouring some dandelion wine into tumblers for everyone. He handed a glass to Connie and she took a sip.

'That's the ticket!'

'Is that wise?' Henry asked.

'No one said I couldn't drink, Henry. And seeing as what we've all been through, I think we're entitled to a little drink, don't you?' Connie raised her glass.

'I'll drink to that,' Joyce replied. 'Come on everybody.'

Everyone raised a toast and the kitchen echoed with the chinking of glasses. Soon they were singing and laughing around the table as they waited for lunch. Through the window, the winter sun shone onto the farmyard where it illuminated a moving flash of white feathers. A loose hen ran across to the stable block, squawking loudly. No one saw it, but it was the other chicken intended for the table; the one that had been accidentally released by Siegfried Weber.

The hen would never know that that one action had changed the course of its life. Some days change your life forever.

The hen ran off into some hedgerow looking for grubs.

Epilogue

Twenty two thousand and eighteen days after that Christmas.

Joyce Fisher watched as her granddaughter, Chloe, tucked into a Kentucky Fried Chicken dinner. She held the drumstick in a serviette and diligently worked her way around it, stripping off the meat. She was eighteen and a student. Joyce guessed that she didn't feed herself very well when she was away at university. She was enjoying the fast food that her gran had bought for her.

Joyce's daughter, Gwen (named in honour of her sister) had insisted that Joyce get a meal too, but Joyce didn't eat much these days. Besides, she'd had a sandwich at home before she came out. She liked to know what went into the food she had. But she was grateful that they'd stopped at the service station. She needed to stretch her legs, use the loo and get some air. She was excited about this trip and was struggling to keep her emotions in check. She'd looked at the photograph on her mantelpiece a lot this morning before she'd set off.

The photograph of Friday Street with John, her mum and her sister. It was faded and dog-eared now, but Joyce had never let it out of her sight since she got it back. She'd looked at their faces and she'd told them where she was going today. It wasn't Friday Street, but she imagined that they would have wished her well.

'Did you have toilet paper?' Chloe's question interrupted Joyce's thoughts.

'Don't ask that!' Gwen didn't like her mum being pestered with inane questions.

Joyce was amused, used to her granddaughter's incessant questioning about what life was like in the war. To Chloe it was all so fascinating. But for Joyce it all seemed such a long time ago now and she sometimes struggled to remember everything. But she remembered the answer to that one.

'All the loo paper had pictures of Hitler on it,' Joyce looked as if she was reminiscing. 'That was the law.'

'Really?' Chloe shovelled chips into her mouth.

Joyce shook her head. 'Not really, you soppy date.'

She watched her granddaughter wash the chips down with a good swig of Coke; knowing that another question was forming in her young mind.

'What happened to the other girls?'

Chloe's need for information was as voracious as her appetite for food.

Joyce chuckled. It would take too long to go into it now. And she'd be talking about people that they didn't know. And some of it would make her sad. And some of it would make her happy. But she thought, as she often did of Esther Reeves, Connie Carter and Iris Dawson. She'd even managed to get back in touch with Bea Finch and Annie Barratt a long time ago. She'd never managed to find Nancy Morrell though. Some of them were names on Christmas cards, others she knew would never write to her again. Lives had moved on; different paths taken. But she often thought of the girls at Pasture Farm.

'It'll be dark soon, we should get a wriggle on.' Gwen cleared her tray. Chloe picked up a final bunch of chips and gave her tray to her mother. Joyce watched as Gwen walked to the tray station. She was proud of her daughter. She was a human rights lawyer. Joyce wasn't certain of what that entailed, but she was proud. Chloe was studying agriculture. Joyce liked to think she got that from her.

Chloe helped Joyce onto her feet, and they walked through the service station, past the boxes full of plastic hoops and teddy bears, past the children coming in with their parents, past the business people coming for a quick coffee. Joyce marvelled at Chloe's striped tights. If only they'd had such a thing in her day.

Gwen drove with Joyce in the passenger seat. Chloe and her mother argued about the choice of radio station. As they always did. This time, Gwen got her way and managed to tune into Radio 4. A man was explaining about how to increase the yield of potatoes. Joyce thought that wasn't how they'd done it in her time at the farm. But she didn't say anything.

After an hour, they reached a turning that led past a new housing estate. There had been an argument about developers encroaching on the land and a small group of identical, new homes with few features and small windows had sprung to life. Welcome to the Gorley Woods Estate said the sign.

Roland Moore

'What were the GIs like, Gran?' Chloe's voice came from the backseat of the car.

'Just like all the stories you've heard. But they were as scared as the rest of us; desperate to make the most of things in case they died the next day.' Joyce scanned the horizon for landmarks. 'I didn't have much to do with them because I was married. Your mother's half-American though,' Joyce said drily.

'Mum!' Gwen squealed in mock horror.

'Only joking.' Joyce smirked to herself.

'But what about that Connie, Gran?'

'Ah, she'd have given any of them a run for their money,' Joyce thought of her old, indomitable friend. 'But she was married too for most of the war. And she behaved herself.'

They took a country lane, past neat hedges. Joyce thought that they rarely had time to trim the hedges in her day. The countryside looked a lot neater now. People had more time for that sort of thing.

Finally, the car slowed down. They had arrived.

A large metal gate was over the front of it, replacing the wooden one that had been there sixty years ago. On the metal, a sticker warned people to keep out and fencing all around made it hard to see inside. Heavy chains were threaded through the front of the plates and a sign promised that guard dogs would be on patrol. Joyce couldn't hear any barking though.

She took a deep breath.

Joyce had come back to Pasture Farm.

She got out of the car. Chloe brought her walking stick and Joyce stepped carefully over the uneven ground. She could see past the gate.

'We should have checked before we came. I told you we should have got permission.' Gwen looked disappointed. 'It looks like it's derelict now.'

'There must be a way to see.' Joyce wasn't going to give up. 'I only want to see.' She peered through a gap in the wooden boards, but shook her head. She needed to get a better view. 'Chloe?'

'Yes, Gran?'

'Will you bring my wheelchair?'

'What do you want that for?' Gwen was starting to get worried.

'I've got a plan.' Joyce shot Chloe a mischievous look. Chloe opened the boot of the car and pulled out a foldaway wheel-chair. Joyce knew she should use it more than she did, but she was reluctant to give up walking. So she liked to use her stick and then moan about the pain in her joints. It was preferable to sitting in the chair all the time.

Chloe pushed the centre of the wheelchair down, locking it into place. She placed a cushion on top and wheeled it over.

'Do you want me to push you, Gran?'

'No,' Joyce looked at the fence. It was seven foot tall and solid, with few places to peek through the metal. 'Bring the chair here, would you?'

'Mum? What are you doing?'

Joyce ignored the question.

Chloe wheeled the chair to the fence.

'Hold it still,' Joyce lifted a foot and tried to position it on the seat of the chair. Her foot wavered in the air uncertainly.

'Mum! You can't be serious?'

339

'She bloody is!' Chloe was impressed with her gran's determination. Chloe held the chair and indicated for Gwen to do her bit. 'Help her, Mum!'

'No, I'm not going to help! Get down this minute. You haven't been feeling well and this is the last thing you need!'

'Help me. It'll only take a moment.' Joyce had one leg on the chair and one on the ground. She wasn't going to listen to her daughter's protestations. She knew what she wanted to do.

Reluctantly, Gwen put out her hand and Joyce took it, using it to push herself up so she was standing on the seat of the wheelchair. Chloe held the chair steady. Gwen looked worried at the sight of her octogenarian mother standing on a wheelchair.

Joyce held onto the top of the fence and looked over.

'What can you see, Gran?'

Joyce stared past the weeds that grew over most of the yard. She stared past the derelict stable block, the pile of wood where the chicken coop had been. Ha, the postbox was still just about standing, its metal box hanging by one bolt on a splintered pole. She stared past to the farmhouse; its windows boarded up long ago.

And then Joyce no longer saw those things.

Instead, she saw radiant golden light in the sky. Summer was here. The fields were newly furrowed; the windows of the house alight with warmth and laughter; tantalising smells of dinner were coming from the kitchen; the yard was free of weeds. From somewhere, she was sure she could hear Bing Crosby singing 'White Christmas'.

And then she saw them.

They were moving across the fields, small shapes against the sunlight; silhouettes dancing and running. But as they came closer, she could make out their faces and see who they were. They were land girls. They were her friends.

Connie Carter, Iris Dawson, Nancy Morrell, Annie Barratt, Bea Finch and Esther Reeves; all as they once were, coming across the fields dressed in their Women's Land Army uniforms and headscarves, laughing, joking, sharing a glorious long-gone summer. They noticed Joyce watching and they started to wave, desperate for her attention, desperate for her to join them in the field.

Joyce Fisher felt herself drawn to them, her heart filling with warmth.

She grinned to herself.

It was good to be back.

THE END

Acknowledgements

I'm very grateful that I've had the chance to tell another story about the Land Girls. I've lived with these characters for over ten years now and seen their journeys play out on television and in these novels – so it is a wonderful opportunity to finish that journey for some of them in these pages. It's been hard letting them go – and watching them disappear into the fields of a final summer's day, but I feel blessed that I can give closure to them. The ending is the one that I had in mind from the time I started to write the series and I hope you like it.

I want to thank my family for their endless loving support and encouragement; Charlotte Ledger at HarperCollins who believed in me and the idea; Emily Ruston and Laura Gerrard for making the manuscript as good as it can be; and Claire Fenby for her great social media ideas.

Thanks too to Julia Wyatt and James Anderson for their support. I'd also like to thank all the actors for their brilliant work on the television series – each of them enabled me to find the voices for their characters whenever I opened the laptop. This book focuses on Joyce Fisher and I kept in mind

343

Becci Gemmell's truthful and visceral performance on TV as I wrote some of the most nerve-wracking scenes for her character in this book. Sorry about putting Joyce through so much, Becci!

Finally I'd like to thank all the readers who have read these novels, reviewed them and supported them. Hope you enjoy this story. Here's to the end of the war.